# *Love and the Downfall of Society*

***A Belle Époque Novel***

MELINDA COPP

Book Cover Design and Illustration by LA Villavicencio

First edition: October 2024

ISBN: 978-1-964546-00-1

LCCN: 2024914867

FIC027200 FICTION / Romance / Historical / 20th Century
FIC027460 FICTION / Romance / Historical / Gilded Age

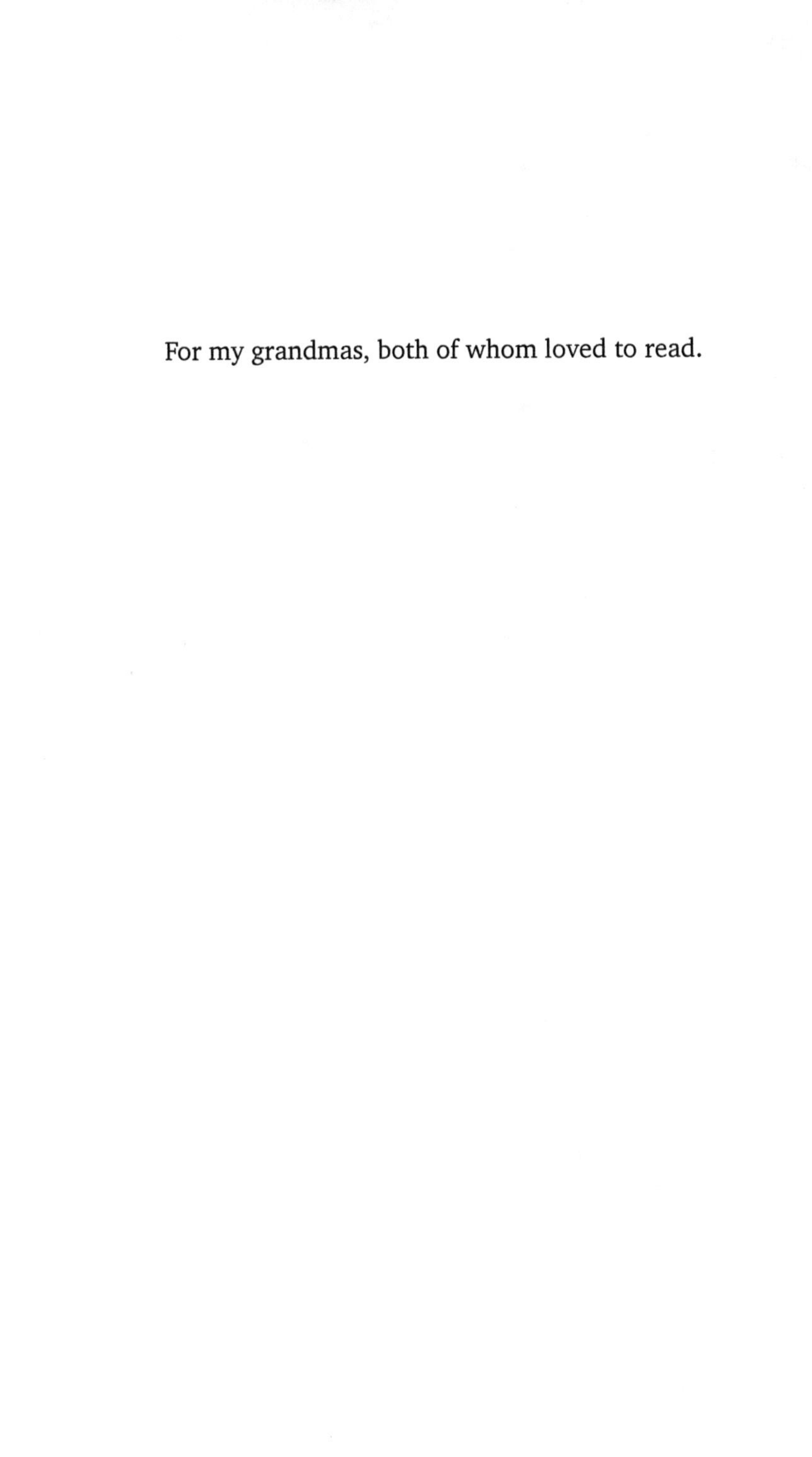

For my grandmas, both of whom loved to read.

When a French man marries he wants to marry as his people always have. He knows there are traditions he can't fight against—and in his heart he's glad there are.

Edith Wharton, *The Custom of the Country*

# Chapter One

## *Paris, May 1901*

*After slipping out* of the house under the guise of a respectable invitation, Charlotte followed her four giggling housemates down the back steps and along the garden path toward the gate. One by one, as they passed through, the women removed their conservatively cut jackets and stashed them between the iron fence and the lilac bush. As Charlotte placed her coverup under its boughs, the soft petals brushed against the bare skin between her glove and the cap sleeve of her borrowed dress. The air felt cool and electric on her exposed décolletage. It was elegant mauve velvet with a touch of black lace trim, and she'd never worn a dress cut so low. But she'd been in the city for four days, she was going out with her new housemates to her first café concert, and it was time to start dressing like the locals.

From the street, the house stood dark except for Madame's rooms and the staff quarters on the top floor. The thrilling promise of Paris nightlife barely muffled the reality that they'd lied to Madame Tremblay about where they were going.

"Will Madame be mad if she finds out we're not really going to a dinner party?" Charlotte asked. The pension on Rue de Fortuny was a place for respectable, professional women—a point that

Madame had emphasized many times since Charlotte wrote to her about getting a room.

"She'll never know," said Nadine, her brown eyes shining confidently. She was an understudy actress at the Comédie-Française and had lived at the pension for the longest. Although they'd so far not gotten past the introductory details of their lives in the few days Charlotte had been in the city, it was clear that, as far as the ladies of the house were concerned, Nadine was kind of the mother hen who lounged about in flowing tea dresses and silky wrappers. Though now it was clear to Charlotte that perhaps Nadine was more like an auntie hen with a mischievous streak. And, with her feathery hat and stunning dress, she knew how to be seen as well as relax around the house.

"Or she'll pretend not to," said Vanessa, tucking an errant blond curl back into her updo without slowing her walk. She worked in the office of one of the big newspapers and was the only housemate who hadn't come to Charlotte's door to introduce herself the day she moved in. "As long as none of us brings home a man."

"I'll bet my can-can shoes that she's had too much whiskey to notice," said Diane.

"Don't dare, you cow. Those can-can shoes are mine, and you know it," Catherine, Diane's sister shot back. They were Americans who'd come to Paris for a vacation and defied their parents by staying and getting jobs. Their French was decent enough underneath the unmistakable accent, and judging from their finery, they were clearly from a wealthy family. However, they completely lacked the pretension and snobby polish that Charlotte was used to encountering in French wealthy people. Charlotte's English was also decent, though she'd gotten quite lost observing a heated argument over a hairbrush yesterday afternoon where the sisters both slipped into their native tongue. By dinner, they were best friends again.

Once they reached the avenue, Nadine expertly drew a cab from the evening traffic to their service with a little wave and firm stomp of her boot.

"Boulevard de Clichy," Nadine said as they stepped into the fiacre. "The Cabaret des Quat'z'Arts, s'il vous plaît."

The cab was barely big enough for all five of them. Crammed inside, the women laughed and talked about people and places that sounded so glamorous.

For years, back at home in Vernon, Charlotte had dreamed of living in the city, dreamed of being a writer, and now she was doing it. Everyone at home, including herself, was shocked when payment arrived from the paper for the story she'd sent on a whim. Her father eyed the check suspiciously and sent a telegram to the newspaper editor demanding to know if it was real. He'd received one back, confirming that, yes, they wanted to publish her little story. Charlotte's mother spent the rest of the day kneeling in church. They were more shocked when, days later, an editor from another paper, called *La Fronde*, wrote to see if she'd be interested in writing something for them, something long enough to serialize. The publisher had read her story, everyone in Paris had, it seemed. And the city was abuzz with a discourse on not only the contents but about the mysterious provincial woman writer. *La Fronde* believed Charlotte would be the next literary sensation, and the publisher—a woman—wanted to get her under contract.

Charlotte gave half of the money to her parents, bought a one-way train ticket and suitcase, paid for two months' lodging at the house on Rue de Fortuny, and had enough left to live on if she was thrifty. Now her home in Vernon felt like a million miles and a lifetime away, which was a thrilling sensation.

Charlotte had started writing as soon as she arrived, determined to sell something else so she could stay in the city. The only reason she'd agreed to come out tonight was that the first installment of her story had just run in *La Fronde* that day. She was celebrating, and she wanted to get to know her housemates. Getting there on her own hard work, experiencing this city, knowing these women—Charlotte was becoming the person she most wanted to be. She knew, jammed into that carriage with her housemates, that Paris would make her even if it wouldn't keep her. And she desperately wished that it would.

When the fiacre came to a stop, Charlotte emerged with the other women onto the bustling street. She waited while Nadine paid the driver.

"Apologies, mademoiselles. I would have gotten you closer to the sidewalk, but…" The driver tipped his head toward a shiny carriage that had blocked a large section of the road.

"Isn't it always the fancy ones," Nadine said.

Charlotte thanked him as he pulled off. Then she and Nadine skirted around the ornate carriage to get to the sidewalk. The door of the luxurious ride was emblazoned with some aristocratic family crest, which made it stand out even more in the humble, working-class traffic that surrounded its gilded edges.

"Is this a fancy place?" Charlotte asked.

"Not at all, but it's great fun. Even the fancy people can't resist the temptations of Montmartre."

Her own success, small as it was, demonstrated that the high society people were at least interested in proletarian life. Still, mingling among them in a place her housemates had promised would debauch her provincial sensibilities was a surprise. "Will they have a special box where they can look down on all of us?"

"Ha!" Nadine laughed. "No. They'll be so close you can touch them."

Nadine took Charlotte's hand and pulled her onto the sidewalk. Around them, couples walked with their arms linked and groups of men called to groups of women, everyone on their way to dinner or dancing. On either side of the wide avenue, the apartments rose above the storefronts. Music seeped from the clubs and the street lamps sparkled. Nadine linked one of Charlotte's arms in hers, while Diane linked the other, and their little group made their way inside the crowded, smoky café.

A brass chandelier hung in the center of the room. The walls were crammed with assorted drawings and paintings. They found a table along the wall under a bronze statue of a goddess-like figure and ordered champagne from a passing waiter. He was wearing more makeup than most women there and winked at Charlotte before hurrying away.

"Your mouth is hanging open," Vanessa said.

"I've never seen anything quite like this before."

"They don't have cabarets in Normandy?" Nadine asked. She'd been born in Paris and boasted about the fact that she'd never made it much further north than the edge of Montmartre.

"If they do, I surely wouldn't know," said Charlotte. "But they can't possibly be anything as interesting as this."

On a small stage at the far back of the room, a woman dressed in a man's suit was reciting what seemed to be a dramatic monologue about meeting a beloved's parents and then having a change of heart. The waiter returned with five flutes of bubbly, golden liquid. Charlotte sipped and took in the crowd, which indeed was an eclectic mix, even for Paris.

Women in towering, ornate hats, low-cut dresses, and necks full of jewels hung on the arms of men in fine suits. Seeing them, she remembered how her housemates had described the place to her earlier that day: gentlemen brought their mistresses here, but not their wives. But there were also mixed groups of working-class people and those dressed with an artistic flair who could be painters or musicians or writers, like herself. Then her gaze fell on a man dressed in evening attire watching her from across the smoky room. When their eyes met, he looked away for a second, like she'd caught him. Then he looked back at her and raised an eyebrow.

He had dark hair and a neat mustache that she recognized immediately. Yesterday morning she'd collided with this same man coming out of a flower shop on Rue St. Dominique with a handful of tulips. She'd glimpsed the tower while she was walking, turned for a better look, and bumped into him like a foolish tourist. He'd put a hand on her elbow to steady her, and he'd watched her intently with a curious heat while she apologized all over herself. This had to be the same man sitting across the room from her now. He smiled mischievously, pinning her with his lusty eyes. Then he winked at her and turned his attention to the man sitting next to him.

Charlotte gasped and turned back to her housemates. She rubbed her fingers along the stem of her champagne flute and tried to fight back her growing smile. He'd truly winked at her. What a delight, even if she wasn't interested. Her cheeks, flushed already from the head, reddened. She did not give in to the temptation to look in the gentleman's direction again. The women ordered another round of champagne. They gave up their table to two smartly dressed couples. Then they ventured into other rooms in the cavernous club, where Nadine promised there would be more entertainment. The crowd was growing, and as they pushed into it to get closer to the stage. The group was only just ahead of Charlotte when someone in the crush of people bumped into her from behind. Charlotte paused to keep from spilling her drink, but her friends kept moving.

Lifting onto her tiptoes, she spotted the feather on Nadine's elaborate blue hat and the red of Catherine's dress. She was about to press on to rejoin them when, as if out of nowhere, he was there. The gentleman who'd been watching her, the gentleman with the tulips, was next to her, smiling with that quirked brow again.

He dropped his gaze and took her in.

"You look lovely," he said as if he knew her.

She laughed and playfully made a show of considering him as well. He was trim but sturdy and broad at the same time, standing two or three inches taller than Charlotte. His suit fit well and appeared to be of the finest quality. The rose on his lapel had only just begun to wilt. "You too, monsieur."

He smiled and nodded toward the stage, where a nun marionette was scolding a child marionette. "What do you think of the show?"

"I'm afraid I've missed most of the context, but the spectacle is brilliant."

"What's your name?"

She hesitated for a moment. She didn't know this man and wasn't exactly sure she needed to be meeting men at all. But he was so compelling. She extended her hand. “Charlotte Devereaux. And yours?”

“Antoine de Larminet.” He took her gloved hand, kissed it, and then held it and watched her for a long moment before releasing it. His dark eyes gleamed with interest.

“I would ask if you come here often, but you seem to be everywhere lately.”

“I was thinking the same thing.” Her skin prickled with delight in this handsome stranger’s presence. “This is my first time here.”

“You were carrying a book the other day.”

“I was. How interesting that you remember.”

“Well, it’s not every day that such a beautiful creature bumps into me.”

“I find that hard to believe.”

He smiled and a lovely flash of white appeared under his dark mustache. “I was in a hurry, but later I remembered you and wished I’d asked you about it. The book, I mean.”

“*Claudine in Paris* by Willy. Have you read it?”

“I haven’t.”

Around them, the crowd burst into laughter. She could still see her friends a few paces ahead, but no longer felt the urge to hurry and join them. She sipped her champagne, letting the bubbles burst in her mouth before swallowing it.

“I saw it in a shop window and couldn’t resist,” she said when the noise died down. “I read the first installment working behind the register at my parents’ bookshop. It was so difficult to put down that I gave a man the wrong change.”

He ducked his head closer to hers while she spoke, so close she could smell the rose on his lapel. His mustache was trimmed in a thick, neat line over his mouth. For a flicker of a second,

Charlotte imagined it brushing along her skin. A man came through the crowd, trying to get past them, and Antoine put a protective hand on her arm so they didn't get separated. The feel of his gloved hand sent a pleasant jolt through Charlotte's middle.

"And where is your parents' bookshop?"

"Vernon."

"Vernon?"

"Yes, it's in Normandy. I've only just arrived in Paris a few days ago."

He seemed to reappraise her. Did she look provincial? Could he see that her dress was borrowed and any sophistication faked? "Ah, well, welcome."

"Thank you."

"Will you stay for long?"

She thought about her room at the house and her meager funds and the promising draft she'd finished that afternoon. "I'd like to."

"Then we must stop meeting at random and do so intentionally." Antoine's gaze was like a thorough caress.

"Must we?"

"Mustn't we?"

She eyed him suspiciously. She'd always been pretty and even back at home, men often flirted. She was used to dodging advances, but something about his felt stickier, almost dangerous. The last thing she needed to find in her first days in Paris was a man this adept at flirtation. "Will you bring me tulips?"

He raised his brow. "Those were for my mother, to clarify. But yes. Absolutely."

"Well, they were very pretty. But, if you don't mind, I'll rejoin my friends now."

"Of course. Though, before you go…" He lifted the rose from his lapel and placed it in her hand. "On behalf of Paris, which is surely more wonderful with you in it."

She thanked him and brought it to her nose because she couldn't help herself. The flower was silvery white and smelled divine. Then her eyes met his.

"Tell me where I can write to you, Charlotte."

Saying yes to this charmer would have been easy. Meeting him twice in two days almost made it feel like fate. But no matter how tempting, she should decline his offer. She needed to work, and a man would only add to the city's countless distractions. Before she could stop herself, she said, "I don't think you should."

His face fell. "Why not?"

"Because…" She wanted to tell him that she wasn't interested but couldn't quite make the words. She shrugged. "Because I'm not a great writer."

With that, she slipped away and didn't stop until she was by Catherine's side. The crowd erupted in another laugh at the scene on the stage, where the nun puppet was now scolding a Marie Antoinette puppet. Catherine smiled and winked at her. Charlotte had only been separated from them for a few minutes. She fingered his rose and ducked her head a little to smell it again, like it was a secret just for her. When she looked up, Nadine was watching her.

"Pretty," she said, eyebrows raised curiously. "Where did you find that?"

"Oh, some flirt gave it to me off his lapel." She dismissed her housemates' questioning looks, even as they oohed and ahhed. But her body still buzzed from the encounter. He could be anyone, though his impeccable dress suggested wealth. She twirled the blunt stem in her fingers, then she tucked the rose in the neckline of her dress and finished her champagne. Wondering if Antoine was still watching her from somewhere in the room, she ventured a look around. But he was gone.

*Antoine slouched in* his velvet wingback chair and set his newspaper aside. He was too distracted to read because his mind kept returning to the woman he'd met the night before. He couldn't stop thinking about the enchanting curve of her neck, her pale décolletage, and the way her wit seemed to be a step ahead of his. He'd recognized her immediately as the bewildered girl from the street. And he hadn't been able to pull his eyes away. But who was she? Not a society lady, though the name sounded vaguely familiar. And, alas, she didn't appear to be the marrying kind. Not that that mattered. He didn't need to look for a wife because his mother was doing that for him.

The light shifted through openings in the heavy brocade window dressings. Soon it would be time for dinner, and it was Thursday, the night his mother regularly hosted guests. So her matchmaking efforts would surely be in full play.

After both his brothers died from the fever, all of his parents' ambitions for continuing the aristocratic tradition fell on him, which primarily meant marrying someone of noble birth. It was an old-fashioned notion; hardly anyone cared about marrying for status these days. Antoine considered himself a modern man, and clinging to aristocratic values was silly in the face of modernity. Although he lived in luxury, he liked the idea of a society built on mobility, ideas, and innovation. But he loved his mother and father, even if they were stuffy aristocrats obsessed with class and legacy.

When his brothers died, it was like all their hopes and dreams died too. His fun-loving parents withdrew into their grief. His mother, who'd been so social, didn't come out of her room for months. Antoine had lost his brothers and his parents too, and when he asked what he could do to ease her pain, his mother said gravely that he was solely responsible for maintaining the family's aristocratic tradition. Antoine, who was a boy at the time, nodded his acceptance fiercely and solemnly. He would have done anything to ease the pain of loss they all suffered, even if it meant marrying someone from a noble family and producing an heir so their outdated ideas of propriety could survive into the twentieth century.

This was a burden Antoine—whose life was otherwise relatively burden-free—had more or less accepted. He could do whatever he wanted, as long as he married a woman who would make his mother proud. And her weekly dinners of late had become increasingly focused on putting him in the same room with women who fit her designs. Today that meant meeting the daughter of Lord and Lady de Montmorency and setting aside any fantasies about Charlotte Devereaux and the expanse of her shoulders exposed by her dress. But why did her name sound so familiar? Antoine was still searching his brain for a memory when the valet, Emile, knocked on the door.

"I can help you dress for dinner, monsieur, if you're ready." Emile was a stout man who'd worked for Antoine's family for over twenty years. They were friendly, but Antoine usually dressed himself. His mother probably sent Emile up to check on him.

Antoine nodded his consent. This wasn't the first time his mother had planned her guest list in hopes of finding him a match, but Antoine didn't expect to fall for the marquis's daughter. Though he should try.

Emile placed Antoine's polished shoes on the floor next to the armoire and began gathering his evening garments. "Madame de Larminet suggested the brocade vest, monsieur, though the wool is clean and ready too."

Antoine laughed. "Better go with the brocade."

Emile nodded and got to work.

An hour later, Antoine was bowing to greet Mademoiselle Louise de Montmorency and her parents, the Marquis and Marquise de Montmorency. When all the guests had arrived, they sat around Antoine's mother's stately mahogany dining table. Thomas and Genevieve Colbert, his parents' snobby friends who were there every week, took their usual seats next to Father. Monsieur Gountaut and his friend Monsieur Canard, who were interesting enough for conversations about music and books, sat opposite Antoine and Louise. There were a lot more empty chairs around the table these days.

His mother's dinner parties used to be energetic and full. But his parents weren't as young as they once were. His father's once commanding presence diminished and stooped further almost every day. Mother's dark hair had turned a dignified silver no less lovely than she'd always been. But she tired easily and napped more than ever. And friends were harder to keep lately. Politics had split society into factions, the aristocracy was aging, and, as Antoine had seen for himself, the most interesting cultural innovations and art were happening in other spaces.

As dinner was served, Antoine played the role of the dutiful son, asking Louise questions and looking for reasons to be interested. She was pretty and well-dressed in an eye-catching green satin gown. She liked playing the piano and riding, something Antoine knew how to do but didn't care for. A true urbanite, he preferred riding about the city enclosed in a carriage with a capable driver at the reins to negotiating huge, unpredictable animals himself. Louise shrugged when he asked if she'd read anything interesting recently. Struggling to find common interests made the conversation dull on their end of the table.

Then Madame Colbert cleared her throat and said to his mother, "I heard your friend, the art collector, is getting married."

Madame Colbert's cheeks were flushed, from either the wine or boldness. Mother nearly dropped her fork. She'd no doubt been hoping that by not inviting Monsieur Swann to dinner, then no one would mention it.

"I'm sure everyone did," Mother said curtly after regaining herself. "It's such an unfortunate turn of events, particularly for someone so charming."

Ever since Monsieur Swann's marriage announcement, it was like the man should be in jail. After the initial shock of hearing the news, Mother, who'd loved Swann's ideas about art and music, refused to see him on his regular visit. She, and probably half of society, shunned him because he was marrying a woman with an unseemly reputation.

"Have you spoken to him about it?" Madame Colbert asked. "The whole thing seems terribly romantic, if you ask me."

"Heavens no. And vulgar is more like it. I happen to know for a fact that his mother wouldn't approve." Monsieur Swann's mother was long dead, but as far as Antoine's mother was concerned, nothing was more essential than a good society marriage. It was even more important than love or happiness. She raised her wine glass to her mouth, but paused before sipping it to add, "He's ruined his life."

"But what if he loves her?" Antoine said. The engagement was only a few weeks old and he was already tired of hearing about it. Antoine had so many warm memories of childhood, of his mother's constant loving presence. And then she said these ungenerous things in front of guests that threw her whole character into question.

"I hardly see how that matters," his father chimed in. As far as he was concerned, love was found in mistresses, not wives.

"Of course, it matters," Antoine argued, heat rising in his chest. This moment needed to be seized. "He has to wake up and face every day in his own life. Why shouldn't he love the person he spends those days with?"

"Because marriage is above all an agreement best entered into by two equally suited parties. People from different classes are too different to ever be fulfilled in something as serious and lasting as marriage." She fanned herself and set down her wine glass. Confrontation flustered Mother, who preferred polite conversation above all else. She cleared her throat and in a softer tone said, "And reputation is important."

"But is it more important than happiness?"

"One doesn't necessarily negate the other," his father said dismissively. He'd already tired of the discussion.

"Who cares what everyone thinks?" Monsieur Canard said, raising his wine glass.

"I agree," Louise chimed in, to Antoine's surprise. "And if his wife doesn't fit in, you'd think that would make her more interesting."

"Interesting is one way to put it," Madame de Larminet said primly. But there was no way she would argue with a guest, let alone the marquis's daughter. "Your mother tells me you've recently gotten a new horse, mademoiselle. Tell me more about it and all this horseback riding you're doing."

Antoine rolled his eyes at his mother's swift change of subject. She didn't care about horses. But it was as clear as ever that his privileged life was something he could enjoy only as long as he followed their rules and traditions.

As they finished dinner and moved to the drawing room, Antoine fixed himself a tumbler of whiskey. Then he settled into an armchair near the fireplace, across from where his mother, Madame Colbert, and Louise were on the settee talking. Antoine swallowed a healthy swig of his drink, steeling himself for another round of dull conversation.

Monsieur Canard, dropping into the other armchair said, most astonishingly, "That Charlotte Devereaux is at it again."

Antoine perked up. "Excuse me, what was that?"

"You know, the story in *Le Figaro* that everyone was mad about last month. The same writer had another piece in *La Fronde* yesterday," Monsieur Canard explained. "Part one of a series."

"The women's paper?" Antoine moved to the edge of his seat.

"Indeed," Lord de Montmorency said, nodding his head. "Claire read it over breakfast and wouldn't stop talking about it until I read it myself."

"You said Charlotte Devereaux?"

"I believe that's it. Claire," Lord de Montmorency raised his voice to get the marquise's attention. "Charlotte Devereaux is the writer that's got you in such a tizzy?"

Lady de Montmorency clucked her tongue. "That's the one. Did you see that, Adeline?"

"I saw it," Louise chimed in enthusiastically. "I thought it was quite funny."

"Funny isn't the word I'd use to describe it," Antoine's mother said.

Antoine remembered the story in *Le Figaro*. It had turned his head upside down. It had been the talk of every salon for days. Was it the same Charlotte Deveraux? Antoine's throat grew tight. "Have we still got a copy of it?"

His mother shrugged and turned her attention back to Lady de Montmorency. "Whoever that woman is, she has some nerve."

Without properly excusing himself, Antoine stood and left the drawing room. Where could he find yesterday's *La Fronde*? The staff never left old papers lying around, and it probably wouldn't be in his father's study because it was for women and his father didn't read it. Or did he? On his way to check the study, Antoine nearly collided with Emile.

"Pardon me, monsieur. Is there something I can help you with?"

"Yesterday's *La Fronde*. Any chance there's a copy still around here somewhere?"

"I'll have a look. The maids often pass them around after Madame has finished."

"Thank you, Emile. If I'm not still in the study, I'll be in my room." Antoine found several papers on his father's desk, but not the one he desperately needed to see. At a loss and relying on Emile, Antoine retreated upstairs.

In his room, Antoine loosened his cravat and slipped out of his shoes. The gears of his mind clicked and whirred, despite the whiskey and wine he'd consumed. There had been something so hypnotic about her. He'd hardly been able to take his eyes off her. And the curls of hair that fell around her delicate ear. He'd smell ed the rose water on her skin when he leaned in to hear her better. So delicious he'd had to resist the urge to taste her. And that quick wit. Had her words—I'm not a great writer—been like a little joke she'd told only herself? No wonder her name sounded familiar. After pacing his room for what felt like ages, Emile's soft knock came at the door.

"Did you find it?" Antoine said in lieu of a polite greeting.

"I did, monsieur. One of the maids had it and has politely requested that she get it back when you're done. Apparently, there's some new series in there that everyone is talking about."

"So I've heard." Antoine took the paper.

"Do you need anything else, monsieur?"

"No, thank you." As soon as Emile was gone, Antoine lit a cigarette, sat in his chair, and unfolded the paper. There, on page two, was her name.

He settled in to read. And from the first sentence, the story gripped him in a subtle and playful way. Every image, every turn of phrase reflected a sharp intellect and wise humor. He laughed out loud. He felt his chest ache with wistfulness and recognition. He was captivated. He was moved. When he reached the end, he took a breath and immediately flipped back to the beginning to read it again.

# Chapter Two

*Nadine, who was* seated next to Charlotte at the table, let out a slow whistle when Madame Tremblay entered the dining room Friday night. The American sisters immediately chimed in with whooping calls of approval. They were all gathered around the table for dinner, which was served every evening promptly at seven. Madame's red velvet gown was trimmed in white lace. Nadine had curled and pinned her salt and pepper hair around a hat that resembled a fountain. Madame blushed and waved away the attention in such an uncharacteristically girlish manner.

Charlotte had never seen Madame be anything but serious. All of their interactions so far had involved either the listing of rules or dignified dinner conversation. Madame Tremblay was a stern woman with rules and standards, not a woman with a feathery hat and tickets to the opera. Charlotte, who wouldn't have thought Madame capable of blushing, joined Vanessa in hearty applause.

"Fancy, schmancy, Madame," Nadine said.

"Stop, mes petites, please," Madame said. "Don't fluster me. The carriage will be here soon."

"Well, you look stunning, Madame." Diane beamed at her. "But what we all want to know is if the gentleman in that carriage has honorable intentions."

They all laughed, except Madame. “Mademoiselles, there is nothing funny about getting involved with a man who won’t marry you, I assure you. But Monsieur Gauthier has no intentions. We’re just old friends.”

“Don’t be afraid of your feelings, Madame,” said Vanessa. “He’s a widower, no? Probably amenable to marriage then. And I saw the way he was looking at you when he came by the other day…”

“He looked to me like he had some intentions,” Diane said saucily.

“Oh, don’t be silly.” Madame was waving off their naughty speculation when Claire, the maid, entered the dining room.

“Monsieur Gauthier is here, Madame. Should I bring him up?”

“No, no. I’ll come down.” Madame fixed her lacy shawl and gave a little wave to the girls as she left. “Behave yourselves, mes petites. I’ll see you at breakfast.”

“Never in my days,” said Nadine when Madame was gone.

“Did you see her giggling like that?” Catherine said, shaking her head. She turned to Charlotte. “She never goes anywhere.”

“Not in all the years I’ve lived here has that woman gone out with a man,” Nadine said.

“Maybe if she falls in love, she’ll loosen up a little,” Diane said.

“Don’t count on it,” Nadine and Vanessa said in unison.

“Was Madame ever married?” Charlotte asked.

“She was, years ago. Monsieur Tremblay died when Madame was still young. This was his mother’s house,” Nadine said. She perched in Madame’s chair at the head of the table. “She took care of his mother and inherited the place.”

“Why did she start taking on boarders?”

“She was probably lonely,” Diane said wistfully. “Rattling around in this old place all day.”

"She never talks about it, so it's hard to say for sure. But she doesn't have any children," Nadine said. "And she always worked. I suppose she needed something to do to keep busy."

"Love will keep one busy," Vanessa said.

"Oh, please. Love will make one crazy," Nadine said between sips of wine. "At least I've heard."

"I don't know anything about love," Diane said.

"Love will make one want to run away from home," Catherine said. "But I'm too hungry to talk about it anymore. Pass me the bread, Diane."

Dinner was red wine, baguette, and roast chicken served family style. Madame Tremblay also served breakfast for the women every day, and there was always something in the kitchen for lunch, though most everyone was gone during the day for work.

This was one of Madame's rules: no night shifts. They kept daylight hours and weren't to be coming and going or rustling around the house all night. Madame made exceptions for Nadine's evening performances because, grumpy as she was, Madame loved the theater and was endlessly proud of Nadine's hard work.

Charlotte already knew the house rules through repetition. Madame Tremblay put them in writing when she was corresponding with Charlotte about the rent agreement, and she repeated them for Charlotte and her mother when they arrived. Her mother had insisted on accompanying her to Paris for both Charlotte's comfort and her own peace of mind.

No gentlemen upstairs was another rule, which her mother had loved, because this certainly wasn't a brothel. Gentlemen with respectable intentions could visit in the drawing room, and

Madame would even serve refreshments. But this was a house for career women, not kept women. Her housemates had warned her that if Madame was home—and Madame was always home—then she was watching and sizing up anyone who came around.

And no extensions on rent. Of all the rules, this was the most likely to put Charlotte out. The woman who'd had Charlotte's room before her was a seamstress who lost her job and couldn't pay. Even though she'd lived there for a year, Madame still refused the extension. The thought of it made Charlotte's heart quicken with worry.

Charlotte's housemates, though, seemed far more concerned with the rules about men. Charlotte occupied a room that once belonged to a woman who'd been made to leave because she took up with a very wealthy, very married man. But Nadine said she'd been so obvious about it, with the jewelry gifts and quitting her job and the fancy carriage dropping her off in the wee hours of morning. Madame refused to accept the woman's rent money from him and turned her out. Lots of other women's pensions had similar rules about men.

Those were the most important rules of Madame Tremblay's house, but there were lesser ones. All other infractions—like sneaking out to cabarets or leaving messes in the kitchen—were minor and not likely to leave Charlotte unhoused.

Even with all the rules, Charlotte was grateful, for the hundredth time since moving in, that she'd found this living situation. Back in Vernon, she and her friend Marie, whom she'd known since childhood, used to pour over the outdated fashion and lifestyle magazines when her father took them off the bookshop rack. Paris was a dream come true. She had new friends, a lovely home, and delicious food. She'd even flirted with a handsome stranger in a cabaret—all part of her charming new life as a writer in the city of light.

After a tall glass of wine and a second serving of chicken, Charlotte was full and tired. Diane was regaling them with a story about an obnoxious table at the restaurant where she worked. Claire brought in a pot of coffee, and Charlotte poured herself a cup. The sharp and bright aroma perked her up enough to finish dinner.

Her luck had been good, but if she wanted to keep this charming life, she had to sell another story. She'd done nothing but write since she got here, save for her night at the cabaret and a few walks around town. But the work she'd been producing excited her. The house was usually quiet during the day, so she'd had plenty of time to work and think. She slipped easily into that magical writing flow that had been so elusive back in Vernon. And when she emerged, she had pages of material that felt very promising. She felt good about her writing. Confident. And from this feeling, she was sure only great work could emerge.

After dinner, Charlotte went upstairs. As she was undressing, she noticed a letter from her mother that had arrived that day. She hadn't read it earlier because she was working, and then it slipped her mind. She opened it now and settled onto her bed.

Her parents' bookshop in Vernon was a small place on a busy corner with a broken-down printing press in the back. The family lived in the upper floors of the building. It was a small, contained life that had been filled with plenty of reading material as an escape. Charlotte took advantage and read as much as she could when she wasn't dusting shelves or helping customers. Her younger brother, who was back from school, was helping them now, and from her mother's update, sounded like he fit well in the role. In addition to news on the family and shop and garden, her mother complained a little about the neighbors. And then, just before closing, she mentioned running into Pierre Fournier on the way to the market. Charlotte took a deep breath as she read her mother's description. She wrote, "He asked after you and was very polite."

Pierre had asked Charlotte to marry him not long before she came to Paris. He did so, she understood, not because he loved her but because her mother had caught him with his hand up Charlotte's skirt behind the shop one evening. Not that they wouldn't have been a solid match. His father was a lawyer and Pierre himself was working to become one too. They had been sleeping together for almost a year, sneaking around and stealing moments alone like it was a game. But as much as she liked having fun with Pierre, Charlotte didn't love him. She didn't love the idea of spending the rest of her life in Vernon as a lawyer's wife. It wouldn't be terrible, and who knew, she may end up back there. But the idea of it didn't make her heart sing the way a writer's life in Paris did.

When her mother caught them, Pierre apologized all over himself and beat a hasty retreat. After the initial shock had passed, Charlotte apologized to her mother too.

"Everyone has seen you together, so although it was a surprise to find you like that, it isn't so much a surprise at all," her mother had said. "But if your father catches you, he'll make you marry Pierre. And if you get pregnant, I'll make you marry him for the child's sake."

Mother knew how a man could distract a woman from her dreams. She'd married young and worked her whole life around the home and business. Charlotte had a better education and many more opportunities than her mother ever had. So although Charlotte had thought of her romance with Pierre as a game, the stakes were actually quite high. She didn't want to get married to the most obvious choice and settle down in her hometown. She had always wanted something else.

The thing she wanted was still nebulous and taking shape, but it wasn't the rest of her life in Vernon. Her mother knew that. Even Pierre knew that. With her mother's words echoing in her mind, Charlotte submitted her story to the paper the very next day, like a wish for something to happen that would set her life on the trajectory she so deeply wanted. And sure enough, it had worked. Mentioning Pierre in her letter now, Charlotte's mother was again reminding her of the stakes. A life in Vernon with Pierre would probably be a fine life. But it wasn't what she wanted.

Charlotte refolded the letter and set it on her desk. The house around her was silent, save for the occasional muffled shriek of laughter coming from Catherine and Diane's room downstairs. As she finished undressing, she imagined Pierre running into her mother. He would have smiled his friendly smile even as his face reddened with embarrassment. He'd been a mess after she'd caught them. Charlotte laughed thinking about it now. He'd felt so bad. Pierre was a good fellow, a satisfactory friend and lover. She hadn't worried a bit about leaving him behind. He was handsome and settling into a reputable law practice—a very eligible bachelor of Vernon. He'd have a new woman in no time.

Charlotte lay back on the bed and opened the novel she'd been reading. It was one of the new books she'd taken from the shop before leaving, Zola's latest about work that had hooked her from the start. But her mother's letter and lingering memories of Pierre distracted her.

She didn't miss him, exactly, but she'd liked the romantic entanglement. She liked having someone to share her thoughts with and something to keep secret. Then there was the man she'd met at the cabaret, Antoine. His rose now sat in a little bowl of water on her windowsill. Unlike familiar Pierre, Antoine seemed exotic and strange. The look in his eyes when he kissed her hand, and the feel of his hand on her arm. He could certainly entangle her. But she was content with her decision not to allow it. He didn't know how to reach her, and Paris was a big city. She'd never see him again.

But she'd been rolling around an idea for a story that seemed to be coming together. She'd even written a few scenes about a charming Parisian man with a rose on his lapel.

Diane's hearty cackle carried through the hall and the lamp flickered against the floral wallpaper. The room had come furnished, as they all did, in simple muslin drapes and soft, sturdy bedding. She had a dressing table and a wardrobe and a wide desk she'd put by the window. There was a faded green velvet settee and a little fireplace that would be nice in the winter. Vanessa, Nadine, and Charlotte were on the third floor. Catherine and Diane's rooms and a small sitting room where the girls liked to gather were downstairs. The dining room and entry were below that. The main drawing room, and Cook's and Claire's rooms were on Madame's side of the house. Already, Charlotte felt comfortable there, like she was exactly where she was supposed to be. The world of her mother's letter, bustling on without her, was too far away to suck her back in.

Charlotte set her novel aside. The metal frame on her bed creaked as she got up. She went to her desk for her notebook and pencil and then settled back into bed. She wrote like that, drafting her fantasies into scenes, long after the noise from the sisters downstairs fell silent.

*The next morning,* Charlotte wrote in her room until she'd filled her last notebook. Forced into a break, she put her hair up, pinned on a little straw hat, and ventured out. She crossed Rue de Prony and made her way past Parc Monceau, where she'd already strolled several times along the lake and among the trees. Every day—on the ones she went out, at least—her familiar territory and confidence grew. On her second day in the city, she'd walked from the house to the Champs-Élysées, exploring and taking it all in. She was sure she'd seen a stationery shop, and so she retraced her route as best she could, toward the intersection with the boulangerie and then down Avenue Hoche.

The grand apartments rose above the tree-lined street, each facade as ornate and lovely as lace. She passed women with baskets, and gentlemen with newspapers tucked under their arms. Everyone coming and going, conducting their business. It had all overwhelmed Charlotte at first. The buildings and crowds—everything was much bigger than she was used to.

And, unlike walking in Vernon, she didn't pass a single familiar face. No one stopped her to tell her this or that gossip about anybody else. No one knew who she was, and no one seemed to care. It was both terrifying and freeing to be so anonymous. Because there were so few people in her town, and there was so little to do or attach importance to, everyone talked about everyone else. Gossip lived well here in the city too. Nadine, Vanessa, and Madame always seemed to be saying this or that about a neighbor. And there was a society gossip column or two in every paper filled. But Charlotte existed pleasantly outside of it, perhaps for the first time in her life.

She found the stationery shop right where she thought she would. Inside, the smell of paper welcomed her. Charlotte marveled at the paper textures and fine leather-bound journals before finding her favorite cahiers. They were ruled, bound in kraft card stock, and simple. She bought four and treated herself to a box of pencils as well.

The paper was more expensive than it was back at home, but Charlotte had assumed some things would be. After paying Madame for the two months, she had some left to live and enjoy herself as long as she didn't go wild. In Paris, it would be easy to do so; lovely treasures filled every shop window. Buying herself a book the other day had been both an indulgence and an exercise in restraint. She had no designs about coming to the city and getting rich. Charlotte knew that a writer's income could be irregular without ever amounting to much. It would be even harder for a woman from the provinces. She had to keep her desires in check. No dress shopping until she absolutely needed one. And her drafts weren't elegant enough for a leather-bound journal.

Pleased to finish her errand, Charlotte stepped back outside. The sculpted wall of the Arc de Triumph was not far off in the distance, and she continued that way. The clouds that had lingered all morning were broken up and scattered across the sugary blue sky. And the creamy late morning light brightened the pale stone buildings.

The closer she got to the Arc, the busier the street became. She skirted around the carriage traffic at the monument and headed down the Champs-Élysées, entering the throng of pedestrians. Women, dressed to be seen in tall hats and colorful dresses, strolled in groups with their equally fashionable children. Couples walked arm-in-arm. And dogs of various shapes and sizes tugged at their leads. Charlotte wasn't ready to go home yet and looked for a café where she could have a cup of coffee and watch people.

After walking a few blocks, she found one with wide blue awnings and tables arranged outside around large pots of flowers. She pulled open the door and stepped inside. A host greeted her with a dignified nod and asked, "En salle ou en terrasse, mademoiselle?"

"En terrasse, s'il vous plaît."

He led Charlotte past the bar and through the open portes-fenêtres to the outdoor seating area. As he placed her menu on one of the little tables lined up along the front wall of the building, she glanced at the gentleman at the adjacent one.

It was Antoine, the gentleman from the café concert, sitting almost directly across from where the host was putting her. He was watching her with a bemused expression.

Charlotte's mouth fell open. Then, remembering herself, she smiled and sat as the host said something about the soup du jour that she completely missed because all of her awareness was on Antoine.

"Charlotte Deveraux," Antoine said, taking her hand for a quick kiss as soon as the host was gone.

"I'm surprised you remember," she said, though meeting him like this was decidedly more surprising. Charlotte sat down and placed her bag from the stationery shop under the table. He'd been here first, so there was no way he'd followed her.

"Of course, I remember." Antoine laughed. Then he clutched his chest as if she'd shot him with an arrow. "How could I forget the name of the most interesting woman in Paris? The real question is: Do you remember mine?"

"Antoine de… Lar… minet." She hesitated for show, as if she hadn't whispered his name to herself a thousand times since learning it.

A server arrived to take her order, and she asked for coffee and a cup of the soup, whatever it was.

"Pardon me," Antoine said to the server when she'd finished. "May I also have coffee, and please, put her order on my check."

"As you wish," the server said. He departed, leaving them alone again, staring at each other.

"Thank you," she said. "For the lunch. You didn't have to do that."

"It's my pleasure." He sank back in his seat and draped his arm over the empty chair across from her. With his dark suit and long limbs, he was like a cat getting comfortable in the sun, eyeing her intently. Charlotte's stomach fluttered imagining that arm draped around her. "It's an honor buying soup for Charlotte Devereaux."

"Why are you saying it like that?" He was up to something.

"Well, I presume you are the same Charlotte Deveraux who wrote the story in *Le Figaro* a month or so ago."

"Don't tell me you read it?"

"Of course, I read it, Charlotte." He beamed at her. "I loved it. And I loved the story in Wednesday's *La Fronde*."

"No, you didn't."

"I really did." He shifted forward and put his elbows on the table. His eyes danced over her with admiration so earnest she tingled.

Who was this man?

He continued, "And I was heartbroken that not only did you refuse my request to correspond, but you also didn't tell me that you are a writer."

"It didn't come up," she demurred. The couple at a nearby table must have overheard them because they were now watching Charlotte and Antoine curiously. Had they read her story too? For a long time, the only people who ever read her work were the people she asked, like her parents and her friends. Being published meant lots of people were reading her, people she didn't even know, which was something she had to get used to.

"You know, I was just thinking I would try reaching you through the paper. That was before you turned up at the table next to mine."

Charlotte wasn't sure what to say. He seemed so genuinely thrilled to know her. "If it's any consolation, I have lived to regret not telling you how to reach me."

"Oh?"

"It's true. I finished the Claudine novel and found myself wanting to tell you about it."

"Me or someone?"

"You, I suppose." She blushed, caught revealing her interest in him, allowing herself to be vulnerable. But something about him made it feel safe and natural and kind of heady to do so. "I was so sure I would never see you again. But I see that's not the case. Paris is smaller than I thought."

"Maybe. Or maybe we're meant to know each other. Maybe fate deems it necessary."

The server returned before Charlotte could respond. But while he served their coffee and her soup, she considered what he'd said. Having an immediate affection for a handsome man was not fate. And she wasn't sure that it was bumping into him repeatedly either.

The soup had white beans and bright green spring vegetables, served with a piece of baguette and butter. When the server left, Charlotte buttered her bread and ventured a glance at Antoine, who was stirring cream into his coffee.

His hands were clean and neatly manicured, not like a man who spent his days working. Shiny gold cufflinks peeked out from the sleeve of his dark blue coat. The fabric of his clothing looked soft and fine. His mustache and hair were impeccably groomed. Not a rough spot on his facade. And it heightened Charlotte's awareness of herself, of the worn spots on her suit, the place where she'd repaired her hat, and the dry skin and ink on her hands. At the same time, she couldn't take her eyes off him. She couldn't stop imagining touching him, smoothing her hands over the fabric of his jacket, feeling the warmth of his body underneath all those clothes, untying that silky cravat and sliding it off his neck. How elegant it would be.

Charlotte tried her soup, which was a delicious mouthful. The creamy bean mingled with the tender vegetables and broth.

"How is it?" Antoine asked over his coffee cup.

"It's lovely. Did you already eat?"

"I did. I had the beef stew. I often come here because it's one of my favorite things to eat in all of Paris."

"Is it? I'll have to try that next time."

"I could order some for you now, if you like. You can have both soup and stew."

"No, thank you. The soup is enough." She ate another bite and watched him watching her. "You don't have to stay. I mean, I don't want to keep you. Since you've already eaten."

He shook his head and smiled at her like she was crazy. "No, my dear. I have the afternoon free. And I intend to extend this fateful meeting for as long as I can. Do you have anywhere you have to be?"

Her new notebooks and pencils in the bag by her feet were all she had to look forward to until dinner. They could wait, couldn't they? She'd written several pages that morning. "No. Not at all."

"Then tell me about yourself, Charlotte. Who is the woman who writes to tease the aristocracy."

Charlotte laughed. "I don't know where to begin."

"Tell me about Normandy." He pulled his chair closer and put both elbows on the table. "That's where you're from, correct?"

"It is. Vernon. A small town you've surely never heard of."

"And your parents own a bookshop there?"

"Yes. It was my grandparents' before them. And so I grew up in the apartment above the shop."

"And you probably read all the books." Antoine crossed his arms lazily without taking his reverent eyes off her.

"I read most of them. There wasn't much else to do."

"Ah, the provincial life."

"It's not so bad," she said a little defensively. "But Vernon is not Paris. What about you? Where did you grow up?"

"Paris. Not far from here, actually. But my family has a country place, south of the city. So I'm acquainted with the small-town atmosphere."

"I assure you, it has nothing compared to this." She gestured at the city around them. "You'll never have reason to go to Vernon."

The server returned again, refilled their coffees, cleared Charlotte's soup bowl, and left the check on Antoine's table. The couple who'd been seated near them earlier were gone now, and the host was seating two gentlemen at another nearby table.

And while they drank their coffee, Charlotte told Antoine about coming to Paris and her hopes for staying. She seemed able to tell him anything. She left out the part about Pierre, though. Perhaps because she didn't want him to think about her in romantic situations, or because she did want him to. And she told him about her housemates and Madame and all the Parisian things she'd done since arriving in the city, which so far hadn't been much.

"I still have a long list of sights I want to see," she said.

"Well, if you're finished here, then I'd love to accompany you."

"Right now?"

"Sure. We can walk toward the tower, toward the river. It's a beautiful day for it." His eyes pleaded with her in the most adorable way.

"It is lovely."

"Then whenever you're ready."

Antoine stood as soon as Charlotte did and placed more than enough money to cover the check on the table. He insisted on carrying her bag of cahiers. And in the most mannerly of ways, he escorted her around the flower pots and out of the restaurant area, back onto the street. He offered her his arm, and she took it.

The sidewalk was just as busy as it had been before she stopped for lunch. But where she'd been anonymous and invisible alone, now she attracted eyes. People noticed him, noticed them. For a moment, she feared that she looked silly and underdressed next to someone so sophisticated. But soon her awareness of everyone around them faded. His arm felt firm under her hand, and the fabric of his coat was indeed a pleasure to her fingertips. No matter how they looked, he felt strangely right.

# Chapter Three

*Antoine and Charlotte* crossed Champs-Élysées and headed down Avenue d'Alma toward the river. As they passed the stylish metalwork gates of the new metro station, Antoine asked if she'd ridden it yet.

"No," she said, peering down the staircase that led under the city. The ornate sign above it had petals of frosted glass so pretty that going underground almost sounded inviting. "So far I haven't had sufficient reason to risk getting lost down there."

Antoine smiled, revealing a perfect line of teeth underneath his neatly trimmed mustache. It punctuated his handsome face so well and the sensation of it brushing against her hand when he'd kissed it at the table tingled on her skin. "Is this your first time in Paris?"

"No. I came once as a child, which I hardly remember, and then I was here last year for the exposition. I didn't see much of the city, though. We mostly attended to bookshop business."

"Does your brother help with business?"

"He does. But everything I've told you is probably so boring compared to your life. Tell me about your family."

"I'm afraid they're not half as interesting as you." He kept doing that—turning her questions about him back onto her. But she hesitated to push him for more. She didn't know him well enough to press him, and it was hard talking and walking along the busy street. His evasions didn't make her uncomfortable, exactly, just more curious.

Because of the height of the buildings and the angle of the street, she hadn't noticed the Eiffel Tower until it was too close to ignore. She might never get used to seeing it, it was so pretty. Beyond the busy intersection, the river glistened under the late afternoon sun. The Pont de l'Alma arched across the water and was decorated with statues of military figures at the base of each arch. The water slipped steadily past the statues' feet while carriages flowed from one bank to another over the bridge.

They walked along the quay until they found an open bench facing the water. As they sat, Antoine said, "I hope the view is worth the walk."

"Absolutely. Though we may have to sit here for a while so my feet can recover. Maybe I can take the metro back to the seventeenth."

"Alas. It doesn't go that way. Not yet, but they have plans to connect the whole city."

"I suppose I can wait here until then," she said, gesturing at the view. A light breeze came off the water, just enough to cool her face. And a long, pretty boat cruised past them on the river. The wooden hull had been polished to a brilliant shine, and women on the deck were dressed in sorbet colors. It was a lovely scene.

"Don't worry. I'll get you home. But I don't want to talk about that yet. Unless you're ready to go?"

He was sitting right next to her on the bench, closer than he had to be for the amount of seating room available. Everything about the way he was turned and looking at her suggested interest. His gaze was like a friendly, loving spotlight that warmed instead of exposed. She relaxed in his company, opened up, delighted in her inappropriate impulse to climb in his lap and feel that mustache with her mouth. "I'm not ready to go."

He smiled like he'd won a great prize. "Good. Then tell me about your favorite book in the whole shop back home in Vernon."

*Antoine hadn't intended* to walk Charlotte to his neighborhood, but he loved this part of the city. This spot, actually, with the tower in the background and the river in the fore, was one of his favorite places to be. It was the first place he wanted to show her when she agreed to walk with him. And now that they were sitting here together, with the river flowing past them, he could sit there forever.

Charlotte was different from any other woman he'd ever met. She was both ladylike in her manners and bold in her thoughts. Once he brought up Zola, she carried on about him enthusiastically for twenty minutes. Her toilette was simple and understated, but lovely in its lack of pretension. She obviously wasn't a wealthy woman, but her suit, though worn, had been well-made. She wore few ornaments or colors so the pink shade of her cheeks and the blue of her eyes seemed all the more vibrant and lovely. Her small wrists and hands emerged from her gray linen suit and gestured for emphasis as she talked. She had ink stains on her fingers, a mark of her work that made her strangely more alluring to him. He wanted to memorize every detail.

And her mind. It whirred like an electric fan. Antoine had read most of Zola's work, but she managed to crack it open for him even further.

"I am talking too much," she said apologetically. "I'm carrying on."

"I like it."

"Well, tell me about your favorite writer."

"You're my favorite writer," he said in complete earnest. He'd never read a story quite like hers.

"Stop. I am not."

He shrugged and didn't revise his answer.

"Then tell me about yourself. What was it like growing up in Paris?"

Antoine both wanted to tell her about his life and didn't. Not because he wanted to deceive her, but because he suspected that fessing up to his aristocratic lineage would shift things between them. It often did. People of all classes and backgrounds treated him differently when they found out. Some distanced themselves because of it. Others latched on as if he were an opportunity. He wanted more than anything, sitting here with Charlotte, to be just a man. Just a person. And he liked her so much that he was afraid to find out how the shift would manifest itself in her. Not only would he be different in her eyes, but through her reaction, she would become different in his.

That, and she wrote about aristocrats as stuffy and cruelly ridiculous. Antoine wasn't ready to be that in her eyes. And so even though he felt compelled to tell her everything, he evaded the defining truth of himself.

"Growing up in Paris was okay. But my favorite memories of childhood were spending time in the country. We had a lovely garden and woods to explore."

"I never would have guessed you for an outdoorsman."

"Well, I wouldn't go that far. I was usually sitting in the garden reading. Or looking for places in the woods to hide with my book. But I greatly appreciated the natural setting. The flowers. All the green. I can remember wanting to stay there forever."

"The countryside does have an expansive feeling. Did you hunt and ride?"

He laughed. "Like I said, I'm not much of an outdoorsman. I have both shot and ridden a horse, but I'd really rather not."

"So almost like city living against a different backdrop, then?"

"Maybe." He considered this. "The quiet solitude also had something to do with it. You know, the slower pace, and all that."

"Did your family go every summer?"

"We did—that is until we didn't anymore."

"Why did you stop?"

Antoine thought back to that darkest time in his past. "My brothers—I had two of them—passed away when I was thirteen."

Her face fell. "At the same time?"

He nodded.

Charlotte gasped and touched his arm. "Oh, no. That's terrible. What a sad thing for your family."

"They were the outdoorsmen. If I merely loved the country, they seemed to transform in it. I think sometimes that all those memories attached to the place made it difficult for my parents to bear the reality of them gone." He stopped short of telling her about the land and tenants his family still had there.

"That must have been very difficult." She withdrew her hand from his sleeve then, and he immediately wished she hadn't. It had been a casual, natural gesture of comfort. But all afternoon he'd longed to touch her; her arm in his wasn't enough.

"With them gone, all my parents' aspirations have fallen on me. The pressure to live the way they want me to live is quite heavy at times."

"What sorts of pressures do they put on you?"

The truth sat right there on Antoine's tongue, but he couldn't bring himself to say it. "Oh, you know. The usual things."

She looked at him curiously, and Antoine could almost see her weighing in her mind the desire to press him for more against politely respecting his privacy. His evasion worked, and she gave more of herself.

"My father wants nothing more than for me to come back to Vernon and get married."

"He doesn't approve of your writing?"

"Oh, no. It's not that. He loves that I write. He loves books and reading. But he wishes I did it in and around the confines of motherhood and domesticity."

"Ah. Does he approve of your being in Paris?"

"Both of my parents were shocked when *Le Figaro* wanted my story. They didn't even know I'd sent it. I was pretty shocked myself."

"Surely they're proud of you, even if you're not living the life they want."

"I'm sure they are." She looked at him thoughtfully, establishing eye contact before continuing. "And I'm sure your parents will feel the same way if you don't follow their suit."

Antoine wasn't so sure, but he was done talking about it. However, he still wasn't ready to be done spending time with Charlotte. He gestured at the square behind them. "Are you up for a stroll around the park? Then I promise I'll get you a carriage home."

"Okay."

Antoine stood when Charlotte did and offered his arm. The sensation of her hand on him again was like arriving home, and his heart quickened happily. He carried her bag of paper and pencils in his other hand. They walked along the water and then crossed the street to the little park. Charlotte smelled of vanilla and roses, and he kept his arm in close as they walked so she was practically tucked into his side. A short iron fence separated the sidewalk from the green space, and they skirted around it to the entrance. He guided her toward the statue that stood on a stone pedestal at the park's center.

"What's it called?" she asked as they approached.

"*The Warrior Reforging His Sword*. The artist, Ernest-Eugène Chrétien, is actually from Normandy."

"You're kidding." Her eyes were wide with disbelief. She was adorable.

"I'm not kidding. Have you heard of him? I hear everyone knows everyone up there."

"Ha. My parents probably do."

For a quiet moment, they admired the bronze figure of a man raising a hammer over an anvil, while the pedestrian and carriage traffic that surrounded them almost ceased to exist.

"It's patriotic, about France rebuilding," she said.

"It is. It's been here for as long as I can remember. But I'll be honest, rather than patriotism, every time I look at it, all I think about is life in the time when warriors had to forge their own swords."

She quirked a brow at him.

"You know, medieval times. Before sewers and factories and all the modern amenities that make life easier than…" He nodded toward the warrior. "Blacksmithing."

She looked at the statue thoughtfully.

"I deeply appreciate the fact that I didn't exist back then," he said.

"As do I. Can you imagine how hard blacksmithing must have been in medieval times? I'm not even sure I could get the fire hot enough in this day and age."

"I couldn't. And based on this rendering, they had to do it naked." He shuddered, and she laughed at him.

"I think the nudity makes him representative of all men."

"Oh," he said, feigning enlightenment. "Perhaps you're right."

Her laugh was high and pleasant. He wanted—needed—to make her do that again.

"You know, people are still blacksmiths. And there are jobs today that are just as bad or worse. Modernity hasn't made life easier for everyone."

"Yes. That's true." He'd passed loud factories from the comfort of his carriage.

"Don't worry. I won't hold it against you."

"I hope not." He stepped away from the statue. "Shall we?"

They walked two slow laps around the park, laughing and talking about books and music and other impersonal topics as they went. It was late afternoon now and the light had turned golden yellow. For the first time since lunch, Antoine checked his pocket watch. It was nearly five.

Seeing him with his timepiece, Charlotte said, "I should probably make my way home."

"As should I. But let's catch a ride."

They made their way to the street where Antoine hailed a cab from the stream of traffic.

"Do you mind if I share the ride?" He should just put her in the carriage and walk himself home over the bridge, but he couldn't help taking advantage of the opportunity to extend their time together.

"Of course not." Her smile puffed up his confidence. He liked this woman so much. "I would ask you where you live, but it won't mean anything to me unless you have a map."

Antoine helped her into the carriage. "Ah, but now you'll have to give me your address."

"I suppose this was your plan all along," she said, smiling. "Rue de Fortuny, please. Number seventy-seven."

Antoine told the driver, mentioned a second stop on the left bank, and then got in next to her.

"I don't know the city well, but do I understand that you're taking me home and then coming all the way back down here to cross the river?"

Antoine nodded; guilty. "Ladies first?"

"That's kind of you, but I don't mind if he drops you first for efficiency's sake." Her bright blue eyes sparkled and held his rapt. "You've already gotten my address out of me. Won't it be cheaper if you go first?"

"To be honest, I'm not quite ready to part ways." Her face turned away toward the window. Outside, the traffic was heavy and moving slowly. His gaze fell on her mouth, down the column of her neck, over the front of her conservatively cut suit, to where her hands lay in her lap. They were small and unadorned, except for the faint smudges of ink. He wanted to loop them around his neck.

When she turned back to him, he said, "I've enjoyed our afternoon together, Charlotte. Very much."

"It was a nice surprise." She sounded a little shy now. Her skin looked soft and flushed from being out. Her face so lovely.

He sank in the bench slightly and reached for her hand. When he had it, time seemed to stop. The traffic all around them became a blur. The carriage swayed over the cobblestones. They sat there, looking into each other's eyes, twining their fingers together. Antoine's heart pumped with increasing strength in his chest. Then when her gaze dropped to his mouth, he moved in closer.

With mere inches between them, he said, "I would very much like to kiss you now, Charlotte Devereaux. Is that all right?"

She bit her lip and her eyes flicked to the side, away from his. But she didn't move away. "It is quite all right. Desired, in fact."

And so he closed the slim space between them and brought his mouth to hers. Her breath was sweet with a lingering hint of coffee. Her mouth pliant and soft under his. Without hurry, he moved his lips over hers, breathing her in and tasting her. She was wonderful to be this close to. He wanted so much more, but he took his time, reveling in the sensation of her.

Her hand tightened on his and then released. A second later, it was on his shoulder, and she tipped her head to the side. His pulse quickened at her advances. He moved his hand to the side of her face and parted her lips with his, deepening the kiss with a swipe of his tongue. She met it with confidence, pushing back gently with hers. His body tingled and sparked, and his groin pulsed. But he didn't accelerate what was a delightfully exploratory kiss. Even though he could feel all his urges building inside him. The urge to be as close as possible. The urge to take off her garments one at a time. The urge to kiss her everywhere. With her mouth moving against his, slowly and lovingly, he wanted it all.

Then the carriage jolted over a bump in the road and their mouths broke apart. Charlotte's lips were puffy now and red, and her eyes held a dreaminess. He moved his hand from her face to her back, sliding it down slowly. Neither of them said anything as they took each other in. Antoine's mind had emptied of all thoughts except for those of her.

When she moved her hand from his shoulder to his back, he pulled her in closer and kissed her again. This time, he couldn't help touching, exploring, from her soft hair, down her exquisite neck. He put a hand on each of her shoulders and felt a surge of affection for her, so small and sturdy against him. She was the most precious creature. Resisting the urge to free her from her dress and ravish her, he moved his hands down either side of her, wrapped them around her waist, and held her as close as he could.

Their kiss was deep, filled with promise, but not urgent. And as silly as it was to think so, it reminded him of his first kiss. Not because of skill—Charlotte had some experience and good instincts. But because kissing a girl for the first time was like opening a door in a way. Sometimes it was simply a means to a physical end, going from one place to another. But sometimes, as it was with Charlotte now, it was seeing the world and all it could be for the first time. This was what he remembered thinking about his first kiss years ago, and it was what he was thinking now.

Kissing Charlotte was like coming out of a dark cave to see an expansive, colorful vista of enchanting possibility. Even there in the carriage, bumping through the streets, he knew he was forever changed.

When the carriage came to a full stop, Charlotte pulled away and turned enough to look where they were.

"Oh, no." She straightened up. "We're here. This is where I live."

Antoine, seeing stars after that kiss, gathered his wits quickly and looked past her out the window. The pretty stone facade was more ornate and somehow feminine than those on either side. He immediately wanted to go in and look at every detail of her life. She put her hand on the door.

"Charlotte, my dear, that was the best carriage ride of my life."

She smiled mischievously, her pupils dilated. "It was pretty great, wasn't it? But I have to go before Madame comes to see what's going on out here."

He passed her the bag of notebooks he'd been carrying for her since they left the restaurant, though his reluctance to do so nearly overwhelmed him.

"Thank you," she said and opened the door. "For everything. Really."

She stepped out and straightened her jacket. He called out, "You'll be hearing from me, Charlotte Deveraux."

As she walked toward the house, she turned and gave him a cute wave. Then she opened the door and disappeared inside.

Antoine swooned. Honest to goodness fell back into the seat and swooned. Then he called his address to the driver and the carriage moved off. He was definitely never going to be the same.

*Charlotte closed the* front door to the house on Rue de Fortuny and leaned against it to steady herself. Her heart felt like an apple bobbing on the surface of the ocean, floating away. She wiped her clammy hands on her skirt and went to the little window next to the door to see the carriage pull away with Antoine in it. In a moment, he was gone.

When Charlotte turned, Madame was coming out of the kitchen. "Bonjour, dear. I thought I heard someone come in. Have you been out all afternoon?"

"Oui, Madame. I walked the Champs-Élysées." She held her bag up. "And bought notebooks."

"Oh, good. Then you're familiarizing yourself with the city."

"I am. I found my new favorite stationery shop and had the most delicious vegetable soup for lunch at a café." Charlotte tended to become chatty when she wanted authority figures to like her, and she stopped herself from saying more. But then, with Madame's stoic eyes taking her in, she worried that perhaps all that intense kissing showed on her face. Or that Madame had seen Antoine in the carriage when they pulled up.

"Let's go up. You must be tired," Madame said, revealing no suspicion. Thank goodness she didn't seem to be the interrogation type.

The lower levels of the house were laid out similar to many in Paris, with the kitchen in the back, a small entry at the front on the street level, and the main living areas upstairs. Charlotte followed Madame up to the second floor and accepted her offer of coffee, which Cook was just bringing into the drawing room. Then she went up to her room to change and rest before dinner.

Upstairs, Charlotte closed her door and slipped out of her shoes. Alone, her thoughts raced across the memories of her afternoon. She wasn't even sure what to make of it all. Meeting Antoine again, spending the day together, and that carriage ride. That kissing.

Charlotte lay on her bed, staring at the ceiling, reliving every moment of her afternoon, every detail of Antoine. She didn't even know him. The more she thought about it, the more she realized how little she knew. At the same time, she had felt his heart beating in his chest, felt the brush of his lips on her skin, tasted his breath, tasted his warm skin and the wetness of his mouth. What they'd done had been deeply intimate. Especially after knowing each other for only a few hours. She surprised herself. He surprised her. And she couldn't stop thinking about it. When she sat up and tried to write, she couldn't gain any steam despite her energy. She'd come alive in a way that she didn't know yet how to put into words.

The next day, Charlotte settled into the faded green velvet settee that came with her room and placed her after-lunch coffee on the floor, preparing to read over the pages she'd produced that morning. There weren't many, not as many as yesterday, but there were pages. That was good enough. She stacked them against her lap and started reading and marking them up. Then she marked them up some more. She was just beginning to despair of their messy state when Nadine came dancing through her open door, making a characteristic grand entrance.

"A letter just came for you. Judging by the stationery, it's from someone fancy." She gleefully passed the envelope. The linen stock was indeed crisp and weighty.

Charlotte smiled before she could stop herself and thought of Antoine. She knew it was from him, or at least she hoped it was. What if it wasn't? She'd spent all day thinking about the electric feeling of kissing him, of being so close and somehow not close enough. He was probably why she'd only managed to write three pages.

"You little hussy," Nadine purred as she squeezed onto the chaise next to Charlotte. "Who is it from?"

"I don't know." She slid her finger under the flap and opened the envelope. She unfolded the single sheet and read.

*Mademoiselle,*
*My every moment has been filled with thoughts of you. Can you meet me for a stroll tomorrow afternoon?*
*Antoine de Larminet*

When Charlotte folded the paper again and looked up, Nadine's eyes gleamed with anticipation.

"So? I didn't bring the thing all the way up here for nothing."

Charlotte laughed. Despite her hesitation when Madame was around, she was now anxious to share her experience with a friend. Even if she knew so little about the man. "Do you know Antoine de Larminet?"

Nadine's mouth dropped. "Is that who wrote to you?"

"It is." Seeing Nadine's surprise, Charlotte stiffened, suddenly alarmed at what she didn't know about this man. Did he have some terrible reputation? Had she been roped in by a nefarious character who preyed on her naivety?

"Of course, I know him. Well, I know the name. He's very fancy; the stationery never lies."

"What do you mean by very fancy?"

"I mean high-class fancy. His father's a vicomte."

"You're kidding."

"No. I'm not. Where did you ever meet him?"

"At the café concert. And then again yesterday afternoon when I was walking." She sighed. "I keep bumping into him."

"You know, Madame will have a fit. He's the kind of man who will only marry a woman with a fancy title of her own. She'll say his intentions are less than honorable." Nadine looked at her pitifully. "And she won't be wrong, if I'm being honest."

Nadine was right. Fooling around with an aristocrat would make Charlotte look like a social climbing courtesan, a word that Madame had practically spit out like a mouthful of bad wine. If Antoine was indeed as interested as his letter suggested, it would not be with marriage in mind. Charlotte's heart sank then. Not because she wanted to marry, necessarily, but because she wanted him to be someone she could consider.

"He asks me to meet him for a stroll." Charlotte looked back at his letter.

"Are you going to?"

"It doesn't seem like I should."

"Did you like him?"

She frowned and sank deeper into the plush seat. "I kind of did."

"So meet him for a stroll. There's no harm in that. But be careful. And if it goes any further, at least hold out for something nice. He's got plenty of money." Nadine stared off dreamily for a moment. Then lit up. "Oh! You could write one of your stories about it!"

But an anger flared inside of Charlotte that engulfed any writing instincts she may have about her recent experiences. Thinking over all their chance meetings and interactions, she parsed his words for clues. He had impeccable manners, and he obviously had money. But how could he not tell her that he was a future vicomte? Or did he assume that she knew? And so then did he think she would want to be his mistress? That she was okay with that?

She'd been daydreaming about romance and fate and him. How could fate be so cruel?

# Chapter Four

*The next morning,* Antoine arrived at the breakfast table like a balloon about to float off. All his thoughts were on meeting Charlotte Devereaux later. Since parting company with her, he'd thought of a hundred things he wanted to tell her. A hundred ways he wanted to kiss her. The post hadn't come yet, but certainly her response would arrive, and he'd be in her company in a matter of hours. Not only for the potential kisses, but he needed to tell her about his title. He hadn't exactly meant to deceive her, but he'd enjoyed the fact that she didn't know. Many women in Paris, if they didn't recognize him, certainly knew the name. Charlotte hadn't. But he couldn't keep kissing her without telling her this most important aspect of his life.

Mother smiled at him as he took the seat across from her. She looked fresh and rested in her dark, high-necked dress. The spread was the same as always: croissants, jam, and coffee. The papers were laid out as usual. Morning light streamed in between the parted drapes. The chandeliers sparkle and cast rainbows onto the solemn landscape paintings that lined the walls. But his father was missing.

"Where's Papa?" Antoine chose the biggest croissant from the platter at the center of the table.

"He's gone to the country estate."

"Oh?" Antoine didn't remember his father mentioning any trips.

"Something's come up. Some opportunity he wanted to look into. He'll be back by the weekend."

That sounded vague, but Antoine was too inflated by his new acquaintance with Charlotte to truly acknowledge it or ask questions. He cut his croissant in half, exposing the buttery layers. And then he asked Mother to pass the jam. He spread on a thick layer and took a bite. What was Charlotte Deveraux having for breakfast?

"We're having dinner at the marquis's house tonight. I'll need you ready to leave by six-thirty."

"Oh." It was like his balloon popped. "I'd forgotten about that."

"You and Louise seemed to get along well at dinner Thursday night," she said primly.

"She seems nice enough."

"Nice enough?" The wrinkles in his mother's brow deepened. "You two had more to say than you've had with any other prospective matches I've hosted."

"Prospective matches? Are we still doing that?" Antoine forced a smile to dull his sharp tone.

"You're not married yet, so it seems we are." She shuddered with exasperation, raising her eyes toward the ceiling as if he were a frustrating child.

"And you want me to enter a courtship with her." What was the rush? Really. It wasn't as if his biological clock was ticking.

"That's the idea. Yes. You'll do well not to forget that women of good breeding are getting more difficult to find these days."

The phrase "good breeding" never failed to make him cringe. Entering a courtship with Louise de Montmorency and agreeing to a society marriage like Mother wanted so desperately was the last idea he wanted to pursue. Though this didn't necessarily have to impede the pursuit of other romantic entanglements, something about Charlotte was different. He only wanted to think about her. That's all he was capable of thinking about. Still, his mother had suffered enough in her life. No parent should have to bury two-thirds of their children, and Antoine had witnessed the change in her firsthand. There was a reason that the only wrinkles she had on her face came from scowling and not laughing.

"I'll be ready for dinner in plenty of time."

This wasn't an answer, per se. But it was an escape from the clutches of this conversation. Antoine stuffed the last bite of his croissant into his mouth and excused himself. On his way upstairs, he passed Emile and asked if any messages had come for him. Emile shook his head, and Antoine deflated even further. Why hadn't Charlotte responded to his letter?

In his room, he sat at his desk, pulled a sheet of crisp paper from the slot, and laid it flat in front of him. If Charlotte wouldn't respond, he would write to her again. He picked up his pen and removed the cap. With the chiseled point poised over the paper, he hesitated. He'd give anything to get out of dinner with the Montmorencys.

Something about writing to one woman while gearing up to meet another didn't feel good. He would have to be honest with Charlotte about his situation, but it all felt too new for that conversation. He needed more time.

Even though he desperately wanted to know her, he was also aware of the fact that contacting her, asking to see her again, was incredibly presumptuous. He wished he could be just a man writing to an enchanting woman. But the implication would always be loaded. A note was more than a note, especially to a woman from a different class. There was something unsavory about romantic gestures, even early ones, that could never end in marriage.

But that kiss! He had kissed women in carriages before, but none had ever turned him out like this. He started writing.

*Charlotte was coming* in from a walk when an envelope on the little table inside the door caught her eye. Claire often put letters here if the recipient wasn't at home to receive them. Charlotte recognized the paper and handwriting immediately. She tucked it under her arm and went straight up to her room to read it. Vibrating with anticipation and out of breath from climbing the stairs so fast, she went to her desk for her letter knife, cut open the envelope, and unfolded the paper that Antoine's hands had so recently dispatched. Her heart thumped hard as she read:

*Charlotte,*
*I was disappointed not to hear from you. It cast a pallor on my whole day. And my walk this afternoon felt dull in comparison to the one we took together. It seems Paris and my life achieve full color only in your company. When can we meet again?*
*Antoine*

Charlotte placed the letter into the back of her journal along with the first. She hadn't written Antoine back, and she wasn't going to now. After his letter arrived and Nadine revealed his identity, Charlotte swore Nadine to secrecy and closed herself in her room. She furiously wrote two scenes involving a sneaky, underhanded man, even though they didn't seem to fit in any of the stories she'd been working on. While many women might have been thrilled to attract the attention of such a wealthy and powerful man, she was not. Not at all.

She couldn't fall for a man like Antoine. And she had to treat their encounter as a minor indiscretion, not a life-altering kiss.

All that charm about her being his favorite writer, all those devastating smiles. He probably did this to women all the time. She'd fallen in with Paris's biggest flirt! Well, she may have been caught up for a moment, but she was no longer ensnared by his designs. Although writing him and telling him off would be more mature and direct, she felt silence in this case better communicated her disappointment.

She wished her friend Marie were here. The only person who knew about Antoine was Nadine, but she was busy with work and Charlotte had barely seen her since she delivered enlightenment with that first letter. Charlotte didn't want to tell any of her other housemates about him—not because she didn't trust them, but because she didn't want to make it any bigger than it already was. She wanted her feelings for Antoine to be over. Past.

Antoine's third letter arrived the following morning along with one from a paper Charlotte was waiting to hear from. Charlotte was in her room when Vanessa brought them up. Unlike Nadine, Vanessa passed the mail to Charlotte without seeming to notice the quality of the paper.

"Everything okay?" Vanessa said. She was dressed for work in one of her dark suits and an understated straw hat. "You've been quiet lately."

"Oh. Yes." Charlotte looked down at the envelopes. The one from the paper was larger and thicker than the one from Antoine, containing her manuscript, either marked up with editing suggestions or rejected and returned. "This is a response to a story I sent, so I suppose I'm a little nervous."

"Do you want me to stay while you open it? I know how hard rejection can be as a writer," Vanessa said. "I have a meeting, but I have a minute if you need a friend."

"I'll be okay. But thanks."

Vanessa smiled and left Charlotte with her two letters in her hands. She wasn't sure which one to open first, but she also knew the one from the paper could possibly contain good news. She cut it open and read what amounted to a very kind rejection of her work and a request that she send something else in the future. This was disappointing, as she'd hoped this story might fund another month in Paris. But she still had time to try and place it elsewhere. She set that letter down.

Antoine's handwriting on the other stirred all the memories of him that she'd been trying to settle. The way the light had fallen on his smiling face that afternoon by the river. The way it felt to walk next to him. The pressure of his mouth on hers. The feelings were still so powerful, even if they could never move her to be with him.

*Charlotte, my dear, for a long day I have been stalking messengers in hopes of a word from you. I fear the worst—illness, injury, all manner of disaster. But I know most likely that I may have unintentionally angered you, or that something has set you against me, whether true or false. Or that I may have presumed. My instinct is to send flowers—massive amounts of them. Tulips of every color. But I fear making it worse. In any case, I would prefer a dressing down to silence. Please, Charlotte. Write to me.*

Presumed. That was the operative word. Everything about their situation was based on presumption. Charlotte was guilty of it too, presuming he was a regular man, and now presuming his intentions were less than honorable. They hadn't talked about any of this, and she had no idea what he was thinking in those regards. If he was thinking about it at all. Were her presumptions preventing some other truth from being revealed?

More likely, and this was perhaps what she feared most, her presumptions were only a few steps ahead. Not responding was better than leading him to think that she might be amenable to that. She didn't even want him to ask. She couldn't let him think she'd be open to the idea of being his mistress when she wouldn't.

Charlotte didn't feel superior to the people who chose that lifestyle. The only reputation she was prepared to attach to her name was literary in nature. But the way her housemates gossiped, it seemed almost everyone in Paris was either a mistress or had one, and no one cared about marriage or bad taste or broken hearts. Here she was again presuming.

Antoine hadn't asked Charlotte to become his mistress, and she wasn't going to give him the opportunity. She wanted to remember their little encounter in its pure, passionate state, contained in that cab and unspoiled by reality. A flame extinguished before it could catch and burn everything in her life down. A flame that could burn on forever in her imagination as perfect and intense. Charlotte put Antoine's third letter in her journal along with the others and went down to see if lunch was ready yet.

The next day, Charlotte received another rejection on a story and a letter from her friend Marie back in Vernon, but no letter from Antoine. Again, the day after that, no letter. She was disappointed, but certain that she'd made the wise choice. Better for things to end like this than drag it out and let it grow into a huge emotional mess. She had stories to finish and send out. She needed to focus on work.

*Charlotte's cab rolled* to a stop in front of a mansion in the eleventh arrondissement. She thanked the driver as she exited the carriage and turned to look at the place. It was more a house than an office building, but next to the stately front door was a plaque that read: The offices of La Fronde. Inside was even more homelike with potted palms and floral drapes, unlike any other office Charlotte had seen. It was both welcoming and awe inspiring.

The young woman at the reception desk greeted Charlotte and showed her to another, larger room. They passed four desks arranged in a square. Three of the desks were occupied by other women, two of whom looked up and smiled to acknowledge Charlotte and one who seemed so caught up in her work that she didn't even notice. These women weren't here to socialize; they were changing the world for women one paper at a time. Charlotte took the spare desk that sat off to the side and faced a window.

"Let me know if you need anything," the receptionist said.

"Oh, yes, is my editor here? Anais Blanchet?"

"Yes. Her office is upstairs." She nodded toward a staircase at the back of the room.

As the receptionist left her, Charlotte considered knocking on her editor's door now. They'd never met in person, even though they'd exchanged several letters. And Charlotte had another story in her bag that she hoped Mademoiselle Blanchet would want to publish. But then she decided it would be better to type everything first, so she could hand her the story that was due and suggest the new one at the same time. She got straight to work, feeding a clean sheet of paper into the machine, lining it up, and setting her hands on the keys.

For the first two installments of her series, Charlotte had typed her handwritten drafts on her father's machine in the bookshop office. Mademoiselle Blanchet had offered to let her use one of their machines when Charlotte moved to Paris. This was Charlotte's first time in the building, and her first time seeing the famed publication up close. Everyone knew *La Fronde* as an extension of the publisher Marguerite Durand's outsized personality and feminist spirit. Charlotte had been relatively ignorant of Durand and *La Fronde* until Vanessa, who worked at a different publication, filled her in. Almost everyone who worked there, from the front desk to the loading docks in the back, was a woman. All the writers and photographers and artists were women, and they published articles and stories about the world from a distinctly feminine perspective. And they covered more than clothing and gossip. This was revolutionary in publishing and business.

Charlotte typed away, making final adjustments to her sentences as she went. She wasn't the fastest typist, but she liked the sounds of the machine and the weight of the buttons under her fingers. Someday, hopefully soon, she'd have one of her own sitting on the desk at Madame's. All the while Charlotte worked, she didn't see one man.

She stopped only to shake out her hands and when Marguerite Durand strode through and caught every eye in the place. She was a stunning woman, dressed in a pale gray suit with a ruffled pink blouse underneath. Her hat, which she was unpinning as she walked through, had pink and orange feathers.

When she'd typed the end, Charlotte stacked her pages against the table and stood up. Two of the three women at the desks had gone, and the fourth desk was now occupied by another serious-looking woman a little older than Charlotte. How was it that every woman in Paris managed to look so sophisticated while Charlotte felt so simple in comparison? The woman smiled, nodded at Charlotte, and then returned to her typing. Charlotte followed the stairs up to a narrow hallway that was papered in a colorful floral pattern. Both sides were lined with office doors that were painted green. When she found one with her editor's name, Charlotte knocked.

A muffled "Yes?" came from inside, and Charlotte stepped inside. The dark-haired woman with glasses smiled expectantly from behind her desk. Anais Blanchet, based on her letters, was a stickler about commas and had a masterful way of pushing Charlotte's writing in small ways that made it so much better. Charlotte didn't have to meet Anais Blanchet to know she admired her, and she didn't want this last installment to be the last thing she wrote for her either.

"Oh, Charlotte, come in and sit," Mademoiselle Blanchet said when Charlotte introduced herself. "I didn't know that was you out there typing. Please call me Anais."

The office was small, but it had a big window looking out over the courtyard. Her wide wooden desk was clean and uncluttered aside from a typewriter and a stack of newspapers. There was an abstract pastel painting in a simple frame on the wall and a low shelf filled with books. When Charlotte handed her the typed pages, Anais said, "So this is it, then?"

"That's it. The dramatic conclusion."

"Well, I'm excited to read it. We've had a lovely response from readers."

"That's nice to hear." Charlotte recognized her chance. As hard as it could be to put herself out there and pitch her work, she knew she needed to take advantage of every opportunity she got. "I have another story, a shorter one, that I was hoping you'd also consider."

"Oh good. Yes, we'd love another story from you. Do you have it with you now?"

"I typed it on your machine after I finished the other one. I hope you don't mind." She passed the stack of pages across the desk.

"Not at all." Anais quickly looked over the top of the first page, where the title and Charlotte's name and address were centered on the page. She nodded approval. "I can't read it now, unfortunately. But I'll look at it tonight."

"Of course," Charlotte said, barely containing her thrill that she could sell another story to a publication she was so excited about being a part of. She'd been reading it daily since she arrived in Paris, and had fallen quite in love with it. She'd recognized all the names on the doors. After watching everyone in the office all morning, she could easily envision herself a regular here, borrowing the typewriter, existing and working among such smart and dedicated women. She wanted to know them all.

"Have you met Marguerite yet?"

"You mean Madame Durand?"

"Yes," Anais said, nodding as if a person as prominent as Marguerite Durand was accessible to a person like Charlotte. "I think she's still here, and I know she'd love to meet you."

"She would?"

"Let's go see if she's still around." Anais rose from her seat and Charlotte followed her back out into the hallway. They walked to the end, where a door that looked like all the others stood ajar.

Anais knocked on the jamb and stepped inside. This office was three or four times the size of Anais's and decorated like a comfortable drawing room with landscape paintings in gilded frames, a colorful plush carpet, and potted palms. Madame Durand was seated on a striped chaise longue with her feet tucked under her skirts and a newspaper in her lap. She uncurled herself and stood when Anais introduced Charlotte.

"*The* Charlotte Devereaux. It's lovely to finally meet you." Madame Durand held out her hand to Charlotte. "Your stories have had everyone in my salon talking for weeks."

"I'm so flattered," Charlotte said.

"I don't have much time before my next meeting, but please sit for a moment."

Charlotte and Anais settled onto the couch across from Marguerite. Her blonde curls were arranged in a pile on her head, and she's removed her ornate hat.

"Charlotte brought me another story to consider for the paper," Anais said.

"Oh, that's good news." Madame Durand's eyes glimmered with kindness and genuine interest. She asked Anais something about another story that they were working on. Charlotte watched them the way she'd watched the other ladies all morning. She'd seen enough business interactions at her parents' bookshop to know that most of the time business was conducted by men. Madame Durand was older than both Charlotte and Anais and strikingly beautiful in a way that Charlotte assumed a woman could only grow into. She was impeccably dressed and styled, feminine in every way, and still running her own widely read publication. Charlotte continued to be impressed, but also enlightened. Why couldn't everywhere be more like this? After her side conversation with Anais concluded, Madame Durand turned to Charlotte. "How long are you in Paris?"

"I'm not sure yet, but at least through July."

"How wonderful. Paris is lovely in summer. Where are you staying?"

"In the eighth, in a women's pension on Rue de Fortuny."

"That's wonderful." Madame Durand apprised Charlotte again. "I have loved your stories, you know. Absolutely loved them. You must come to my salon this Wednesday evening. So many people want to meet you."

"I can't imagine why," Charlotte said modestly. She was still getting used to the idea that people were reading her work and having opinions about it.

"Well, you're the provincial young woman who managed to make us all stop and think. And laugh!"

The receptionist came in then, with a stack of mail under her arm and a tray of coffee and madeleines balanced on her hand. "Marguerite, your two o'clock meeting is here."

"Give me just a minute and then send him in." She turned back to Charlotte. "Please come Wednesday. After dinnertime. I'd love to have you, and you'll meet enough people to keep you busy the whole time you're in the city."

Charlotte got a little jolt of pleasure from Madame Durand's insistence. It felt good to be wanted. And an invitation like this could definitely help her career. "I wouldn't miss it."

"Good! Now, mademoiselles, I must shoo you out. I need to win an argument with a man."

They left Madame Durand's office as a gentleman with a self-satisfied air was going in. Anais walked Charlotte back out to the reception area, and before they parted ways, Charlotte asked her if she'd be at Madame Durand's salon.

"Not this week, but I've been a few times before," she smiled warmly. "It's mostly society people. So wear your best dress and be ready to join in the discourse."

# Chapter Five

*Antoine watched the* ball soar through the morning sky and ran across his side of the court to put himself in position. As it fell, he pulled his arm back and swung, hitting the ball right where he wanted to, sending it back to Guillaume. They'd been playing together since they were kids, and this was their third game that morning. Guillaume was getting tired, his late night wearing on him, and Antoine only needed to score one more time to win best of three. He rarely beat Guillaume, but he was going to beat him this morning. With much exertion, Guillaume returned the ball. Antoine met it with a backhand volley, landing the ball just out of Guillaume's reach, and scoring the game point.

"That's it, my friend." He smiled like a wolf at Guillaume, who was panting and seemed ready to collapse.

"Let's go get a drink," Guillaume said as he tried to catch his breath.

Antoine's first thought was that he had to go home and check the post. But he hadn't heard from Charlotte in a few days, and there was no reason to hope today would be different. "How about lunch?"

"I'm in for both." Guillaume Allard was Antoine's oldest friend. His father came from humble beginnings to make a fortune investing, and his mother, who had a vaguely aristocratic background, was a dear friend of Antoine's mother. Like Antoine,

Guillaume's family was wealthy enough that Guillaume led a leisurely existence.

They walked toward the showers, stopping an attendant for a glass of water on the way. The summer heat was just taking hold of the day, but the early morning fog had blown off, leaving the blue sky empty and bright. After cleaning up and getting dressed, Antoine was hungry, and Guillaume looked as if he'd make it after all.

The club restaurant was a small affair, an afterthought to the modern courts. But the menu included both sandwiches and American whiskey, so Antoine and Guillaume often found themselves there. They sat at a little table by the window, where they could look out on the green space that secluded the club from the rest of the city.

After the server had taken their order and departed, Guillaume said casually, "Any word from your lady writer?"

"No. And it's been nearly a week."

"It sounds like I should stop asking." Guillaume sipped his whiskey and met Antoine's eyes. He'd been there at the cabaret when he met Charlotte, and he was the only person Antoine had told about their afternoon together.

Antoine nodded. "I believe you should, sadly."

When Antoine didn't hear back from Charlotte after three letters, he stopped himself from writing to her again every time the impulse struck—a thousand times probably. Instead, he'd gotten drunk. He'd played tennis every morning and a few times long into the afternoon. He'd gone to three different cabarets. Everywhere, he kept waiting for Charlotte to appear. She did not. His longing to see her again and talk to her and kiss her was like a physical craving that nothing else seemed to satisfy.

"Maybe she's gone back to the provinces."

"I don't know for sure, but I'm afraid it has to do with the fact that I didn't tell her who I am."

"What do you mean?"

"I didn't tell her I'm in line to be vicomte."

"You spent an afternoon with her and failed to mention your title? That must be a first."

"Very funny. I don't lead with my title, Guillaume. It didn't come up. She didn't know. She didn't ask. And I didn't come out and say it."

"And you think she's found out?"

"I don't know. She lives with other women and could have mentioned my name. Someone could recognize it." He sipped his whiskey thoughtfully. "I'm grasping, maybe, but you don't understand. She walked into me on the street. Then she was at Quat'z'Arts. And then she sat down right next to me at Maribelle's. Right next to me, Guillaume. She was everywhere. Christ, her story that everyone couldn't shut up about was in the newspaper. And I've never met anyone quite like her. You'll think I'm a fool for saying it, but there was a connection. A real connection. I've never felt quite like this about anyone. And I know she felt something too. You don't kiss like that if there's not something there. You can't possibly. Now suddenly she's gone. Nowhere. Unresponsive."

"Maybe you misread it. Most women would only be more interested because of the title, not less."

"But she's not most women. And I can't marry her."

"Maybe she came all the way to Paris to become an aristocrat's mistress."

Antoine was fairly certain she had not.

Their lunch arrived. A croque-monsieur for Guillaume and ratatouille and baguette for Antoine. And for a few minutes, they ate without speaking.

Charlotte was exactly the kind of woman Antoine would marry if it were up to him. He would probably never get bored. But that would be impossible. No, Charlotte hadn't come to Paris to be some rich man's mistress. He knew he should feel fortunate for his station and wealth, and he did. He understood, as his father had said so many times, that he'd come to appreciate it more with age. But there was also a particular weight to knowing that he couldn't always have what he wanted because of all those privileges. Not that it mattered now that Charlotte hadn't written him back.

Antoine bit into his bread, which was almost crusty and warm enough to make him forget his woes. Almost.

"Well, then, what about the marquis's daughter?" Guillaume asked after devouring almost half of his sandwich in a few bites. "That's a far less complicated situation, I assume."

Antoine laughed. Far less complicated indeed. But he'd been so preoccupied with thoughts of Charlotte that he'd almost forgotten about Louise. "That ball has been on my side of the court since Mother and I had dinner with them last week."

"You haven't seen her since?"

"No." Courtship protocol meant he should have visited by now. And Louise was fine. Dinner with her family had been fine as well. All aspects of his mother's marriage plans were lined up right in front of him. All he had to do was take the next step. In that respect, it was probably good that Charlotte had brushed him off. Even if his disappointment was so deep that it felt like heartache. "I suppose it couldn't hurt to do so."

"Probably couldn't."

"Not that you'd know anything about it," Antoine said. Guillaume's parents, more nouveau riche than aristocratic or traditional, were much more relaxed about his prospective marriage. They'd never pressured Guillaume to find anyone suitable or titled. When they did ask about his romantic affairs, it was to gauge his heart, not his prospects. Guillaume had no idea how lucky he was that his mother believed love was supposed to go with marriage.

"Ha." Guillaume smiled like he knew exactly how lucky he was. "Your backswing's improved. All your recent heartsick court time shows."

"Then I suppose that's something."

Later that afternoon, Antoine's father returned bright-faced and weary from his trip to their country estate. Antoine spoke to him only briefly when he came in, and then didn't see him again until dinner, which wasn't unusual. Antoine looked almost exactly like a younger version of his father with the same brown eyes and dark hair. But they weren't close or similar in personality. Antoine only expressed interest in the family affairs because he felt like he should. And his father did little to engage him. They both seemed perfectly content to stay out of each other's way.

But once the soup was served at dinner that night, his father, clean and rested, cleared his throat and said, "I have an announcement. A bit of good news."

Antoine looked from one smug parent to the other; whatever his father was about to reveal his mother already knew. "Let's hear it."

"I've accepted an offer on the country estate," he said with a tone of finality.

Antoine flinched. "I wasn't aware it was for sale."

"It's been in the works, you could say."

This was unexpected. Since his brothers' deaths, his parents' grief seemed magnified at the country estate. His was too. But it had been in the family for hundreds of years. It was the land that made them who they are, that came with the title. They had tenants on that property, families that had been linked to theirs for generations. "And now it's done?"

"It is done."

The surprise paralyzed Antoine's brain. He'd heard of other titled families selling out, but his parents were so hell-bent on tradition that he never dreamed they'd do something like this. "So who did you sell it to?"

"A property developer who has grand plans for tearing everything down and building a factory. To be honest, it was so painful to think about that I didn't really ask for much detail."

"Too painful? People still live there. They farm that property. What are they supposed to do?"

"They'll have to move, I suppose. Or maybe help with the building. Whatever they want."

All those people. Even though Antoine wasn't involved in the family estate business, he didn't know the tenants and their families. And Antoine knew exactly what happened to tenants when the landed gentry sold out. Forced out of their homes by some indifferent owner, their way of life rendered obsolete, they ended up in coal mines and slums.

His father took his mother's hand where it was resting on the table, presenting a united front. Then he continued, "By selling, we can buy a smaller country place if we like. And your mother and I will be able to afford to travel more without sacrificing our standard of living."

"Our standard of living? Father, how can you be so obtuse?" A mad heat rose through Antoine's chest. "Those people could starve. They're farmers."

His father squared his shoulders. "Well, adapt or perish. Isn't that what you're always saying? Modernity."

"That's not something you can fairly throw in my face when people are involved. We owed it to them not to sell, especially not to someone who intends to tear everything down."

"What's done is done, I'm afraid," Mother said. "Whatever happens now can't be helped."

Antoine looked down at his soup.. His anger spun in his mind until it became self-conscious. He was sitting in an elegant dining room, in the wealthiest neighborhood in Paris, eating with silver utensils off Limoges dishes, in a bespoke suit, while people in slums a few miles away were hungry. It wasn't fair. He thought of Charlotte and her story about the out-of-touch aristocrat and felt ashamed. Ashamed of his parents and who they were and every privilege that had been handed to them. He was part of society's scourge, the exploitive class. He was a part of the problem, and he was too small and comfortable and lazy to fathom a solution.

"I believe I've lost my appetite. If you'll excuse me."

"What?" Mother's mouth fell open. Father's brow furrowed in bafflement.

"I'll be in my room." Antoine got up and left the table, leaving his parents speechless.

"*Madame Durand invited* me to her salon," Charlotte said, beaming from the toile bench in the little drawing room where all of her housemates were gathered and drinking wine.

The women shrieked in delight. Madame Durand was an outspoken supporter of proletarian and women's causes. She was eccentric and flamboyant and had been known to walk a large exotic cat around the park. But she also kept upper-class company. Her ex-husband had been in government, and she had a child with a married aristocrat, according to rumors.

"Does she invite everyone who works for her?" Diane asked, refilling her wine glass. "Maybe I should work there?"

Diane had recently changed jobs, but Charlotte was beginning to suspect that was a frequent occurrence.

"It must be such an amazing place to work," Vanessa said dreamily. "And probably all the important people in publishing will be at the salon."

"I bet everyone will be doing drugs," Nadine said with a mischievous smile.

"I hope not," Charlotte said primly, and Nadine cackled.

"It's a salon, not Moulin Rouge. It will probably be a little dull," Diane said. She was more the dancing type than the intellectual conversation type of woman, not that there was anything wrong with that. Diane was barefoot and draped over the armchair where Madame always sat when she joined them on this side of the house. Then she perked up. "You'll need to go shopping."

"You'll need a fashionable dress. Not just something new, but something that makes an artistic statement," Catherine said, just as gleefully as her sister.

The American sisters had come to Paris largely for the shopping and were always thrilled to have an excuse to do more of it. It was hard not to when everyone in the city was so fashionable. And they were right. Charlotte's Vernon wardrobe wouldn't suffice for an evening at Madame Durand's.

"Something that defines your style, both as a writer and a successful woman," Diane agreed.

Of all her housemates, Charlotte had spent the least amount of time one-on-one with the American sisters because they worked long hours and often danced the nights away at this or that cancan venue. They talked about so many dance clubs that Charlotte couldn't keep them straight. But with their urging, what to wear became Charlotte's most pressing concern. She wouldn't know anyone but Madame Durand, and she needed to make a good impression in a room full of fancy people. But she also needed to remain true to herself. And stay within her tight budget, of course.

The next day Diane and Catherine took Charlotte to their favorite department store. Charlotte had never shopped in a department store before. Countless displays of clothes and hats and jewelry surrounded them, and the place was huge. It was all very convenient and overwhelming at the same time.

She found a ready-to-wear navy blue satin dress that was pretty and versatile enough that she could change the appearance (and get lots of wear out of it) with accessories. When Charlotte tried it on in the dressing room and looked at herself in the mirror, her first thought was of what Antoine might think of it. She quickly dismissed this thought though. He'd stopped writing, and although she couldn't seem to help herself from looking everywhere, she hadn't run into him again. And so she was facing the stark reality that she'd never see him again after all. That a woman like her could only bump into a man like him once or twice. She'd had her chance, and she'd made her decision. And so she pushed thoughts of him away and imagined all the people she might potentially meet at the salon instead.

The dress was too long and more expensive than she'd hoped, but not by too much. And it was the first new dress she'd had in ages. She couldn't keep borrowing dresses, and she'd known when she arrived that she'd eventually need to buy something. Now was the time. She'd just have to be conservative with her money, even more conservative than she was already. And hopefully, she'd sell a story soon. A seamstress raised the hem while they had coffee and a croissant in the store's café.

On the day of the salon, Charlotte put on her new blue dress and her only pair of dangly earrings. Then Catherine helped her curl and pin up her hair. They'd wrapped it in rags that morning, and all day Charlotte had worked with her hair in knots.

"Are you nervous?" Catherine asked, looking for a place to start unwrapping.

"Yes. Well, not about my hair." She watched in the mirror as Catherine pulled away a strip of cloth, leaving behind a coiled tendril of her dark hair.

"Well, smile as much as you can," Catherine said thoughtfully, pulling another coil of hair loose. Her long, blonde hair was braided and draped around her shoulders. She was dressed in one of her many frilly tea gowns. She and her sister had more clothes than Charlotte had ever seen a person own. "You're a lovely, intelligent woman with lots to offer. She wouldn't have invited you if that weren't the case. You'll probably be surprised."

"Thank you. I should write that down so I remember it when I feel like a provincial fool later."

"Ha." Catherine snorted. "I understand why you're nervous. Believe me. I came here all the way from America with only a classroom understanding of the language. It's hard to put yourself out there and go after what you want. And this is your first night out on your own in the city, right? I'd be nervous too. But it's never as bad as we worry it will be. You'll probably meet so many interesting people. And if they're snobs, then don't be afraid to find another wallflower and introduce yourself."

Catherine pulled the last strip of cloth from Charlotte's head, and there was a pile of waves quite different from her sleek, straight hair. With all that volume, Catherine started twirling and pinning it all strategically into a hill on Charlotte's head. When she was done, it looked far more sophisticated and elegant than Charlotte could ever accomplish on her own. She was grateful for the help. Without her friends to help her get ready for this, she probably wouldn't go.

It was going to take an inordinate amount of courage for her to get through the night once she arrived. She planned to talk with Madame Durand for as long as she could without being clingy, meet as many people as possible without clamoring for introductions, and then make a quiet exit. She could be in bed with her book before midnight.

When she was dressed and ready, Charlotte took a cab from Rue de Fortuny to the ninth arrondissement. The short ride carried her past the Palais Garnier, which sat like a cake on a platter in the middle of the city. She tried to think about it instead of how much was riding on this evening for her, career-wise. She needed to make a good impression. She needed to sell more stories. And because this was her first real opportunity to make professional connections in person, she inflated it with an exorbitant amount of importance in her mind. The part that made her most nervous was that she had no idea what to expect. She'd been to salons before, but not in Paris. Not hosted by Marguerite Durand.

When the cab stopped, she paid the driver and double-checked the numbers above the door. Then she took a deep breath and knocked. A moment later, a gentleman who appeared to be the butler opened the door and welcomed her inside.

"Madame Durand is in the drawing room to your right," he said, gesturing with his gloved hand. He had a grandfatherly, stuffy air that revealed little about himself or the house. What could this man have seen and heard, being employed by such an interesting, eccentric woman? "Let me know if you need anything."

"Thank you, monsieur." She smiled and stepped inside. The foyer was not much bigger than the entry of the house on Rue de Fortuny, but the finishes and decor were more luxurious. Instead of disappearing into the ceiling, the white marble stairs wrapped up and around the open second floor. Two men were leaning on the banister above, deep in conversation; they looked up when she came in and then went back to talking. An electric chandelier sparkled overhead. Down the little hall, there was another group of people talking. Music played on a record player somewhere and a soft din of conversation and laughter filled the house.

A smartly dressed couple on a settee glanced at Charlotte as she passed on her way into the drawing room, where most of the guest were congregating. There was a table of card players, a drink table where a woman in a black and white server uniform was pouring glasses of champagne, and a large group gathered in a seating area near the fireplace. Madame Durand was holding court in an armchair for a group of mostly women. She was dressed in an elegant red evening gown with ornate earrings and a small feathered clip in her hair. Although Charlotte hated to interrupt what seemed to be a lively conversation, she approached them and presented herself.

Madame Durand cried, "Ahh," upon seeing Charlotte and rose from her seat to kiss Charlotte on both cheeks.

"Join us, my dear," Madame Durand said, waving Charlotte to an open space on a couch nearby. The man sitting there shifted over a little to make room. Then Madame Durand addressed her group. "Everyone, this is Charlotte Deveraux. She's been writing a serial for us, and she wrote that story in *Le Figaro* that everyone was talking about a few weeks back."

And to Charlotte, she named everyone in the circle. "Monsieur and Madame Aubert are my neighbors and comrades. Monsieur Lefevre is the head of the printers union and my esteemed guest. His wife is playing cards. Severine, my dearest friend and a journalist I'd love for you to know, Charlotte. The best in France. Next, of course, Monsieur Patenaude, who is an editor at Palace Books and whom you should absolutely speak to about a collection of your stories. And, last but not least, these ladies are brilliant actresses: Camille Forche and Genevieve Meunier. Now don't worry, Charlotte, if you forget all of that. We're a friendly bunch. And welcome to society, my dear!"

Charlotte smiled and waved bonjour to everyone, then took the seat they'd made for her and listened as the conversation picked back up. They were talking about labor laws, a topic Charlotte only knew at surface depth. But they didn't stay there for long. The conversation shifted and flowed as people came and left from the assembled group. Several other people came after Charlotte, presenting themselves to Madame Durand and then either hanging around or wandering off to see who else was at the party.

When the people between them on the couch left, Monsieur Patenaude moved down and held out his hand to Charlotte.

"I liked your story very much."

"Thank you. That's wonderful to hear," Charlotte said.

"Don't tell Marguerite, but I haven't read the series in her paper yet." He winked at her conspiratorially. "But I have all the papers on my nightstand and plan on reading them in the days leading up to the final installment. I do that often when there's a series I know I'll like."

He spoke with an undercurrent of excitement about literature, which Charlotte recognized and appreciated immediately.

"You're very talented, and your work has started a conversation. As a publisher, I'd be a fool not to ask if you have enough stories for a collection."

"Well, no, not yet. But I've been working so much since coming to the city that I'm probably not far off." This wasn't exactly a lie, she hoped. She had three stories, not including the ones from *Le Figaro* and *La Fronde*, that she felt really good about. Selling a collection seemed like something she was nowhere near ready for, like a distant dream. But maybe it shouldn't be. Selling a book could help stabilize her income. "How many exactly would I need?"

"Well, that depends on the length, but a book needs a hundred and fifty pages or so to make it worth the effort." He reached into his coat pocket and produced a card. "I'm giving you this before I forget. If you want to put something together, I'd love to take a look at it."

Charlotte, whenever she was faced with opportunities like this, could never tell if it was her hard work paying off or luck. Maybe it was both. "I'll do that, monsieur. Thank you. You have no idea how thrilled I am."

"Well, I'm thrilled to get to you first."

Monsieur Patenaude's petite, bejeweled wife came up to him then. She touched his arm, taking his attention away from Charlotte. "Are you ready to play, dear. It's almost our turn."

While they talked, Charlotte fingered his card and then tucked it into the little pocket on her skirt. How quickly could she get together a hundred and fifty pages of stories? She had the two pieces that were already published. Those should go into her first collections, and her contracts allowed it.

"Charlotte Deveraux, it was a pleasure chatting with you. But the card table is calling me."

"The pleasure was all mine." Charlotte smiled again at the Patenaudes and stood as they left the seating area.

"Don't lose my card," Monsieur Patenaude said over his shoulder as his wife led him away.

Charlotte, finding herself unengaged in conversation and elated by the publisher's enthusiasm for her work, went to the refreshment table. The server had just brought out a fresh pot of coffee, and Charlotte poured herself a cup, thinking she might try to get a cab home as soon as she finished. She'd accomplished everything she had hoped for the evening, and she had a lot of work she wanted to do in the morning.

She was stirring cream into her coffee when a small commotion of guests arriving drew her eye to the door. She hadn't expected to see any familiar faces among them because she hardly knew anyone in the city. But standing there, eyes on her, was Antoine de Larminet.

# Chapter Six

*As soon as* Charlotte's eyes met Antoine's, his smile faltered and his eyes flashed like a hook had been set. And the small longing that had taken up residence in Charlotte's chest unfurled. Antoine was devastatingly handsome in his black suit and white bow tie. His dark hair combed to the side and his brown eyes filled with his compelling humor. Seeing him again was like being in that cab, pressed together in a passion so perfect and consuming. Her body hummed. Whatever was between them had not been extinguished by her nonresponse to his letters. Thinking it could be now seemed like a joke. Charlotte, frozen in the spot where she stood, didn't know what to do.

Madame Durand welcomed Antoine and his friends into the throes of her salon. One of the gentlemen with Antoine introduced the others to Madame and the guests in her vicinity. Antoine seemed to be trying not to look at Charlotte because every time he did, his eyes flicked away. He carried himself with ease and confidence, and everyone seemed eager to meet him. It was because of his social status. Everyone wanted to meet the aristocrat in the room. The man who'd kept her company for hours and kissed her witless was not like other people. He was not like her. She sipped her coffee and turned her back to the scene. She'd established the silence, and so she should maintain it. She needed to get away.

Charlotte found an empty spot on a sideboard for her coffee and set it down. It was delicious, but she couldn't finish it. She needed to find the butler, but if she couldn't, then perhaps she could hail a cab on the street. She'd seen Nadine do it. Then as she turned toward the door, he was there, standing in front of her like he was ready to catch her.

"Charlotte Deveraux." He took her hand, warming it through her glove, and kissed it, eyes locked on hers. "I saw you from across the room, plotting your escape from me."

He said it quietly because curious faces watched them from seemingly everywhere. She bowed when he released her hand and greeted him properly and with as much indignation in her tone as she could muster. "Vicomte de Larminet."

"Indeed." His face fell as her subtle strike hit. But it didn't deter him. He nodded apologetically and looked her in the eyes. His were so dark and pleading. "I'm terribly sorry for any confusion, Mademoiselle Devereaux. But before we talk about that, which I hope we will before the night is over, I want to introduce you to my friends."

Before she could protest, Antoine had drawn her to his companions, who were talking to a small group that included the Patenaudes. When he had their attention, Antoine said, "Guillaume, this is the writer I've been telling you about."

Guillaume, whom Charlotte recognized from that first night at the Quat'z'Arts, smiled at her knowingly and kissed her hand. "It's lovely to meet you, mademoiselle."

"And this is Marquis Renee de Conradines, who I happen to know is hooked on your series in *La Fronde*."

"I'm thrilled to make your acquaintance, mademoiselle. When Madame Durand told me you were writing for her paper, I was hoping I'd get to meet you," Renee said, kissing Charlotte's hand. Then to Monsieur Patenaude he asked, "Have you met Mademoiselle Deveraux?"

"I have," Monsieur Patenaude said, winking at Charlotte. "She's already promised me a collection."

"You work fast!" Renee turned his attention back to Charlotte. "So tell me, mademoiselle, are you in Paris now? I thought you were from somewhere up north."

"Yes to both, monsieur. I am from Vernon, but I've been in Paris for a few weeks."

And just like that, Charlotte was swept into a conversation with Antoine's friends about her work and plans. They were friendly and interested, charming like Antoine, who listened and watched intently. The brief disruption their arrival had caused was over, and they'd been fully incorporated into the salon, which seemed to be ramping up instead of slowing down with the hour.

When the conversation shifted away from Charlotte, Antoine, who was still at her side, said close to her ear, "Now that you've changed your mind about leaving the party, let's get you a drink."

Charlotte forgot all about her bed and her book. With a light hand on her back, he led her to the refreshment table and asked for a champagne and a whiskey. When he handed her the delicate flute, his fingers touched hers for a brief, heavenly moment that made her desperately thirsty.

"I suppose I shouldn't be, but I am surprised to see you here," Charlotte said.

"I have been a little worried I'd never see you again." He said it earnestly, and the look in his eyes revealed a desperation that felt so similar to hers. She was both relieved and crushed to see her feelings reflected in him. And why did she still like him so much? She needed to keep in mind that he'd deceived her.

"Is that why you're here, in my publisher's house?"

"No. I promise. Guillaume and Renee and I had dinner at a restaurant, and Renee mentioned stopping at a salon when we finished early. I had no idea. Though as soon as I realized, I hoped."

"And here I am, despite all my efforts to avoid you."

"Is that what you're doing, then?"

"Avoiding you?" He was baiting her into a conversation that could get her into trouble. People were watching them. "I'm afraid I barely know you, Monsieur le Vicomte."

His eyebrows shot up. He looked around the room for potential listeners, then he leaned toward her ear and said barely above a whisper, "My dear, Charlotte, you have my deepest apologies for misrepresenting myself. But you must understand that although I may have withheld this single detail of my life, I presented myself honestly in every other way. And I never meant to deceive you."

She looked away. "Deception is deception."

"It is. And I'm sorry. But I didn't mean any harm. I like you Charlotte. Very much. And I wanted you to see me as only me. Not as a title. Just as a man who very much enjoyed spending the day with a woman."

"You know it's not that simple."

"I know."

"I never would have…" She trailed off for a moment but met his gaze. She'd kissed a few men, none of whom she ever considered marrying. But kissing a man who wouldn't marry her because of her class was something different. "If I had known."

Antoine drew his mouth into a line and nodded. "Understood."

"It won't happen again."

"As you wish." He moved a hand like he was going to touch her, but then stopped. "Mademoiselle. Charlotte. Tell me we can still be friends."

"I think acquaintances might be more appropriate."

"My dear, I think we left appropriate somewhere along the Champs-Élysées a week ago."

She laughed. She couldn't help it. He was so chastened and seemed so genuine, without losing his lightheartedness. She couldn't resist. "Perhaps we should pretend like the Champs-Élysées never happened."

"If that's how you'd like to proceed." Antoine took a deep breath and let it out. His relief endeared him to her even more. He continued, "But for goodness sake, it's the twentieth century. Please don't ever call me Monsieur le Vicomte again. I will inherit the title one day, but it's not mine yet."

She laughed again, but couldn't let him out of trouble so easily. "Acquaintances, then."

"Mademoiselle, you destroy me. Shall we rejoin the group?"

She followed him toward where his friends were talking with Madame Durand and completely forgot about wanting to leave.

*The fire crackled,* and Antoine, who'd set the group loose on the topic of *Les Misérables*, drank the last swallow of his second whiskey. Madame Durand put on a vigorous salon but lacked in waitstaff. Antoine lamented this now because refreshing his own drink meant getting up from his seat next to Charlotte.

"I read something quite critical of Hugo's relying so heavily on coincidence to further the plot," Renee said. Antoine, who loved Hugo, had heard him make this same argument before. "That it weakens the novel's power, and I can't say I don't agree."

"I respectfully disagree," Charlotte chimed in, sitting up straighter in the seat. A light flush had risen on her cheeks. Antoine had never seen anyone so marvelously and adorably flustered. "I think the coincidences give the novel an almost magical quality, like the forces of the universe are at work on Jean Valjean. And in a way, it solidifies his character's representation of humanity, as well as Javert as morality and Thénardier as sin."

Renee, who perked up in the armchair, said, "You know, I never considered it that way. But I see what you mean. It adds a mythic quality to the whole story."

Charlotte nearly jumped from her seat in delight. She had completely charmed his friends with her wit. Guillaume was quite taken with her. Though the old boy kept a respectful distance. Even Renee, whom Guillaume had described as a snob on more than one occasion, was captivated. She was the rarest sort of woman whose beauty was both physical and infused in her personality. Her laugh was like a little bell ringing. She was well-spoken with the slightest hint of an accent that was pleasant rather than rough. Confident and witty. Well-read. The kind of person you could talk to for the rest of your life and never get bored.

When the conversation lulled, Charlotte announced, "I'm afraid I must be going."

"So soon?" Antoine said. "It's not even midnight."

She smiled and set down her now-empty champagne glass. "Midnight and I haven't been friends in ages."

Charlotte rose from her seat, and all the men rose too. She bowed and extended her hand to Guillaume and Renee in turn, who expressed their regrets at her departure and hopes that they'd have the chance again.

Then she turned to Antoine and said a benign goodnight.

"I insist we send you home in the carriage."

"Oh, that's not necessary." She stepped away from the group.

"I insist as well," Renee said, backing up Antoine. "We won't need it before you're done. Please."

Charlotte looked between the two men and acquiesced. "Thank you. That's much appreciated."

"I'll see you out," Antoine said, following her.

"Thank you. Just let me say goodnight to the hostess."

He lingered while Charlotte spoke to Madame Durand, who kissed Charlotte on both cheeks and eyed Antoine suspiciously when he said he was sending Charlotte home in the Marquis Renee de Conradines's carriage. Charlotte didn't seem to notice. They found the butler in the otherwise deserted foyer. He was reading the evening edition of *Le Figaro*, which he set aside at their approach. And when he left them alone to call up the carriage, Antoine took Charlotte's hand.

"I'm so happy you were here and that you didn't run from me when you saw me come through the door," he said.

"I will admit I wanted to."

"I deserve that." He tried to catch her eyes, but she was looking down at her hands. "And now?"

"And now we part ways." Finally, she looked at him. "It was a pleasure to see you, Antoine. Thank Marquis de Conradines for me again for the use of his carriage."

The butler returned. The driver was bringing the carriage around now. Antoine desperately wanted to walk her out, kiss her goodbye, or even hop in the carriage and ride with her home. But he hesitated. The butler would see her off, and the gentlemanly thing to do, the thing she wanted him to do, was say goodbye. Antoine nodded and kissed her dainty hand. Then the butler opened the door for her. Charlotte thanked him and passed through, looking back as she walked away. She smiled wistfully at Antoine, and then the door closed and she was gone.

Antoine suppressed the urge to push open the door and follow her. He returned to his friends, refilled his whiskey, and pasted a smile on his face to fake interest for the rest of the evening.

Even later, after the marquis's carriage had returned from Rue de Fortuny and they were all leaving Madame Durand's salon, Antoine was still thinking about Charlotte. Leaving his meetings with her up to chance was no longer an option. Guillaume and Renee were quieter and more subdued on the ride home than they'd been on the ride there, breaking the silence only to reminisce on a moment or share a bit of gossip. Just before his stop, Antoine suggested to Renee, as casually as he could, that Charlotte Devereaux would make a delightful addition to the guest list for his upcoming ball.

"That's not a bad idea," Renee said passively. He was drunk now and probably tired.

Guillaume, on the seat opposite, was looking at Antoine like he'd lost his mind. "Louise de Montmorency is sure to attend. That means your intended fiancée and intended mistress in one ballroom?"

"The marquis and his family are invited," Renee said to clarify just how sticky a situation Antoine was asking for.

"It's not like that. Charlotte is a friend."

"A lovely friend," Renee said almost suggestively.

"A lovely friend for me." Antoine scowled.

"Ha. Friend indeed. You look like you're ready to kill me!" Renee patted Antoine on his knee. "Don't worry. I already have my hands full with my wife and my mistress."

Guillaume, stifling a laugh, turned toward the window. He didn't have mistresses or a wife. Guillaume had petite amies. A long history of girlfriends; some lasted for a weekend, some for several months, but always one at a time. He fell in and out of love like a planet circling the sun, over and over again.

"So you'll invite her then?" Antoine pressed for a definite answer as the carriage rolled to a stop in front of his house.

"I believe I will." Renee straightened on the bench. The streetlight outside cast a shadow across his face. "And not only because she's lovely and smart, but also because the presence of anyone from the lower classes will scandalize my mother and sisters."

*Charlotte was reading* in her room the next afternoon when Madame called up about a delivery for her. She set her book aside and went down, along with all her housemates who couldn't resist finding out what had been delivered. In the foyer, a young man dressed in a well-worn blue work coat and scuffed boots held a bulky box in his arms. Madame was standing there, arms crossed, regarding it in her characteristic way: with suspicion.

"I have instructions to put it on Mademoiselle Deveraux's desk," the courier said. "That's if she has one, madame."

"What is it?" Madame asked Charlotte.

"Well, I'm not sure."

"It's a typewriter, mademoiselles. A heavy one. Do you mind showing me to your desk?" He bent, obviously straining under the weight.

"Oh, of course," Charlotte said. She started up toward her room, and everyone, including Madame, followed.

Charlotte cleared her notebook and drafts from the center of her desk and the courier placed the box. For a moment, everyone stood there looking at it, unsure what to do.

"Is there a note or a card?" Charlotte asked.

"There is, mademoiselle." He pulled an envelope from the interior pocket of his jacket and passed it to her.

The stationery. Antoine. And here she was with everyone watching her, waiting to see who'd sent this extravagant gift. She said to the courier, "Let me get you a tip."

"Oh, no, thank you, mademoiselle." He held up a broad, boyish hand. "I'm under strict instructions not to accept it. Not to worry, the gentleman has compensated me well. I'll show myself out."

Madame started to follow him and then stopped, watching Charlotte as intently as the others. Everyone was waiting for her to open the gift. So Charlotte set the envelope down and released the hook on the front of the box. She lifted the lid and there was a shiny black typewriter, similar but sleeker and newer than the one at *La Fronde*. Vanessa gasped like a piece of beautiful art had just been revealed.

Madame clucked her tongue and said, "My goodness, that looks noisy."

Nadine whispered, "Ooh, la la."

"So who's it from?" Catherine asked.

Charlotte hesitated for a breath, then she slid her finger under a corner of the envelope flap and worked it open. She didn't need to read the letter to answer the question, but she unfolded and read it silently while her audience stood there watching.

*Charlotte,*
*The machine is a token of friendship—mine and Renee's. Your wit and conversation last night were a pleasure. When Renee learned you were toting your drafts across town to borrow Durand's typewriter, he insisted that would never do. He's right, of course. A writer of your skill and potential deserves the best.*
*Sincerely,*
*Antoine de Larminet*

"How nice." Charlotte refolded the paper. Her body warmed with the knowledge that they must have talked about her after she left the party. She held the letter against her chest. Her audience gazed at her expectantly. "Last night at the salon, I got into a conversation about my work with two gentlemen who were apparently impressed. They say it's a token of their friendship."

"Impressed and rich, I'll say," Diane said. "Good for you."

After riding in that luxurious carriage, calling them rich almost seemed like an understatement. And now this expensive gift.

"Will you keep it?" Catherine asked, watching Madame, whose scowl hadn't softened.

"Of course she'll keep it, silly," Diane said. "Why wouldn't she?"

"You know how gentlemen can be," Madame said. "An elaborate gift can be a symbol of intentions."

"Oh, no. This was all above board, wasn't it, Charlotte?" Nadine smiled at her encouragingly. "Charlotte's not the kind of girl for funny business."

Perhaps chastened, Madame withdrew her assertion. "Of course, Nadine, I know that. But now that all the fuss is over, I'm going back to my shopping list. Otherwise, there won't be anything to eat all week."

Madame made her way out of the room, followed by the housemates, who had also lost interest. All except Vanessa, who lingered after the others had gone.

"That's an awfully nice present," she said, wanting to know more.

"It is, isn't it?" She wasn't sure what else to say. Nadine was still the only person she'd told about Antoine. She wasn't hiding it from her friends, exactly, but talking about it seemed to make it a bigger deal than she wanted it to be. "You can borrow it anytime you like."

"Thank you," Vanessa said, still lingering. "I should tell you something, though. It's a small thing, something I'd almost forgotten about. But now that this gift has arrived, I feel I should say."

"What is it?"

Vanessa smiled like a cat with a mouse. "Well, by any chance, was this gift from Antoine de Larminet?"

Charlotte took in a sharp breath. "Shit, yes. Why?"

"Let me show you." Vanessa nodded toward the door. Charlotte followed her while Vanessa explained. "It's nothing really. At least it won't look like much to anyone who sees it. I just think you should know."

Vanessa's room had similar furnishings and layout to Charlotte's, but her window faced the back of the house instead of the street. Unlike Nadine and the American sisters, Vanessa had more books and papers than clothes. Charlotte hadn't had a chance to properly look at Vanessa's books, but this probably wasn't the time. Vanessa pulled a paper from the stack next to her bed. She searched the pages for a moment, and then put her finger on whatever it was she wanted Charlotte to see.

"Here." Vanessa passed the paper. "It's the gossip column in *Le Petit Parisien*."

There in the text was Charlotte's name. Her eyes found it immediately. She scanned for the beginning of the sentence, passing Antoine's name as she went. Her whole body tingled as she read: "The future vicomte and Paris's favorite aristocrat, Antoine de Larminet, was quite cozy on Madame Durand's settee with the provincial writer Charlotte Devereaux. Whatever story she was telling held him rapt." She kept reading, but everything else amounted to nothing more than a roll call of guests and who was seen with whom. Charlotte hadn't noticed anyone taking notes, but the place was full of journalists after all.

"It's just the two lines," Vanessa said, bringing Charlotte back to the room.

"Yes. But 'quite cozy'?"

"Not how you would describe it?"

"Not exactly. I've encountered him before, around. He's quite handsome. But we aren't cozy. We're… friends. Acquaintances really."

"I believe you."

"Others may not, though. Do you know the writer?"

"I met her once, but only in passing. He's in line to be a vicomte, so he's often in the papers. Seen here or there with so and so, that sort of thing."

"I'm sure that's the only reason the writer mentioned me. But does it look bad, do you think?"

"Oh, no. That's not why I mentioned it. It doesn't look bad or look good or anything. It just means that people are looking."

"It does." Charlotte nodded and held up the paper. "Do you mind if I keep this?"

"Not at all." Vanessa smiled.

As she walked back to her room, Charlotte read the column from start to finish. The whole thing seemed to be grasping at intrigue that wasn't there. But those two innocuous lines tugged at her like a warning. If she continued a friendship or relationship of any kind with him, people would notice. She tucked the paper onto her bookshelf and ran her hand over the cool metal keys of the typewriter. She opened the desk drawer and thumbed a clean sheet from the stack she kept there. She fed it onto the roller and lined it up. Then she did the one thing she told herself she absolutely wouldn't: she wrote to Antoine.

# *Chapter Seven*

*Charlotte entered the* park at the gate next to the Rotunda on Rue de Prony. The trees rustled in the breeze overhead as she walked along the path. As soon as she came around the little bend toward the lake, Antoine was there. His slim, dignified form leaned against the concrete bridge railing, right where he said he'd be. Antoine was unexpected for an aristocrat. He wasn't a snob. He wasn't small-minded. He wasn't dull. He didn't act superior or dismiss people. He was curious and intelligent. But there was something vaguely regal about the way he carried himself. His manners were refined and at times almost laughably polished. Watching him eat at the café had been a marvel. An etiquette guide come to life. Like he was not only raised to think he was better than everyone else, but he was also born in a body that behaved that way.

Charlotte wasn't a peasant, but she came from a working-class home. People in her family put their elbows on the table. They didn't pay attention to silverware placement. Antoine may have been standing there, waiting to meet her. But they were from different worlds. In her daydreams, she'd imagined herself as much more than friends with him. From a courtship to the bedroom to a deep love that they would undoubtedly form... only in her dreams. She knew better. But her heart sang in his company. Standing next to him set off wildly inappropriate urges like a flame catching and creeping up through her. Everything he said delighted her. She longed to feel his mouth on hers again. And so here she was, meeting him because he'd asked her to, even though doing so only stoked the flames. It was like she couldn't help herself. She fussed with her dress and then fanned her face as she walked.

Her eyes fell on the monument to Guy de Maupassant as they always did when she passed it. It was her favorite one in the park, not only because she loved de Maupassant's short stories, but because she liked the way the sculptor had added the young woman lounging on a pillow below the bust. Her gaze is cast out toward the distance, like an aloof lover or maybe a contemplative fan of the writer. Supposedly, the woman represented a character from Maupassant's novel about a working-class artist recklessly falling in love with a countess, an irony that made the sculpture somehow symbolic this afternoon.

Antoine turned then; he must have heard her footsteps approaching on the gravel. He lit up with a smile, truly delighted to see her. And Charlotte was once again trapped in his charming net. He came toward her and took her hand. Raising it to his lips, his eyes met hers for a moment before he kissed her. His breath on her bare skin sent a shiver up her arm.

"It's such a pleasure that you've come." He was dressed in a navy blue morning coat with a white carnation on his lapel. The rich smell of his soap or whatever it was he'd applied to his body made her head light.

"Merci."

"I thought we could walk." He offered her his arm.

She took it and fell into step with him as they climbed the stairs on the footbridge over the water. The smooth fabric of his jacket and the sturdiness of his arm were a pleasure to hold. Being on this man's arm was unlike any other she'd experienced. It elated her with temptation.

"It's a lovely afternoon."

"And I was thrilled to receive your letter." He smiled down at her.

"You mentioned that in your response."

"Well, I mean it." The way he was looking at her brought that word from the gossip column to her mind—rapt. He beheld her with his eyes, regarded her with such open affection. No one had ever looked at her like that. And he wasn't the only one rapt. His presence set her adrift on some current of delight and desire. The edges of her arguments blurred. Her thoughts slowed and focused only on this one man. Rapt, indeed.

"How could I not write after such a gift? It seemed impolite not to." All morning, she'd admired the typewriter there on her desk and kept finding herself gazing at it even while she was doing other things, like getting dressed or brushing her hair or even reading. The keys were cool and ready under her fingers, and the sound of them hitting the paper as she worked became the sound of her thinking. And it made her feel like a real writer, like she was really doing it here in Paris. Perhaps even more so than seeing her name in print. Oddly enough.

"Ha. I should have sent the typewriter earlier then, is that what you're saying?"

What was she saying? Certainly not that there would be any more kissing now that he'd sent a present. What she couldn't say, couldn't ask, was about his intentions. As unlikely as a real courtship between them would be, as much as she'd written off the possibility, it wasn't impossible. For a moment, as they passed out of the trees, the sun framed his profile and the curve of his hat in a light that reached into her soul. She didn't want to be friends with this man; she wanted to be much more than that. There was a chance he would consider her. Maybe if they fell in love? Her words caught in her throat.

When she didn't answer, he patted her hand where it held the crook of his arm. "No problem. The air is cleared between us, right? That's all that matters."

"I suppose. It was a lovely token of friendship." She stepped wider than she had been to put a few inches between them. "Friendship."

He nodded. "That sounds better than acquaintance. Though friends is not quite what I'm interested in."

"I do have another reason for wanting to speak with you, though." She ignored his insinuation.

"What's that?"

They were walking along the water now, and the path was more crowded with people. No one seemed to notice them or be paying them any mind, but apparently, it could be hard to tell. Would any of these people recognize him? Or her? Charlotte steered him off the main path onto a more secluded one, and when they were several paces away from the traffic, she asked if he'd seen the write-up of Madame Durand's salon.

He pulled his mouth into a line. "I believe I did."

"My housemate showed it to me, otherwise I might have never known." Although her feelings on it were complicated and mixed, they depended ultimately on his reaction. "I've never had my name mentioned in a gossip column before."

"It's not the sort of thing I usually pay attention to. My mother saw it, though."

"What did she say?"

"Not much. But she made it clear that such write-ups could jeopardize her plans."

"What plans?"

"Her designs for my marriage." He said this with a dismissive wave of his hand, as if whatever his mother's plans for the most important decision of his life were, they weren't relevant.

But suddenly Charlotte's throat felt like it might close up. "She's designing your marriage?"

"Well, she's found someone she thinks is perfect. We've met a few times now, and she's not a bad choice. She meets my mother's demands for sure. Now she's pushing for a commitment—my mother, not Louise."

"Louise?" Charlotte couldn't believe it. After everything—the serendipitous meetings and the life-altering kiss and the breakup and the apology and the typewriter and fighting her feelings—there was another woman. A woman he intended to marry.

"Yes. But what's the rush, you know? I'm not in any hurry. Especially since meeting you." He put his hand on hers again, and it was so warm and comforting, even as everything coming out of his mouth sounded so awful.

"Antoine." Charlotte pulled her hand away, releasing his arm and putting distance between them. "I'm not sure what to make of any of this."

"Well, I had an idea." He spoke with the same earnest care that she found so compelling. "And maybe it's crazy, but what if we spend more time together? Let the papers see us. Let everyone talk. An attachment to you will delay things, put my mother off for a while. And it will give us a chance to get to know each other. To see if we could be more than friends."

"But not a real attachment? Because you're marrying someone else."

"Yes. Eventually. Not anytime soon if my plan works."

"I must say I don't see the point."

They'd reached an empty bench, and he gestured toward it. He took her hand again as they sat and turned to face her. His eyes glimmered flirtatiously. "Charlotte, I think about you every waking moment, and being here with you now is a thrill unlike any I've ever known. I want to spend time with you. I want to know everything about you. Everything, my dear. Without the distraction of a marriage. At least not yet. Charlotte, you have enchanted me."

"But you're not interested in marrying me?"

"I can't marry you, Charlotte. I'm my parents' last, only hope for a society marriage. It's important to them, and so it's important to me. I want to do it for them."

"Do what, exactly?"

"Marry someone from the nobility. Carry on the tradition."

His words sounded like a cruel joke, and Charlotte's stomach churned like she'd be sick. It was true that she wanted to be more than friends. But all her little fantasies about the handsome wealthy man sweeping the everyday girl off her feet really had been childish fairy tales. Reality was far more unseemly. But this was how it was with the upper class. They arranged marriages to appear respectable, but those marriages were open and non-monogamous. But monogamy was important. Charlotte's parents were in love and happy even in humble circumstances, and she wanted that for herself too. She could get used to being an aristocrat's wife in a proper marriage. But she wouldn't be an aristocrat's mistress while he married someone else. It had to be the fairy tale or nothing.

"Well, Antoine, as tempting as that is, I must decline." She scooted away from him and pulled her hands into her lap. "The tradition in my family is marrying for love, regardless of class or wealth or status. And I refuse to have my name sullied in the papers only so you can go on to marry another woman."

"I hardly see how an association with me would sully anything."

Her mouth dropped open. "You shameless man! I am making a name for myself as a writer. As a talented observer of the human condition. As a critic of outdated societal ideas. And becoming known as your mistress runs counter to everything I want to be known for."

His face reddened and he swallowed hard. "You're right. I'm sorry. I've embarrassed myself."

"You have. Appearances are important. You of all people should know that."

"You're right. I do know."

They sat quietly for a moment, facing the park. A little troupe of young women riding bicycles passed in giggles. The breeze rustled the trees and a chorus of birds sang from their discreet perches. The lush green grass spread out before them. But the natural beauty couldn't draw her away from her thoughts. The pictures in her mind of what their lives could be like together were so clear and perfect, and yet there was no way any of it could ever come true.

"I meant everything I said. That you've enchanted me. That kiss in the carriage haunts me."

"I like you too, Antoine. That's why it's hard for me to learn that you're so… stupid about our situation." That was the only word for it. Marriage for status was stupid. She'd never understand it. If two people were in love, why did class or birthright matter? Not that she was in love with him. That would be a disaster.

"Can we still be friends?" Antoine asked.

"I suppose." She wanted to remain friends, and so she hid her disappointment behind a smile.

"No kissing, though?"

"No kissing."

"I can introduce you to everyone I know with even the slightest connection to publishing."

"My career could use the boost, Antoine. But I still can't kiss you again."

*The rejection hit* Antoine like a kick in the heart. It was a foolish idea to see her as a way to stave off his inevitable marriage. But he had been so blinded by the promise of spending more time with Charlotte that it had, at least for a moment, made sense in his mind. She was right. Appearances mattered. He did know that better than anyone.

"I should be going," Charlotte said, rising from the bench. "I want to write a little more before dinner."

"I see." Antoine stood with her. "And so my plans to spend the rest of the afternoon with you have been foiled by none other than the present I sent."

"Ha! You've no one to blame but yourself, it seems." She hadn't lost her humor, but she had cooled toward him. His proposition had shifted something between them.

"I'll walk you."

She looked at him wide-eyed and said, "That's quite all right, Antoine. Madame is adamant that her house is not a brothel. Supposedly she threw the last woman who lived in my room out when she became the mistress of one of the lawyers at the firm where she worked, and I need a place to stay."

Brothel. That definitely wasn't what Antoine had intended. "Then I'll walk you to the edge of the park. Surely that will be acceptable."

"Yes. That's fine."

Antoine held out his arm for Charlotte, and she took it. But she didn't walk as close as she had before, held herself a little farther away. All he could think about was how to pull her back in. He couldn't marry her, but he didn't want to live without her either. He could carry on as friends for now, but he couldn't stop asking her for more. Presenting it as an opportunity to delay his marriage perhaps wasn't his best idea.

They were walking back toward the water when someone said Antoine's name. Thomas Colbert, who frequented his parents' dinner parties, was coming up the path toward them. He had a dressed-up woman on his arm who wasn't his wife. And not his usual mistress either.

"I thought that was you," Thomas said as they reached each other.

"Ah, Monsieur Colbert. We missed you at dinner last week." Charlotte dropped Antoine's arm so he could extend his hand to Thomas. Antoine had recently received an invitation to Madame

Colbert's birthday party. But he shouldn't mention a man's wife in front of the woman who was quite obviously his mistress. "Where have you been?"

"With me," the woman said boldly. "I'm Leah, his favorite way to pass the time."

Antoine kissed her hand. Then he turned to Charlotte, who was watching the scene unfold. "And this is my friend Charlotte Devereaux, the esteemed and gifted writer."

Charlotte gave him a suspicious look and allowed Thomas to kiss her hand. Leah nodded pleasantly and kept a hand on Thomas as if he might get away if she stopped touching him. Antoine disliked the idea of gauging a person's character based on their clothing. It didn't matter how people dressed. But Leah's gown seemed ostentatious for a walk in the park. Her lipstick a little too bold. Judging by the diamond necklace she wore, Thomas expressed his affections with elaborate gifts as well. Antoine asked about Thomas's mother instead of his wife's party.

"As fit as ever," Thomas said. Leah squeezed his arm and raised her eyebrows to signal that she wanted to go. Thomas got the hint. "But we won't keep you. We can catch up properly at dinner next week."

"Let's do that."

As they walked away, Antoine offered Charlotte his arm again. But she either didn't see it or ignored the gesture, expanding the distance she'd been keeping by another several inches.

"How do you know that gentleman?" she asked when the other couple was out of earshot.

"Oh, from around. His mother has been friends with my mother for some time, and I suppose I've always known Thomas."

"I take it his favorite hobby Leah is not his wife."

"No. She isn't. His wife is named Genevieve. She's a lovely woman; much more subdued than Leah seems to be."

"I see." Charlotte, if she'd been cool after his botched proposition, was icy now. Antoine's disappointment deepened. He had come to see her in the highest of hopes, and now she was upset for reasons that were surely complicated and likely valid. When he commented on the statuary, she said nothing more than, "Huh."

At the gate where they would part ways, Charlotte said, "Thank you again for the typewriter. And although I love it and fully intend to keep it, please don't send any more gifts."

"Charlotte, Thomas Colbert is a fool, and I'm sure that woman is too."

"'That woman.' You mean of course his mistress. The woman he sees outside his marriage."

"I hardly see what Monsieur Colbert and his mistress have to do with us."

"Oh, Antoine. I saw how you looked down at her. You think less of her because of her position. Because she is that man's mistress."

"I didn't think that."

"Well, the face you made suggested otherwise. And his face was just as embarrassing."

"If my face revealed anything, it had to do with the invitation I recently received to Thomas's wife's birthday party. I wasn't sure if I could mention it or should mention it in his mistress's company. I was trying to be sensitive to the situation."

"I see. Because it was an awkward situation, you're admitting that. Uncomfortable even."

"I suppose it was."

"Well, I won't live my life like that. I won't have your aristocratic friends looking at me like I'm some kind of possession or worse an interloper." Her chest heaved as she spoke, and her words came out strained. But then, as if she remembered herself, she straightened her back and took a deep breath. She scowled and then turned to leave him. And before walking away, she called over her shoulder, "Thanks again for the typewriter. And enjoy the rest of your day."

She hurried across the street, and then a broad delivery wagon blocked his view. When it moved out of the way, she was gone.

Antoine stood there on the sidewalk. What just happened?

When an empty cab rattled past, Antoine raised his hand to hail it. He got in, and as they pulled away, he searched through the grimy window for Charlotte's blue dress and dark hair. Her rejection and dressing down stung. But at the same time, everything up until that moment when he posed his question had been like a dream. She was always so wide-eyed and agreeable. So interested. Her heart seemed to be as stirred by him as his was by her. The visible signs of growing affection could not be faked or truly hidden. Had he ruined his chances? Or had he merely lost one battle?

The cab turned down Champs-Élysées and slowed with the heavier traffic. The sidewalks bustled and the world clicked on. The newsstands and hawkers conducting their business. People moving in and out of shops on errands. Antoine admired their sense of purpose. The commerce happening, making the world go around. He'd never had a job. His father oversaw work, but didn't do much of his own. Antoine didn't have anything like that in his life. Aside from his growing stack of books to read, he didn't have a project. He didn't have a career or aspirations like Charlotte did.

Charlotte. No wave of affection had ever hit him so hard. Seeing the pleasure on her face over the typewriter had charmed him. She was so excited. So delighted. And all over a machine to do more work. Antoine was almost jealous of her.

But he wanted to bring her that level of delight again. He wanted to make her life easier. He wanted to make her happy. No matter how they looked to everyone else, his intentions were honest and driven by pure affection. Love could win outside the bounds of a marriage and traditional domestic and romantic arrangements. And even though she was mad at him and she'd refused him, by the time the carriage rolled to a stop at the gate of his house on Quai d'Orsay, Antoine was only more determined to keep showing Charlotte Devereaux how much he liked her.

He paid the driver and walked around the corner, along the gate that surrounded the family mansion, to the service entrance on the side. A work carriage was parked there with the phone company logo painted on the side of the tool cabinet. The two surly-looking draft horses that were attached to the front of it pawed at the gravel as Antoine passed. He made a wide arc around them and hurried to the door.

Inside, the voices of the men at work echoed through the hall. A wire wrapped from somewhere up in the house to somewhere down into the kitchen and moved as if someone were tugging at either end. Antoine followed it.

His father was in the hall upstairs, watching a man in coveralls tinkering with something along the baseboards of the floor. A shiny new telephone, with a dark wooden stand and round black receiver, stood on the sideboard like a flag. Either the modern world had colonized them or his parents were surrendering.

"I thought I heard you come in, Antoine," the old man said. He puffed out his chest with pride, obviously chuffed with his new toy. "You're just in time to step into the twentieth century!"

"Say it isn't so." Father had never once mentioned to Antoine anything about a telephone, though they'd been speaking even less than usual since the sale of the family property. Probably one of his friends got one and so Father had to get one too. "You're awfully joyous so far ahead of cocktail hour. Have you started early?"

"Bah. I thought you'd be thrilled."

"I'm only surprised. You and Mother are such staunch supporters of the olden days."

Father scowled and then ignored the barb. "We'll be able to call anywhere in the world before long, right from here."

Antoine almost asked if Father planned on making friends outside of Paris society, but he didn't. Pushing the point would only be cruel when the old man was in such a good mood, so Antoine headed upstairs to his room, where he would write to Renee to double-check that Charlotte had been invited to the party. As he reached his door, a tight ringing sound came from downstairs followed by a whoop of joy. If only Father would also modernize his ideas about how the world should work.

The next morning, Antoine was sprawled across the leather chaise in his room when a commotion carried up from somewhere in the house. Even though they'd finished yesterday, as far as he knew, he assumed it was the workmen returning to the telephone installation job and kept reading his book. It was Zola's latest, one Charlotte recommended, and he'd had trouble putting it down since he started it after breakfast.

Then something about the way the voices rose in pitch got him up. When he opened the door, a man was shouting downstairs. And was that a child crying?

Antoine followed the sounds of the commotion down to the service entrance, where the butler and his father were engaged in an argument with a man and his family. They were dressed in faded and mended clothing, their faces tan from outdoor work. It was the DuPonts, farmer tenants who'd stayed on their property since before Antoine was even born. Monsieur Dupont's father and grandfather had farmed there too. One of the most productive farmers on the estate.

"We've nowhere to go!" Monsieur Dupont shouted and threw up his hands. "They're forcing us out and we've nowhere to go."

"Surely you must have family somewhere," Father said. He looked absolutely dumbfounded by Monsieur Dupont's complaint. "Or you can rent a place in the city? There's work to be found here, surely."

"What do you know about work, monsieur? Not a thing!" Madame Dupont spit these words. Then her wild eyes landed on Antoine. As he realized what was happening, his brain and mouth couldn't form words that felt adequate.

"My children will starve, while yours is a layabout who won't have to work a day in his life. What a life you all must lead here in your fancy house."

"What is it that you want?" Antoine said.

"What do we want?" Madam Dupont screamed. Her handsome, weathered face reddened. "We want our livelihood. We want credit for the work we've done on that land for all these years. Generations of labor, and you've taken it away because of some royal decree made hundreds of years ago that makes you better than us. We want our dignity!"

"Please. Come in and let us serve you coffee. And something to eat," Antoine said, gesturing for Emile and his father to step aside. To wide-eyed Emile, he said, "Please see that the kitchen sends up a few trays to the drawing room."

He brought the Duponts inside. Even though seeing the mansion in all its splendor could offend the Duponts' sensibilities, Antoine risked it and took them to the same room where they saw all esteemed guests. The rich velvet drapes and brocade tapestries contrasted starkly with the patched, rough fabric of their workwear. And their wide-eyed survey of the room suggested they'd never seen anything like it.

"How much time do you have before they're forcing you out?" Antoine asked when they were seated and served refreshments. Although they were the ones who'd come, the Duponts weren't the only ones being turned out. Other families would be in the same dire straits.

"The end of the month," Monsieur Dupont said solemnly. The child seated at his side sniffed and wiped her tears on the back of her hand.

"Then let us come up with a solution," Antoine said, trying to sound confident. "Please, give me some time to figure out how to help."

They had to do something. He didn't know what, but surely Father would agree. He and Mother stood wordlessly aside through the duration of the visit. After the Duponts had aired all their grievances, and Antoine had soothed them with genuine promises to do better, they went on their way.

When they were gone, Father finally spoke. “I don’t know what they expect. And you’ll regret making promises to them like that.”

“So you intend to do nothing.”

“There’s nothing to do.” He turned and led Mother down the hall. So much for the twentieth century.

# Chapter Eight

*Charlotte's desk chair* squeaked under her as she reached her arms above her head and stretched. She had been working all morning, happily and productively typing away at her typewriter, piling up the pages in neat stacks, shuffling them around, and grouping them together. It was glorious. Now all she needed was the post to arrive with an acceptance. Because almost every day she'd received a rejection for one of the stories she had out on submission. There was no shortage of magazines and papers, and her strategy had been to try them all. But for all this trying her rejection pile kept getting higher.

She had assumed that, after her first few successes, it would be easier than this. That she'd not be rejected quite so much. That maybe the magazines would be excited to include her in their pages, the way *La Fronde* had sought her out and seemed thrilled to have her. Not quite the case, it turned out. And so her confidence and excitement about her work swung wildly between best writer in town and ready to give up for good. Being a writer was hard. But there was nothing else she wanted to do, and nothing else that she was particularly good at.

She opened her window and the warm breeze blew in, fluttering the muslin curtains and rustling the pages on her desk. She'd had no word from Antoine. And although she hadn't written to him either, he seemed to infuse every word that her fingers tapped on her gleaming new machine. Handsome aristocrats and bookish, polite gentlemen with mischievous, bright eyes kept populating her stories. At least on the page, she could torture these handsome gentlemen for being so bound up in class superiority.

Antoine's words still rang in her head. *Marry someone from the nobility, carry on the tradition.* He probably had no idea how snobby he sounded. Skewering this sort of foolishness in her stories felt cathartic. Getting over Antoine in real life was not quite as fun.

*You've enchanted me, Charlotte.* The tingly feeling she got standing next to him. The way she wanted to know every word he said, every thought he had. The way she wanted to stare at him, take in every detail. The weight of his simple, respectful touches lingered on her skin. That kiss in the carriage. And then those words hollowed her out like a scoop: *I can't marry you, Charlotte.*

Charlotte's stomach grumbled; she'd had little more than coffee and bread all day. She rose from her desk and stretched again from side to side. Then she shook out her wrists and hands. Typing felt different from writing by hand, strained different muscles. She slid on her house slippers and left her room for the first time in a few hours.

The hall was quiet—Madame was perhaps out on errands. Nadine was at practice. Vanessa and the sisters were still at work. Cook and the maid were probably around somewhere, and the groundskeeper was out in the yard. But Charlotte descended the stairs in that quiet luxury of having the place nearly to herself. The wooden treads under her feet were worn from traffic over the years, but polished and spotless, the way Madame always kept them. Charlotte had been there for almost a month now and had yet to find a speck of dust. It was nice to live in a place so well cared for. Not all boarding houses in the city were so clean. She'd heard stories from Vanessa and Nadine about terrible living conditions and neglectful landlords. And on her walks, she'd passed more than a few buildings that even from the outside seemed to be falling apart around the inhabitants.

When she reached the hall near the front door, she stepped out onto the foyer and checked the spot on the table where the mail was kept, just in case she'd been so enthralled in her own imagination that she missed the sound of its arrival. But the table was empty, except for the vase full of lush white lilacs cut from the garden. The sweet fragrance filled the air. Charlotte sniffed the blooms with a deep inhale and then went down to the kitchen.

The kitchen, with heavy stone walls and small arched windows along the ceiling, was like a scullery in some medieval castle. A pot of something simmered on the big stove that smelled like a pleasant broth. Perhaps the start of that night's dinner. Charlotte peered into the bubbling liquid, breathing in the homey, delicious aroma. As she turned, Cook came around the corner from where the dry storage shelves were stacked with bags of rice and flour and baskets of potatoes.

"Good afternoon, Mademoiselle." Cook was a friendly woman close in age to Charlotte's mother, who was fifty-one, and Madame, who was forty-nine. She was plump, as cooks often were, with graying dark hair and a heavy brow. "Is there something I can get you?"

"I'm just looking for a snack to keep me busy until the mail comes."

"Start with this." Cook placed a peach in Charlotte's hand that felt fuzzy and perfectly soft in her hand. "I just picked it up from the market, and it's still warm from the sun."

The fruit's skin was indeed warm. Mottled magenta and pale orange, it appeared to be the most perfect peach. The ideal. Charlotte raised it to her mouth and took a bite. Juice poured out and ran down her jaw. She bent over to prevent it from dripping on her dress, and Cook passed her a clean dish towel. Charlotte nodded her appreciation and wiped at the mess on her face.

"It's delicious," she said around chewing and swallowing. "It's perfect."

"Isn't it? I've already eaten two of them, they're so good." Cook moved away, around the long sturdy table that sat in the center of the kitchen. This was where Charlotte often found Cook's cookies and pies and other recent creations when she came poking around. "I've got some cheese and meat cut for later. I'll fix you a plate to tide you over until dinner."

"Thank you so much." Charlotte reached the pit of her peach and the flesh fell away to expose the hard, ridged middle. "Will there be a peach galette in the near future?"

"They might not last that long." Cook brought a small plate of brie and sliced, cured meats to Charlotte. "Better take one with you."

"I will. And thank you for the food." Charlotte tossed the clean pit from her peach into the compost bucket under the sink. "I'm sure you're busy?"

"I am. If you want to have dinner then you'll leave me to this soup." Cook winked at her, picked up a wide wooden spoon off the counter, and dipped it into whatever was simmering in her pot.

Charlotte, carrying her plate and peach, made her way back upstairs. She was passing the first floor when a knock at the door drew her back.

"I'll get it," she yelled down to Cook, unsure if she actually heard. Then she set her snack on the foyer table and looked through the frosted window next to the door. A man stood outside, though she couldn't make out any of his features in the blurred glass.

"Bonjour," she said as she pulled open the door.

"Good afternoon, mademoiselle." The young man standing there was dressed in a fine uniform, like he'd come on behalf of some noble house. Like he was in the wrong place, in other words. When Charlotte gave him nothing more than a confused look, he continued. "I'm here on behalf of the Marquis Renee de Conradines with an invitation for a Mademoiselle Deveraux."

"You're kidding."

"No, mademoiselle." He produced a large envelope from behind his back and held it out to her. The paper was as pale blue as the sky over the city.

Charlotte thanked him and took the envelope. The well-dressed courier bowed and left, while Charlotte closed the door behind him. The creamy paper and embossed details made the envelope seem heavier in Charlotte's hand. She opened it and slid the card out. It was an invitation, written in ornate, swirling calligraphy, to a ball at the home of the Marquis Renee de Conradines. It was indeed addressed to her. But why?

He'd obviously liked her when they met at the salon, but she never imagined that it could lead to further invitations. Especially not to a ball. She didn't even have anything to wear. Well, maybe she could style her new blue dress to make it more formal, but her housemates' faux jewels might not cut it at an aristocrat's ball. She slid the card back into the envelope, picked up her snack plate, and started back up the stairs. The words for her regrets were just coming together in her mind when another knock came at the door. Again? Was this what went on down here all afternoon while she was upstairs working?

"Can you get that if you're still there, Mademoiselle Charlotte?" Cook yelled from downstairs. "I'm straining my broth, dear, and my hands are a mess."

"I've got it." Charlotte put her food and her invitation on the table and went to the door. This time she opened it without checking the window. Another courier, a less fancy one, was standing there with a box wrapped in the prettiest cabbage rose floral paper.

"A delivery for Mademoiselle Charlotte Deveraux," the courier said. He was a young man and his pants were faded at the knees.

"May I ask who sent it?"

"I don't know, mademoiselle. I deliver for the store. They don't tell me anything about the boxes, I just carry them across town."

"I see." She took the proffered box. "Thank you. Let me get my purse. It's just upstairs."

"Tip's paid, mademoiselle. My boss insisted the sender wouldn't pay if I took a sous from you."

Antoine. He had to be the sender. "Merci."

The young man nodded and went on his way.

Standing there with the box, Charlotte decided not to open it until she made it to the privacy of her room. With more to carry than hands, she placed her plate on top of the box and wedged the peach between it and her chin. And she started back upstairs, slower and steadier.

When she reached her room, she pushed the door open with her hip and stepped inside. She put her plate of food on her desk and set the box on the edge of her bed. It was a lovely package. Ostentatious, even. Good thing no one had seen her receive it. The typewriter had been easy enough to dismiss as a gesture of kindness from those concerned with her career. This, whatever it was, would surely be harder to hide. It looked like a package a gentleman with intentions would send to a woman. It was like a bouquet of roses in box form.

Careful not to rip the pretty paper, Charlotte unwrapped the package. Inside was a blue box with a lid. Lifting it revealed a spray of gold and purple feathers shooting from the front of a burgundy silk hat. It was well-made and elegant. Quite a bit more formal than anything else she owned. This was a hat for a woman like Madame Durand. Someone more stylish. Charlotte set it on her bed and tipped the box. She pushed the tissue paper to the side. No card. And so it was an anonymous gift, arriving minutes after her invitation for an occasion where such a hat would be quite handy. A hat that would make her dress formal enough for the ball. The colors didn't match exactly, but they complemented each other. It would probably look lovely.

But had Antoine sent the gift? Or Renee? Surely it couldn't be anyone else. Either one might suspect she had nothing to wear. Or that her accessories wouldn't cut it. Probably either man would be kind enough to send such a gift. But only one of those two gentlemen had motive to do so anonymously. Charlotte put the hat on her head and went to the little mirror on the top of her dresser. She couldn't see her whole head or much of the hat up close. Though she could tell the colors enhanced hers. She stepped back a few paces, the way she always did when trying to see herself in full in the glass. The hat stood well over a foot higher than her head, But it was fabulous. The prettiest hat, for sure, that she'd ever worn. A hat she'd never imagine picking out or procuring on her own. It was like someone else's idea put on her head, and she didn't hate it.

She slid the hat back into the box. To hide it, she moved a stack of sweaters off the bottom of her armoire and tucked the box inside. It only just allowed the door to fully close. But even hidden from view, that hat was on Charlotte's mind for the rest of the day. She was so busy thinking about it that she barely noticed when the post brought her two rejections.

In the days leading up to the ball at Renee's, Charlotte's anxiety about it grew. She'd make a fool of herself. She wouldn't look sophisticated enough. Not rich enough. She wasn't rich at all. And despite all those etiquette books she'd consumed back in Vernon to smooth out any rough provincial edges, she probably wasn't all that sophisticated either. The morning of the event, she sat at her desk unable to string even a few words together. Then after lunch, as if to put Charlotte out of her misery, Nadine set her hair in rags and drew her a hot bath with enough lavender oil to relax everyone in the house.

Even though her dark blue evening dress could have worked, she fell in love with a simple embroidered black sheath in the collection of dresses that Nadine offered to lend. The decoration had an oriental flair, which made it fashionable, and the dress was in decent enough shape, even though it had probably been to more fancy events than Charlotte had in all her years. The only issue was a small tear on the hip seam.

"If you can fix it," Nadine had said, "you can have it."

And so Charlotte stitched along the delicate fabric as carefully as she could. She'd never been much of a seamstress or good with a needle at all. But the repair was a straight line of stitches. No problem.

Nadine, who had the night off, helped her pin her hair into an elegant updo that made the perfect nest for the burgundy hat.

"This is quite a confection," Nadine said when Charlotte brought it out from her hiding place in the armoire.

"It is, isn't it?" Charlotte held the hat at arm's length and gave it a small shake to rustle the ostrich feathers, which were dyed to match the silk hat. "Do you think it's too much?"

"Not at all. Especially not for a ball in a mansion on Quay d'Orsay! Now let me help you into the dress."

Charlotte rose from the stool and went over to where the dress was lying spread out on her bed. The embroidery work shimmered, and her repair was hardly noticeable on the dark fabric. She wiped her sweaty palms down the sides of her petticoat and stepped into the dress while Nadine held it for her.

"Are you nervous?"

"Nervous would be understating it. I feel like I'm ready to faint."

"What for?" Nadine shifted the fabric around Charlotte's waist and then began fastening the buttons up the back.

"I won't know anyone."

"Is Monsieur de Larminet going to be there?"

Charlotte met Nadine's eyes in the little mirror and blushed. "He will be."

"Ooh la la," Nadine sang. "You like this gentleman, don't you?"

"I do. Perhaps too much. But that doesn't mean I'm interested."

Nadine raised her eyebrows but didn't say anything. She had a way of doing so that encouraged one to keep talking and revealing secrets.

"But it's not like we'll be spending the evening together. I'm sure he'll be with his friends or family or whoever. And it isn't exactly my crowd."

"How'd you get invited to this ball, again?"

"I met the Marquis de Conradines at the salon at Madame Durand's." Charlotte recited the words she'd been telling herself all week, all the reasons why Renee had invited her to such an event, both for herself and in case anyone asked. "We had a good conversation about books. He's rather well-read. And so he invited me, it seems."

"Huh," Nadine said, sounding half-convinced. "It seems."

The only item she purchased was a gently worn pair of shoes in a secondhand shop. All of hers were scuffed and worn, even more so from traipsing around the city. With higher heels and shiny patent leather, they were more ornate than any shoes she'd ever owned. When she was dressed, Charlotte faced the mirror. Her hair in a lovely pile, the colorful hat, the elegant, understated dress—it all came together in a pretty picture. One that Antoine would hopefully notice and appreciate, even among the countless other women in pretty dresses who would undoubtedly be in attendance. Even though she refused to be more than friends with him, the truth was that she still wanted him to want her. She wanted him to be enchanted.

Nadine, who was tidying up her brushes and the curling rags, turned to face Charlotte.

"You're lovely," she said. "And these things are all about being seen. At least for everyone else. For you, you'll get to see all the fancy people dressed up. That will be the best part, seeing what everyone is wearing."

Charlotte nodded. She kept thinking about Balzac's Lucien from *Lost Illusions*. Charlotte never loved that book, but ever since that invitation arrived, the story kept bubbling to the surface of her mind. In it, Lucien is a talented writer from the provinces who comes to Paris and gets a society invitation much like hers. He spends nearly all his money on new clothes that are so ostentatious and loud that he stands out even more while trying desperately to fit in. He becomes a laughingstock. He goes on to make a name for himself, but ultimately loses everything from his last sous to his reputation and friendships. Charlotte was nothing like Lucien. Her situation, despite the similarities, was quite different. But she kept thinking about him nonetheless, bumbling across town in clothes he wasn't equipped to wear.

After thanking Nadine and slipping out of the house without attracting much attention, Charlotte hailed a cab like a true Parisian and was on her way across town. The thing about Lucien was that he became obsessed with living a life of luxury. She didn't want anything more than to write. She didn't care about money, aside from needing it to live. She didn't care that her dress was borrowed and had been repaired by her own unskilled hand. She just wanted to write and to support herself in doing so. But she also wanted to stay in Paris. She wanted to stay at the pension on Rue de Fortuny. She wanted more time to live the life she was so happy and so productive in. She didn't care about anything else. But then there was Antoine. And even though money and luxury weren't important, thoughts of Antoine had grown increasingly so.

The cab carried her through the city, across the bridge where she'd sat with Antoine that blissfully uninformed afternoon, onto a street along the river unlike any part of the city she'd seen so far. The wide, quiet street was lined with large, stately homes. Each one seemed to outdo the last. Antoine would be there tonight. There was no doubt of that. But this wouldn't be like the cabarets or salons of mixed company; she was stepping into his high-society world. And the weight of that was nearly crushing any excitement or positive anticipation.

When they came to a stop, in front of what was surely the most palatial house so far, Charlotte gasped. It was huge, lit up like a work of art in the fading daylight, surrounded by a tall iron fence that said to everyone who passed that they could see how lovely it was without getting close enough to touch.

She paid and thanked the driver, who whistled and nodded at the mansion. "Fancy place, Mademoiselle. Don't forget to eat. They'll have good food, I imagine."

Charlotte laughed as he pulled away. The carriage pulling up behind her was far shinier and sleeker than her ride. The servants at the gate watched her expectantly, eager to check her name on the list, perhaps more so because she arrived so humbly. She smiled and gave her name, and the servants smiled back upon finding it. They seemed as relieved as she was. Then they welcomed her in.

There were several small groups of people milling about the garden, which was formal and highly designed with little benches and rows of box bushes shaped like soft balls. A fountain with a statue of a mermaid on a rock trickled in the center. And the house, glowing from within, rang with music and laughter. Charlotte made her way through the garden, up to the steps. She paused to take a deep breath, and then she climbed the stairs and stepped through the wide front door.

Inside, the music filled the foyer, where two wide and curving staircases rose above another fountain and mermaid sculpture. More small groups of guests were talking and laughing, some on the stairs, some under them. A few turned to look at her when she walked in, only long enough not to recognize her, and then they went back to whatever they were talking about. Another servant greeted her and passed her a flute of champagne from a precarious-looking tray of several. Charlotte took it gratefully. She'd need it.

Two sets of doors to the ballroom were open. Not a single familiar face so far. It wasn't her clothes that made her stand out, exactly, though her dress was far simpler than the others. There was something inherently different about her and these other people. This was a broad brush to paint the room with, but provincial proletarian Charlotte was different from these upper-class Parisians.

This was not her kind of party.

These were not her people.

And yet she was here. She'd come all this way and might as well stay for a while. She took a large gulp of her champagne and slipped into the crowded ballroom.

Making her way along the walls, Charlotte maneuvered around the crowd at the door to a little clearing near an ice sculpture of a dolphin jumping out of the sea to the left. People were dancing in formation on the clearing at the center of the wide, deep, and elegantly appointed room. The silver chandeliers, tall mirrors, and silvery tones in the wallpaper made everything sparkle. It was unlike any room she'd ever been in before. A pianist played on a raised platform in a far corner. When she found a spot to stand, her eyes followed nearly everyone's in the room to the dance floor. Women in elaborate hair pieces and a rainbow of gowns twirled and bowed with the line of gentlemen in dark formal suits. One couple in particular caught her eye, and when the gentleman turned around, Charlotte nearly spilled her champagne.

It was Antoine.

Smiling and holding perfect posture and time, he twirled a young blond woman one way, and then the other. Who was she? They were smiling at each other. When the dance steps brought them together for a few steps, he whispered something close to her ear. She laughed, and he smiled down at her. Warmly, though not as warmly as when he looked at Charlotte. Still, he was flirting.

# Chapter Nine

*Charlotte swallowed the* last of her wine and turned to find more. She found a glass on a convenient server's tray, took a hearty swallow, and stole another glance at the dance floor. Antoine's back was to her, but the blonde woman was now facing her. She was pretty and adorned in jewels that looked as if they cost as much as a year's rent. Maybe more. Was this Louise? It had to be. Charlotte's chest constricted. How foolish to think she'd have his attention at a party like this. He may not even speak to her. No. He wouldn't be that rude. But he'd also be expected to dance several rounds with his intended fiancée.

Charlotte decided she'd find Renee to say bonjour and merci and au revoir and then she'd leave. There were enough people crammed in this room that she could easily avoid Antoine for long enough to do that. Searching the room again, Renee wasn't present. But a buffet table as long as a carriage was set up in a place sufficiently far from the dance floor. Food might help calm her nerves, and she wasn't the sort of woman who could pass on a free gourmet meal. With the cab driver's words in her mind, she headed toward it.

The spread was arranged on several tiers with three overflowing bouquets of fresh fruit and flowers down the center, towering over plates of oysters, shrimp, and small bites that weren't as easy to identify, at least not for her. There was a croquembouche, a rainbow of macarons, and tarts. Elaborate spreads of cheese and meats laid out in patterns of flowers and what looked like an owl. Vegetables and dips in every color. Nuts and berries. Tiny sandwiches. Her mouth watered at the sight of it all. She'd been so nervous about this night for days that she'd hardly eaten a thing. She fixed herself a plate, trying a little of everything, popping bites into her mouth as she went.

"I thought that was you."

The smooth voice in her ear startled Charlotte. It was Antoine.

She chewed and swallowed and nodded at him, buying time to decide what to say. "Did you recognize the hat?"

It came out a little colder than she intended, and his eyes flickered and dimmed. It almost broke her heart.

"I'm sorry." She softened. "I don't mean to be so abrupt. But I saw you dancing and was sort of hoping I could avoid you for the rest of the night."

"Why is that?" He stepped closer to her side and grabbed a plate off a stack.

"For appearance's sake."

"Charlotte, I see that you're eating, but may I have the next dance? In front of everyone?"

Wasn't he witty. She couldn't dance with him, not here. Not in front of all these people.

"You know that isn't a good idea. You said so yourself." She turned and faced him, plate wobbling a little in her one hand, champagne in the other.

"Charlotte, what do you mean? You're a guest at the ball. Of course, we can dance."

"Ah, as you were dancing with a woman when I arrived. Was that Louise?"

This knocked him off a touch. He straightened his shoulders. "If it was a blonde woman in a light green dress, then yes. That is Louise."

"What will she say about you dancing with me, then?"

He tilted his head closer and smiled tightly, as if this could hide the fact that she'd put him on the spot. She had every right to. He'd more or less propositioned her. She could ask questions.

He leaned in close and said, "She and I aren't engaged yet. But this is a society party. I will have to dance with many women tonight, per society's standards for my conduct. My mother is here and many family friends. But I can also dance with you. And I won't stop asking until I have you out there on the floor."

"What will people think?" Charlotte found a bare spot for her champagne, freeing one hand to reach for the serving tongs. She deserved another macaron.

"They'll know we're friends." He smiled devilishly. "Which is exactly what we want them to think."

"That's what we are!" She nudged him with an elbow. Her plate was so full now she had to stop looking at the buffet. Antoine had almost filled his plate too.

"Let's sit, then, friend."

She followed him to a clean table surrounded by empty chairs, each elegantly adorned with a bow of silvery tulle. They sat next to each other, but she scooted her chair a few inches away from his, creating space.

She unfolded her napkin and put it into her lap while Antoine sliced a bite of canapé with the most sophisticated manners. Where did he even get the silverware? She must have missed it. The discussion about dancing dropped while they ate.

After a few minutes of watching her and chewing, he dabbed his mustached mouth with his napkin and smiled at her appreciatively. "I like the hat."

"Merci. As you may know, it was a gift. And because of your other recent gift, I assume it was from you."

"It was. But I didn't want to be obvious. I'm not trying to change your mind about anything we discussed at the park. I completely understand your position. But I find I can't help myself."

Charlotte put a piece of shrimp in her mouth and chewed it slowly. Just sitting next to him, in the sphere of his cologne and attention, made the world more vibrant. The pianist played the room into a swirl of dancing and laughter. It would be a pure, dizzying pleasure to dance with him in this beautiful room. Could she do it without falling even harder for him?

"I suppose one dance couldn't hurt. In thanks."

"I hope you'll wait until I've finished my dessert."

They ate in companionable silence, taking only a few minutes to finish their plates. He introduced her to an older lady and gentleman as they ambled past, and Charlotte smiled politely. The man was dressed in full regalia, and the woman's wrists were covered in heavy jewels. Nadine had been right: the best part of going to a ball was seeing what everyone was wearing.

"Ready?" Antoine said when their plates were empty. "I think this song is almost over, and we can join in the next one, if you like."

She swallowed and nodded. Her heart kicked up in the hollow of her chest. "Where do we put our dirty dishes?"

"Just leave them there. Someone will come and clean it up for us. We're guests."

She took his hand and followed him through the crowd, around the tables, to the dance floor. As the song ended and the pianist started into a simple, ethereal waltz, they situated themselves among the other couples. Although Antoine was right, probably everyone danced with everyone, it was also a public space. Far more overtly public than anywhere else they'd ever spent time and been seen together. Her awareness of herself and her otherness heightened with every glance from the other dancers and spectators around the room.

In position, Antoine bowed and took her hand, then walked her into a circle formation with the other couples and bowed again.

But when his hand met her waist and held her, it was as if everyone else in the room disappeared. The simplicity of her gown no longer mattered, if it ever did. Her secondhand formal shoes. The spray of feathers on her head didn't quite disguise these subtle indicators of her class. These other women in their fancier dresses with their refined manners and kept lives disappeared. None of it mattered with his arms around her. How was it possible to feel so much with someone she couldn't have? And would he ever change his mind?

Antoine was a confident, strong dancer. And her heart fluttered as she spun in and out of his arms. When he pulled her in closer than was perhaps appropriate, his black cravat was right at eye level, and the spicy scent of his cologne blurred her thoughts. She wanted to run her hand along his jaw and thread her hands through his neatly combed. hair. When he dipped her, and she relinquished her weight into his outstretched arm, she almost lost her breath. When she made a small misstep, he easily recovered her. She could dance like this with him, to this same music, all night without ever tiring of the experience. His moves were seduction set to music. She had danced with men before, of course. Waltzed dozens of times at parties back at home. Never had she been romanced in this way. It was like she'd been ignorant of the true power of body language until Antoine swept the ballroom floor with her. When the music stopped and he bowed to her for the final time, she was panting and warm, like she'd run through a snowy field and come into a warm kitchen.

He smiled at her, flushed and panting as well. Then he took her hand. Instead of raising it to his mouth, he pulled her close and whispered in her ear, "Meet me in fifteen minutes at the top of the stairs. I want to show you something."

"What will I do in the meantime?"

"Here." He reached into the interior pocket of his jacket, produced a silver cigarette case, and passed it to her. "You can smoke out back. Renee's probably out there."

He bowed and took off into the crowd. Charlotte twirled the cigarette in her fingers and shook off her daze. He was gone, and the absence felt like a chill of reality after such an engrossing dance. Dancing and so many people had made the room stuffy. Then she noticed the seam she'd repaired had come loose. It must have happened when they were dancing. She tightened her grip on the cigarette case and cut across the dance floor while the pianist was taking a break. The door to the terrace was closed, but outside several people were partaking in the night air. Beyond the wide stone terrace, the garden was lit only by a few torches spread out across the property. Darkness had fallen. The gibbous moon clung to the sky, embedded in the cosmos. Charlotte opened the cigarette case and immediately there was a well-dressed gentleman there to light it for her. She accepted his assistance and smiled in thanks through her first puff.

"Ah, there she is," someone called across the terrace. Renee was leaning against a low stone wall, surrounded by friends. He raised a hand to beckon Charlotte over.

"You've caught me in the act, I'm afraid." She raised her hand, cigarette pinched between two fingers.

"You're in good company." Renee laughed and pulled her in for a kiss on each cheek. Then he introduced her to the men in his little circle. No one she knew, and no one Renee gave any indication she needed to know further. She was perhaps too worried about positioning the tear in her dress out of their view to make for good company. And they must have assumed she was Parisian because their faces fell a little when she told them she was from the provinces. The conversation was cordial enough, but as they carried on gossiping about some American investment gone wrong for a gentleman they referred to only as Dunce, she was alone in her thoughts.

That dance with Antoine had shaken her resolve that they could be merely friends. He was difficult to resist. And what could he possibly want to show her on the upper floors of his friend's house? She finished her cigarette and thanked Renee again for inviting her, in case she didn't bump into him again before she left. She wasn't sure how much longer she could hang around and not talk to anyone. Antoine surely couldn't abandon the festivities for long, not with his mother and future fiancée watching.

Back inside the ballroom, she plucked a flute of champagne from a passing server's tray and went out into the foyer. Antoine was nowhere to be seen. The music had begun again, and dancers were assembling. Had it been fifteen minutes yet? It had to be close. Charlotte slipped through the ballroom, past the ice dolphin, and back out to the foyer. The water in the fountain trickled, and the sound combined with voices and carried off all the marble surfaces in the vast room. More guests were mingling here now that the party was in full swing and everyone who was coming had arrived. Charlotte stepped lightly, hoping no one would notice her going upstairs like she was up to something. She wasn't up to anything. Though perhaps Antoine was.

Her heels clicked on the marble steps, and when she reached the top, Antoine was leaning on a wall, just down the hall far enough to be out of sight from the foyer. He stood up straight when he noticed her coming and smiled. She came to a stop in front of him.

"So what must you show me in this stranger's house?"

"You'll see." He led her down the hall. The walls were adorned with paintings of men wearing solemn expressions and military uniforms. They passed several tall doors before coming to the last one at the end. It was wider and taller than the others, and the knob clanked when Antoine opened it. Inside, the gaslight sconces were lit and glowing high on the walls. And a small fire was going in front of a pair of deep, cushioned chairs.

The walls, from floor to ceiling, were lined with bookcases, all filled to the edges with what had to be thousands of books. More books than in her parents' bookshop. The room was bigger than the town library in Vernon and the library at the convent where she'd gone to school. Like all the other areas of the house, it was done in intricate, detailed wooden moulding, stained a dark honey color, which gave the room a warm glow. And the books! The books seemed to go on forever.

"Are we allowed to be in here?"

"They left the lights on. Surely we aren't the first to sneak away tonight."

"Is that what we've done? Sneak away?"

"I suppose you could say that." He was still standing close, his shoulder five inches or so taller than hers and close enough to touch. Both of them stared up at the books. A spiral staircase led up to little balconies on either side of the room. There appeared to be a sliding track that must have made the books in the tallest places accessible, but it wasn't immediately clear how it worked. The ceiling, two tall stories up, had a skylight. The room was a marvel. She didn't have to ask why he wanted to show it to her.

"Have they read all these books, do you think?"

"Maybe through the generations. Renee reads quite a bit, probably not this much though."

"Do you have a library like this in your house?"

He looked down at her, locking her eyes with his. And he seemed to understand something about what all this wealth and excess—not only the library, but the whole house, all of it—was like for her. "We have a library at the house, yes. It's not quite as marvelous as this, but it is full of books that have accumulated over generations. More books than I could read in a lifetime. This is probably the best private library in town."

"You're very lucky," she said. "You and the marquis and everyone else here, I'd be willing to bet."

"That's true, Charlotte. But you're lucky too."

"Antoine, I'm wearing a dress that ripped on the dance floor because it's been worn so many times, and not by me."

"Yes, but Charlotte, you're talented. You have an amazing ability that everyone at this party would love to have. They're all so dull compared to you."

That didn't mean she could have what she wanted. She couldn't have him. "I work hard for my successes. Luck had nothing to do with it."

"You're right, at least a little. But I think luck does have something to do with it. Getting your story in front of the right editor at the right time is a kind of luck."

"It's not the same kind of luck as being born to a wealthy family that everyone respects and opens doors for because of a title."

She turned to the shelves and examined the books closer. They'd all been bound in fine leather and embossed in gold lettering, much more elegant than most of what came and went through her parents' shop. There were books here that she knew by heart. Books she'd heard of and books she hadn't. Books that had been translated. And books that looked so old she was afraid to touch them. How were they organized? How could a person even organize such a large personal library?

"If you were to spend the rest of the night here, what would you choose to read?" Antoine was watching her.

"I would probably spend all my time looking for something and never decide on one. What about you?"

"*Les Mis* is my favorite book. I'd probably pick that one."

"*Les Mis*? It's a solid choice." She gazed up at the shelves.

"I liked what you said about it the other night. About coincidence."

"It's one of my firmest stances."

"Well, I'd never heard anyone say it quite like you did. And it made me love you a little."

Charlotte's mouth fell open, and she covered it with a hand. This man was not afraid to wade into dangerous conversational waters. Waters that would likely sweep her away. "Why did you bring me here?"

"Because I knew you'd appreciate it. And I wanted a moment alone with you. How have you been, Charlotte?"

"I've been working a lot." She looked up at the shelves. If she wasn't going to run away from him, she at least needed to change the subject. "Typing away at my new machine, I suppose."

"And how's it going?"

"Well enough." She didn't mention the growing pile of rejections. He might think less of her if he knew about all that.

"Any new stories coming out that I can await?"

"No. Well, not yet."

"Have you been back to Madame Durand's salon?"

"I haven't. Have you?"

"No."

They were standing close to each other still. Every time she moved to look at a different shelf, he followed her like he was tethered to her. His voice was smooth and mesmerizing in the quiet space. And she adored being with him to the point of losing her head. They weren't even talking about anything of consequence, and she didn't care as long as they were talking. She liked it. Liked being so near to him, even though maybe she was stealing his company from someone else.

"Are your friends and family looking for you?"

"You mean have they noticed I'm not downstairs? I doubt it." He raised his arm and set an elbow on the bookshelf, leaning into it and over her. He was so close she could smell the hint of champagne on his breath. "Everyone is enjoying themselves and no one cares about what I'm doing."

"I find that hard to believe."

They were even closer now, facing each other. The memory of their passionate carriage ride tingled on her skin. His face so handsome in the shadowy gaslight. His clothes so perfect. Everything about the evening felt surreal, like she'd stepped out of the cab into some sort of wonderland. The exquisite house, the lavish spread of food and drink, the guests in ballroom attire, the magical library, Antoine in his impeccable suit—it was like a dream. Perhaps she'd had too much champagne.

Antoine raised his hand and tentatively moved a stray curl of her hair away from her eye. "Your hair looks lovely tonight. You look lovely."

"Thank you. You look lovely too." They were so close, staring into each other's eyes. One move and they would be kissing. Making that move, though, would erase all the work she'd already done to distance herself from him. Everything she'd said about being just friends and not being the sort of woman who could enter into the kind of relationship he was offering her. It made her chest ache to think about kissing him again, pressing herself to him, and not being able to have him. Because it mattered, didn't it? Love mattered more than what everyone thought. At least, in that moment, inches from Antoine, it felt like it did.

Then the metal clunking sound of the elaborate doorknob turning drew their attention. Someone was there, coming into the room. Simultaneously, as if choreographed, both Charlotte and Antoine took a step back, putting a meter or more space between them just as the door swung open.

"Oh," the woman who'd opened it looked quizzically between them. Then her eyes, wide with the surprise of finding them, narrowed with suspicion. "I didn't know this room was taken."

The woman was older than Charlotte, maybe in her late thirties. And she was dressed in a fiery red satin dress. The man with her, who was tall and thin, stood there as unopinionated as a piece of furniture. Charlotte didn't recognize them. Did Antoine?

"It isn't. I was merely showing my friend here the marquis's impressive library. We were just leaving." He looked cooly at Charlotte, and when she didn't move, he held out an arm to direct her toward the door.

"Oh." Charlotte squeaked, catching on. "Yes. Thank you for showing me the library, friend."

She walked to the door and nodded at the woman and man, who nodded back. The man, who was dressed in a black brocade suit, didn't seem to register the interaction at all, but the woman smiled coyly and stared at Charlotte as if she were memorizing every detail.

"Your dress is ripped," the woman said as they passed through. Then the man pulled at the library door and it closed with a thud of finality.

"What just happened?"

Antoine laughed. "Nothing of consequence. But your dress is perhaps getting worse."

"It's fine. I'm going home now anyway." She started walking back toward the staircase, embarrassed and eager to get away from the scene of the crime. "Why do I feel like I've just been caught doing something I'm not supposed to do? Do you know those people?"

"We're allowed in the library. But I didn't want you to feel as if I'd put you in a precarious position. Or lead you to do something you might regret. So I thought it best to leave."

"There was some tension building in there before we were interrupted."

"There was." He smiled at her, maybe relieved that she'd mentioned it. "I wasn't sure what to do. I mean to say, I know what I wanted to do. But I didn't know what I should do."

"Getting out of that very seductive library seems like a good choice."

As they stepped down onto the staircase, into view of everyone in the foyer below, several curious eyes watched them descend. It was like being on a stage, with an audience gazing up at her. Antoine was grinning and trying to hide it, looking at his feet instead of anyone in the room. But what were they looking at? What did they see? What would they say about this moment later? This wasn't a world Charlotte knew well enough to judge, but she was familiar with the way gossip could circulate around a community. No place had a whisper network like Vernon. When they reached the ground floor, she stopped him.

"I must be going, I'm afraid."

"Yes. Leaving actually sounds nice."

"You can't come with me." She whispered in case the piano wasn't loud enough to drown out their voices.

He grinned, always ready to flirt. "I'm sorry to hear that. But I wouldn't presume. Please, let me have a carriage called around for you."

"I came in a cab, Antoine. I don't have a carriage."

"Of course not. I meant that you could borrow one. Mine or someone else's. It's fine. Please."

Antoine asked the servant attending the door to bring up his carriage for Charlotte.

"Of course, monsieur," the uniform-clad man said with a bow. He didn't go himself, but sent another, younger uniformed attendant off.

"Can we walk in the garden while we wait? Out front?"

The man nodded. "Please help yourself, Monsieur de Larminet. Look for the carriage to pull up to the gate. Yours is the only one called up. It shouldn't be long."

"Thank you," Charlotte said. She followed Antoine out the wide front doors, into the cool night. The music carried through the open window, and guests were milling about in groups and couples throughout the landscaped yard. The streetlights and lights in the house cast a faint glow over the scene.

"Are you sure you want to leave already? I can give you my coat to cover your dress."

"It's fine." Was he crazy? That was all she needed was to wear his clothing in front of the woman he planned to marry. "This is a place to be seen, and it turns out I don't love being seen all that much."

"What do you mean?"

"I don't know. I'm conscious of what people will think. I don't want anyone to see me."

"You'd rather let your words on a page represent you?"

"Exactly! Meanwhile, I wish to remain invisible."

"I don't think you should be concerned what these people think of you, to be honest."

"I know, but I do. I know they're judging me because I'm different. My gown isn't from Worth. I don't even own any fake jewels, let alone real ones. And I stand out because of it."

"Standing out from this crowd isn't a bad thing." A carriage rolled to a stop outside the gate. "Let me walk you out."

He helped her climb aboard the carriage. Then as it pulled away, he stood there and watched her go. Only when they'd pulled out onto the street and he was out of sight did she settle into the plush velvet seat. The interior was finished in leather and polished wood; different from the marquis's carriage, but just as ornate. Charlotte, smoothing the tear in the side of her dress, didn't know enough about luxury transportation to know which of the two was better appointed.

# Chapter Ten

*The next morning,* Charlotte was in the kitchen where everyone except Madame Tremblay had gathered to intercept Cook as she arrived home from the boulangerie. The croissants were so fresh and warm, that they didn't even bother taking the box into the dining room.

"You have to tell us everything," Vanessa said.

"Yes, you weren't out that late." Nadine spread jam on a pastry.

"I know. It was all a bit overwhelming, to be honest." It had been. She'd arrived home after everyone had gone to bed. Now she was happy to have them there to talk about it. "I didn't know anyone, and the people were a little intimidating."

"So you made an appearance by sticking to the wall?"

"No, I wouldn't say that either. I danced a waltz with a gentleman I am acquainted with. And I saw the most stunning library I've ever seen." She was getting ready to tell them all about it when Diane interrupted.

"So you're telling us that you danced with someone and then he took you to the library?" The women leaned in, all eyes on Charlotte.

That moment in the library when they almost kissed zipped through her mind. They'd been so close she could practically feel him on her. She regretted not doing it, regretted that interruption. "Yes, but not exactly. We're just friends."

Nadine cleared her throat, and Charlotte's eyes shot right to hers. Vanessa looked between the two of them with her brow furrowed even deeper than usual. But Nadine didn't say anything, despite the knowing gleam in her eyes.

Then the heavy wooden door that led from the kitchen to the courtyard behind the house swung open and the groundskeeper came in. He held up his hand where an envelope was pinched between two fingers. "A letter for Mademoiselle Devereaux."

Everyone's eyes snapped to Charlotte now. She feigned surprise, even though the sender was obviously Antoine. She recognized that stationery. Probably Nadine did too. "The post is here already?"

"A special courier just came and went, mademoiselle. Must be important."

No. No, it wasn't. But she couldn't say so without attracting more attention to whatever was in that envelope. And sending a special courier—again!—gave all of this more weight than she was comfortable bearing. What could it be like to have someone in your employ that you could send all around the city delivering notes at all hours of the day? Imagine that. "I'm sure it's just a thank you note, from last night. Those aristocratic types are very polite like that. I'll open it later."

"No you don't, missy," Vanessa said playfully. "We want to hear every detail of whatever you're being so evasive about."

Charlotte looked at Nadine, who shrugged. Oh, she might as well. "Okay, fine. I've been receiving gifts and correspondence from Antoine de Larminet."

She paused while they all gasped and squealed.

"But I assure you that there is nothing between us. I've made it very clear that I am not interested in being a mistress to an aristocrat. Never." She took a deep breath when her argument reached this all-important, must-cling-to truth: "We're friends."

"Are you sure, honey, because that is not an arrangement to be dismissed lightly," Nadine said. "I know you've got your artistic integrity to think about, but that man is very wealthy."

"It might be worth the sacrifice," Catherine said.

"If you're not interested, then can you introduce him to me," Diane said. "I'm kidding, obviously, but only if you like him. If you don't, then maybe I'm not kidding."

"I'm absolutely sure. There's nothing between us." These words rang hollow and false even as she said them. Now that everyone knew her secret, all she cared about was getting upstairs and reading his letter.

"So how did you meet him?" Vanessa asked as she bit into her croissant.

Without hesitation, Charlotte told the story she'd already practiced in her head so many times, downplaying the romance and leaving out the kissing. Her housemates, rapt if she'd ever seen it, ate and listened, nodding along. Even without all the romantic parts, it was a cute, coincidental friendship. They got along so well and saw the world just differently enough to make everything so much more interesting. And the desire that swirled between them every single time he was near could be left out of the story. But it was there, undeniably. He looked at her in the same enchanted way that she felt about him. And he held back at the same time too. Even in the awkward moments, like at the ball when they came back downstairs and everyone had been watching, there was something there between them. A mutual not knowing what to do next.

"So what's he got to say now?" Catherine said when Charlotte had finished her truncated version of the events that led her to Antoine.

The envelope in her hand felt smooth and cool. She'd told him, over and over again, that they could only be friends. Her housemates leaned in expectantly. She ran a finger under the seal and popped it open. Then she slid the folded paper free and unfolded it.

*Dear Charlotte,*
*I was thrilled to see you last night at the ball. Your company, while brief, was the highlight of my evening. And that light shines again this morning, a torch I will carry with me throughout today. I could not wait to contact you, to keep the lines of this friendship open and active. I have an appointment this afternoon that I dread but can't escape. Tomorrow, are you available for lunch in a café and an afternoon in the park? I will come to you, on your side of town. And you can hold me captive for as long as you like, for whatever your pleasure.*
*Love, Antoine*

She read it silently under the gaze of her housemates, her face growing hot. She couldn't read it aloud verbatim. Even without saying anything out of the ordinary, his words somehow managed to sound like sex. She'd have to summarize. "He's asked me to lunch."

The women oohed and ahhed. Then began their questions.

"Where at?" Nadine asked frankly.

"Yeah." Diane chimed in. "His place or at a hotel?"

"At a café. One without curtains and private tables! I would insist."

"Is this the man who sent the typewriter?" Catherine waggled her eyebrows.

"Yes."

"Are you going to let him buy your lunch?" Vanessa asked pointedly.

"No. In fact, I'll meet him for a stroll in the park. That will be less intimate with all the people around."

"You're sure you're not interested?" Catherine winked. "We can all keep it a secret until he puts you up in your own apartment."

"Stop it! He's not putting me up anywhere. There's no secret to keep. Except for, maybe, we don't have to tell Madame Tremblay."

*Maitre Benoit Favreau's* office window looked out over the street below. Antoine had admired this view since he was a young man accompanying his father on his errands, stopping off here at Favreau's for a drink and conversation about topics that Antoine always felt too young to understand. Now he was here behind his father's back, hoping to find, if not an ally, a sympathetic ear.

"Have a seat." Favreau settled into his worn leather desk chair while Antoine sat in the wingback across from him. Then the old man regarded him expectantly.

"I appreciate you seeing me, and I hope you won't think me impertinent or sneaky or anything like that. But I'm here to ask about my parents' finances. They've sold off the viscounty, as you know, and I want to know why."

"Why don't you ask the vicomte yourself?"

"I have, but he evades my questions. I am quite concerned, though I have no idea what I need to be concerned about. Are they broke? Are they hoarding money? What on earth made them decide to sell?"

"You know it's not really a viscounty anymore. Just a piece of property. So it's not like you're losing a title."

"It's not about that. I'm surprised he gave it up, is all. Tradition has always been so important, and then he comes home one day and tells me he's done this. I don't understand it. And the tenants are being displaced."

Favreau leaned back and the chair under him squeaked. His hair had thinned and gone completely white, though his face was as spry and thoughtful as ever. "You know I can't say exactly what he's thinking. But since you're his son, and I believe your curiosity is warranted, I can tell you what it looks like on paper."

"I'm not sure there's a difference." Antoine sat forward in the seat.

"Your father has, it seems, lost interest in activities like keeping an eye on the estate or maintaining aging assets."

"So he's not selling for any particular need?"

"Not really."

"All the people who lived there, who worked the land. They're in dire straits since my father sold. And I'm as forward-thinking as the next person. I know the estate economic model is no longer as lucrative as it once was, or even viable. But it feels to me as if the right thing to do would be to divide the profits among the people he is displacing, rather than spend the money on trips and other luxuries."

"You can't exactly tell your father how to spend his money." He adjusted his pince nez. "But you should mention it to him. Tell him your concerns. It sounds unreasonably generous to me, but your father might hear you out or be willing to compromise."

Unreasonably generous? Perhaps Favreau wasn't the friendliest ear for this discussion after all. Still, he needed to know what his options were, even if Favreau wasn't the right person to help him.

"What about legal recourse? Is there anything I could do if he disagrees?"

"You're planning to threaten him?"

"Not necessarily." Antoine waved his hand. "I don't even know if there's anything I can threaten him with."

"I'm not sure that even France can force a man to turn over the money he got from selling his own property." Favreau shifted in his seat and looked hard at Antoine. "Don't tell your father this, but I don't begrudge those people for wanting some recompense. The same thing has been happening all over France. All over Europe. It's a small chance, but there may be room for a civil suit."

Antoine leaned closer to the desk. This was why he'd come to Favreau. Even when he wasn't on your side, he could help you see how to get around the problem.

Favreau pulled a sheet of paper from a sheaf and scribbled something down with his fountain pen. "This gentleman might be able to help."

*Antoine arrived at* the park a few minutes early, and he walked to the place by the bridge where he'd met Charlotte before. The sky was overcast so not many people were out. He'd brought an umbrella just in case it rained, and he leaned it against the base of the stone bridge. Then he turned and watched the path for Charlotte to appear, not wanting to miss a single glimpse.

A couple came along and passed him as they climbed the bridge and crossed. They gazed soulfully into each other's eyes and barely noticed Antoine until they were close enough to touch him. His presence startled them from their amorous daze. The man nodded a greeting to Antoine and the woman smiled and blushed. They seemed not to have a care in the world when they were together like that, locked in each other's sights. Not that Antoine had any cares about Charlotte, at least not any insofar as his affections for her. Or her affections for him, for that matter. She clearly enjoyed him. Responded to his presence. And Charlotte was easy company. But while this couple could fully exist together like that, he and Charlotte had something in the way.

Antoine didn't want to be friends with Charlotte Deveraux. He wanted to remove every garment from her body and worship her. He wanted to lie naked in her arms, blissfully spent, and hear her thoughts on the world, on art, on whatever she had in her mind. He could play friends for a while, but he wanted more. As much as he could get. Even if he had to wait. Not because she was some prize to win, but because he'd never felt this way about anyone else in his life. As long as he was alive and capable, he'd try to win her heart.

His gaze fixed on someone coming up the path. Someone in a skirt. Definitely a woman. She was too far off in the distance to know if it was Charlotte. But as she moved along, he recognized the breezy, leisurely gate.

His whole life, or at least since his brothers died, he'd believed that marrying for status and tradition was a fine life for him. He always trusted his parents when they told him a proper partnership could only be made with a wife of equal birth. And he always knew that, even if that marriage was loveless, love could be had through mistresses. But he'd never imagined that when he found that love—and he was falling in love with Charlotte—that there might be a hitch. That the object of his love might refuse to be kept a mistress while he married someone else.

He read the papers. He looked out at the world. And it was moving to a place more socially equitable. No one outside a small, aging circle of snobby aristocrats cared who he married. Even so, he'd made the promise to his parents many times. Now, watching Charlotte walked toward him, he wondered for the first time if he could go through with it.

Charlotte waved girlishly as she approached, an adorable, enthusiastic gesture. Her presence brought him happiness he could feel with his whole self. How could he possibly live without this?

He bowed and took Charlotte's small, precious hand in his. Then he raised it to his mouth for a quick kiss and a lingering moment of eye contact. Her gray dress, upon closer inspection, had a subtle lavender coloring that brought out her eyes. She smelled of rosewater and soap, and everything about her delighted him. Every little detail. "How have you been since I saw you last, my dear?"

"I've been fine, Antoine. Fine." She was smiling, but her happiness seemed delicate.

"Is something wrong?"

"Not really. Another rejection. I missed it in the post yesterday, so it was waiting for me first thing this morning. Sometimes when

I haven't written yet, a rejection can derail my day a little. Make it difficult to get any work done."

"I'm sorry to hear that. Surely, whatever fool editor rejected your brilliant prose should be fired. I've no doubt he'll live to regret it one day."

"That's actually a helpful way to think about it. Very cheerful, in fact."

"Shall we walk?" Antoine gave her his arm and picked up his umbrella as they started down the path. "The fool probably doesn't know a good story from garbage."

"You're probably right."

"But you have other stories out there, right? Making the rounds through the decision-makers, I imagine."

"I do. But it's so hard to get my hopes up over and over again, only to be disappointed."

"What's the problem?"

"I don't know. With some stories, I think they're good. Though I suppose they aren't quite good enough. And others I feel like I'm circling around something but not quite getting it. Though really I have no idea."

A woman walking two little French bulldogs passed them, one of which barked and made Charlotte jump and then laugh. When the woman apologized, Charlotte said, "Oh, that's quite all right. I've been barked at before."

As they moved on, Antoine continued. "Maybe you're too close to the work."

"Hmm? Yes! I'm too close. I need to distance myself somehow."
"Maybe an outside opinion?"

"Yes, well, maybe that too. Vanessa offered to read my drafts, but she's been so busy lately I don't want to bother her. I keep hoping that some editor will see something and take me on and help me get to where I need to be, rather than having to find it myself. I suppose that's some level of privilege speaking. Why should anyone help me when there are so many out there who are simply better writers?"

"How about if I read your drafts for you?"

"What? No. I couldn't ask you to do that."

"But I'd love to help. I love your work, Charlotte. And I read. Maybe I can see something you can't." The prospect of helping Charlotte in this way thrilled Antoine. Anything to make her feel better about her work. Anything to read more of her words, get closer to her thoughts. This wasn't just about getting her in bed, though perhaps it couldn't hurt him there either.

"You'd do that for me?" They'd wandered onto one of the smaller paths, and she stopped walking to face him. Her eyes questioning. She seemed so genuinely surprised.

"Of course, I would. You act like it's a giant hassle when it would please me to read every word from your mind."

"Stop. No one wants to read anyone's failed drafts." She put a hand on his lapel, stirring up a wave of warmth that made his whole body throb. Her lips were like a plush bow of the softest ribbon. Her eyes like pools of calm, deep water. They were standing so close now. They always ended up like this.

"I do. It can't be easy, toiling away alone at your desk. A writer needs readers. Let me help you, Charlotte."

Mischief flashed in her eyes and she looked around to see if they were alone. Then she looked up at him. "I want to kiss you, Antoine."

This was great news. Unbelievable. "Right here?"

Charlotte grabbed his hand and pulled him behind a massive oak tree that stood not far off the path.

"Right here." She pushed up on her toes and brought her mouth to his. This was unexpected, but Antoine soon caught up. He still had the umbrella, but he wrapped his free arm around her and held her close. The smell of rosewater enveloped him in a lusty haze. Her mouth felt like coming home and tasted sweet. When she parted it, he pressed deeper and swept her tongue with his. What started slowly, built fast, and Antoine's whole body came alive against hers. He needed this woman, and if they didn't stop kissing like this, they would be doing much more in no time.

"Charlotte." Antoine pulled away, so dizzy he saw stars. But Charlotte didn't stop kissing his face and jaw. "Charlotte, please."

She gasped to catch her breath. "I'm sorry."

"Don't be sorry."

"I don't know what came over me."

"I think I know."

She laughed and straightened herself.

"If you'd like to continue, we could do so behind this." He pushed open his umbrella, which was nearly as big around as she was tall.

Charlotte laughed again, and then she pulled him back to her and kissed him. Slower this time, without the sense of ascent, she moved her mouth over his, while he hid them from the opinions of the rest of the world with his umbrella. After a moment, just before things started to ramp up, she pulled away and looked at him.

"We'd better stop."

"Should we?"

She smiled wryly and maneuvered around the umbrella and back out onto the path. With a hint of defeat, Antoine closed the umbrella. Clearly, they were done testing its capabilities for the afternoon.

"I think we should do it."

Although it wasn't clear exactly what "it" she meant, Antoine nodded enthusiastically. "I do too. Though I'm not sure the umbrella can cover up that much nudity. We should find a room."

"Antoine!" Her mouth, red from all the kissing, dropped open, but it was definitely with a mix of shock and delight. The flush on her cheeks reddened deeper. "I meant about letting you read my stories."

"Ah! Of course." His face ached from smiling so much. She was too much fun. "I don't know what I was thinking."

"I think I know!"

They both laughed again and then continued on their walk. But she didn't say anything else about the kissing and whether or not there would be more of it. No question that Antoine wanted more. But he didn't bring it up either. It had perhaps been so sudden that Charlotte didn't know what to make of it. She talked about her work a little more, and then she used the gathering clouds as an excuse to end their outing and go home.

"I'll put together some pages for you."

"We can meet here again tomorrow. I'll pick them up then?" He didn't say so, but he'd be bringing his umbrella.

She paused for a moment, considering this. "No need for that. I'll send them in the post."

He stopped himself from arguing this. Stopped himself from mentioning the kissing one last time. Although he definitely wanted more, he was also willing to wait and take what he could get along the way. If she wanted to say they were friends, then that was fine. Friends who kissed like that would suit him just fine. She maybe needed time to get used to the idea. He walked her to the rotunda and asked to escort her the rest of the way. She declined. And when they parted ways, he resolved not to get ahead of himself. Not to get ahead of her. There was no question how he felt, or how she appeared to feel about him. But what to do about it, and what could reasonably unfold between them, left nothing but questions.

# Chapter Eleven

*A summery breeze* carried in through Charlotte's window, and somewhere in the distance, someone was playing the piano. The notes were faint but smooth. Her desk chair creaked under her. She'd spent the past few days assembling pages, making edits on the sheets in pencil, and then retyping the ones she'd fixed up. Now she had four stories, about fifty pages, stacked in a neat pile on the corner of her desk. She'd wrapped and tied them in a piece of red satin ribbon, which seemed more seductive than a simple piece of string. She stopped herself from spritzing it with her perfume, but may have applied some on her person within close range a time or two. Such a fool she'd become for love! And how easy it was to ignore the fact that he might never change his mind. All she had to do was figure out what to write in the note accompanying it.

She pulled out a crisp piece of her best stationery and poised her pen to write. Since that kiss in the park, he'd written to encourage her to send her stories. She shouldn't have kissed him because he still planned to marry another woman, and Charlotte hadn't changed her mind about what that meant for her and Antoine. But she didn't exactly regret it either. Kissing Antoine had been like melting into a pleasant, happy puddle and wanting nothing else. Although she hesitated to acknowledge it, a flicker of hope had sparked in her—hope that he'd change his mind and forget all about his stupid family traditions. She kept her note simple.

*Antoine,*
*I am deeply grateful that you've agreed to read these pages. There's so much I could say, and after going around about it, I've decided not to. I will let the work speak for itself. I look forward to your feedback.*
*Sincerely,*
*Charlotte Deveraux*

She folded the note. Then she packaged her manuscript in a craft paper envelope, tucked the missive inside, addressed it to Antoine, and carried it downstairs to put it in the post. Then she took a walk to forget about Antoine and her pages and the fact that he'd soon enough be reading them.

Later that evening, when Charlotte went down for dinner, her housemates were already seated and gossiping about the ladies in the house next door. Charlotte put a slice of roast chicken and three small red potatoes on her plate as the dishes were passed around. Nadine filled her glass and Charlotte's with red wine. She didn't know which neighbor the women were talking about, but she'd gathered quickly that it wasn't one of the ones Madame deemed respectable. Charlotte found the women she encountered in her neighborhood, and everywhere in the city really, to be fascinating creatures. Overdressed and concerned with such a multitude of sins.

"You heard about that one didn't you?" Catherine said, nodding at Madame.

"I know she left," Diane said. They were talking about one of the neighbor girls who'd come around a few times with Diane. "She didn't tell me why, I didn't had a chance to ask she was gone so fast."

"She was taking gentleman callers," Madame Tremblay said. "I spoke to Madame Placard this morning."

"Madame, that could mean anything from having a boyfriend to prostitution," Vanessa said. "Did you ask her for more details?"

"Lord, no," Madame said breathlessly. "I don't want any sort of details in my mind."

"So what will happen to her, then?" Charlotte asked, genuinely curious. These matters were largely about perception. What happened to the fallen ladies everyone was always talking about? Did they all just die in poverty and misery like Fantine? Or did they bounce from one man to the next? Because that was the risk: that a man would tire of her and her reputation would be ruined.

"A baron's son is putting her up in the second. I saw her this afternoon after work," Catherine explained. "She said it's a nice place, and she was wearing a new dress."

"That doesn't sound so terrible, to be honest," Nadine said.

Madame Tremblay shot her a hot look. "Don't get any ideas, mademoiselle. That's not a life that will lead you to a happy place. You girls need to learn how to take care of yourselves. That's the only secure path for a woman. That's why I opened my doors to you, to help you do that."

"I know, I know." Nadine rolled her eyes lovingly. She always joked, but she did seem to heed Madame's advice. She never brought men around. If she were seeing someone, she'd been doing it in secret and nowhere near Madame's respectable pension.

"What happened to the woman who lived in my room before me? I don't remember her name. The one with the gentleman caller?"

"Her name was Fleur," Vanessa said. "She's still in the apartment. Is that what you mean by what happened to her?"

"I don't know. Is she still with the gentleman she was caught with?"

"She actually isn't," Nadine said. "But she's seeing someone else. And she'd saved quite a bit of his money, sold some jewelry. She said you kind of have to do that anyway because a new man wouldn't appreciate seeing gifts from previous lovers adorning a mistress."

"I've told you to be careful socializing with a woman like her." Madame clutched her fork and knife while she gave her warning, and then she sliced into her chicken breast. "Though I'm happy to hear she's all right."

"She came to see me after a show a few weeks ago. We keep in touch."

Charlotte considered this fate. A powerful, wealthy man's mistress might live well until he tired of her and replaced her with someone younger. But some men kept the same mistress forever alongside the same wife. She'd heard stories about those arrangements too. Would finding herself broke after a man abandoned her be worse than being broke because she couldn't sell a story? There was risk in any romantic entanglement, but she imagined her future life would be alongside a best friend, a companion who didn't need anyone else but her to be happy. That's what her parents had. That was what she wanted. Maybe her parents had limited her idea of what a marriage could be.

Maybe she was too idealistic. But that was what she imagined for herself. Too bad she kept picturing Antoine there.

"No woman needs a man to take care of her," said Madame Tremblay. "Especially not in this day and age. There are better opportunities. People aren't as backward. You all have it easier than I did."

Charlotte wasn't so sure. She'd received two more rejections in the post that morning. She was running out of options for placing her pieces. Even with Antoine's help, it might be too late. She might be heading back to Vernon.

"Why so curious about Fleur?" Vanessa asked Charlotte pointedly. "Thinking of getting into mistressing?"

"No. Not at all." She made a face to emphasize the fact that she would never consider it. They were all watching her. "Just curious."

Being curious was different from being someone's mistress. No matter how tempting, she wasn't going to be that. For the rest of dinner, she listened to her friends gossip and started formulating a plot in her head. A woman gives up her ambitions to become an aristocrat's mistress, but she's flung loose and forced to live on a budget when he dies unexpectedly in a train accident. She ate her chicken and plotted. By the time she got back to her desk, the words poured out of her.

*Two weeks later,* they were back at the café on Champs-Élysées.

"I know you're behind my busy social calendar," Charlotte said after they'd finished discussing her latest stories. Antoine had worked his social connections to get Charlotte, the up-and-coming writer, invited to two different salons and a party.

"But there is always a publisher or two, so consider it professional advancement." This was true, even if he wanted nothing more than opportunities to spend more time with her.

Every time, Charlotte held her ground. There had been no kissing or gentle touches. When he reached for her, she pulled away. She toned down the flirting and refused to dance with him more than one time a night. They were friends and nothing more. Still, he'd been spending exponentially more time with her than with Louise. A name he dared not say in Charlotte's company.

After the party—a large affair at the home of a judge and his extravagant young wife—Charlotte and Antoine were mentioned in two different gossip columns. Nothing more insinuating or damning than a mention. Two names listed benignly in a sentence. So and so talked to so and so. His mother didn't even mention it. But the friendship had become more visible, and therefore riskier in a way, even if they weren't engaged in an affair. Knowing this hadn't made it any easier for him to pull back.

Antoine stacked their empty pastry plates and put his elbows on the table. Charlotte was lovely this morning, as always, in her gray skirt and a green ruffled blouse. And he wasn't ready to end their little meeting.

"Can I tell you something, Charlotte?"

"Of course."

"Do you remember me telling you that my father sold our family's estate?"

"I do remember you mentioning that." She nodded when the server came around with a coffee pot. And Antoine pushed his cup over for a refill as well.

"I'll take the check whenever you're ready," Antoine told the server, who nodded, cleared the empty dishes, and departed. Then Antoine turned back to Charlotte. "Well, I've asked him to give the money to the tenants who are being displaced by the new owners."

"Who are the new owners?"

"Developers. I guess they plan to build a factory."

"And what did your father say?"

"He said no. Absolutely not."

"It's a lot of money, I assume."

"It is, but we don't need it. I've checked."

Her blue eyes flashed with something shocked but fleeting. "So what are you going to do?"

"I'm not even sure there's anything I can do. But I suppose I feel like a terrible son even pursuing it. I've made an appointment with a lawyer."

"Oh, my. You really are pursuing it then."

"I am. So how terrible does that make me?"

"Well, I can't speak for your father. And something tells me that he and I would have differing opinions. But, Antoine, if your family doesn't need the money, but it will help so many others, then your father is wrong."

"I agree. But I'm afraid it will tear my family apart if I go through with it."

Charlotte got quiet then, refocusing her attention on her coffee cup. When she didn't say anything for a few minutes, Antoine broke the silence.

"Does it bother you to talk with me about things like this?"

"What do you mean?"

"I mean money. Class. Is it difficult for you to talk to me about it?"

"Don't take this personally, Antoine. But it seems to me that if things like marrying for love and doing what's right are what's threatening to tear your family and traditions apart, then maybe you should all reconsider what's holding it together. Thank you for the croissant."

She rose, and he did as well. He still hadn't paid, and so he reached for his wallet. But Charlotte was already walking away. When she reached the door, she looked back at him. Her blue eyes simmered. But she smiled, so she couldn't be that mad. Could she?

Antoine was still wondering about it the next day on the tennis court with Guillaume. The sun had been up for less than an hour but the early summer heat was already taking hold of the day. After his meeting with Charlotte, Antoine had gone out with Renee and drank too much whiskey, lamenting the state of his love life. Now sweat was running into his eyes, down his chest and legs. His feet felt heavy and his reactions were sluggish. And Guillaume, who had gone to bed early the night before, was proving to be an apt competitor. Over and over again, he returned the ball as easily as a bird takes flight. Antoine, meanwhile, could hardly hit a thing. This carried on until Guillaume grew bored.

After he thoroughly mopped the court with Antoine, they retired to the locker room, where they showered and dressed in amicable silence. Now they were standing side by side, combing their hair and tying their ties.

"Sorry my game was off," Antoine said.

"I hardly noticed," Guillaume said smugly. But then he cleared his throat and apologized. "I almost forgot that your brothers' anniversary is coming up. That's probably what's distracting you."

Antoine hadn't considered it, but the anniversary was in a few days. That wound had closed, for the most part. Now it was a dull, ever-present ache that persisted all year long. "Maybe you're right."

"My parents are hosting a dinner party," Guillaume said to Antoine in the mirror. "Next Friday. I've invited you."

"Sounds lovely." Guillaume's parents always pulled off a fun evening. Their events were smaller, more intimate, and less stuffy than many others he was expected to attend.

"Louise's family is not invited."

Antoine eyed Guillaume curiously.

"My parents don't know them." Guillaume shrugged and put his comb away. "But if you wanted her to be there, it's probably not too late."

Guillaume was testing him; he knew damn well that Antoine didn't really want Louise anywhere.

"No, that's all right. Though I suppose it's not good to say so."

"Probably not."

They left the locker room and made their way to the exit. The club buzzed with activity, attendants running errands, and people coming on and off the courts. All the same people they saw every time they came, dressed in their stylish whites to be seen as much as to play.

They asked the club attendant in the lobby to call up their carriages. Then they walked out to wait in the garden. Guillaume lit a cigarette.

"You know who would be a good addition to your guest list?" Antoine said, leaning against a gate. "Charlotte Deveraux."

"I have been secretly waiting for you to propose just that."

"I don't know why."

"It's clear you like her. It's not so clear that she likes you. But I hang around with you enough to see the pattern of you getting her invited almost everywhere."

"She's good company, is all."

Guillaume took a long drag of smoke. "And she's still refusing you."

"I haven't asked her for anything but her friendship."

"Sure you haven't."

"So maybe I have. She's a friend, she insists. And a good writer. I want to help her. I want her to be happy."

"Does that mean being with you?"

"I certainly think so. Though I don't believe she agrees."

"Does Louise know about her?"

"There's nothing Louise needs to know, at least not yet. And as we've already established. Charlotte has refused me. Until she changes her mind, there's no reason Louise needs to know anything."

"Sounds like a tangled web."

The carriages came around then. "Will you invite her or not?"

"Of course, I will. I happen to like Charlotte very much." Guillaume waggled his eyebrows suggestively. The urge to hit him came suddenly, then subsided the way it often did with friends. Antoine couldn't even think about another man swooping in and snatching Charlotte away. And if he wanted to see her at Guillaume's party, he had to be nice.

On the morning of June 17, Mother came down from her rooms dressed in black, as was her custom for the anniversary of her eldest sons' deaths. Antoine had been thirteen when it happened; within a matter of days, they'd both fallen ill and were gone. Antoine and his parents' lives had never been the same since. Antoine and Father had already gathered in the drawing room to mark the occasion in quiet togetherness. But Mother was smiling, strangely enough, while she poured her coffee and settled into the settee.

"Your father and I had the lawyer draw up a marriage contract while we were there last week. The papers arrived today."

Aha. She was maneuvering. That explained the cheerfulness. Antoine didn't hate having the power to please her. But the responsibility wasn't so easy to bear either. Especially with the growing sense of doom associated with the idea of marrying Louise. Why couldn't his mother find her purpose in some other pursuit that didn't involve him?

"Are the Montmorencys aware that you're taking legal action?"

"That was my question for you. Can the Montmorencys anticipate an engagement? Soon?"

"I assume you've given them every indication that it's in the works."

"Stop talking around it, Antoine. Isn't it time to propose?"

This was the first time she seemed to be moving past the deaths of his brothers. After the tragedy of their passing only hours apart, this day came and went each year. And it was always a cruel annual reminder that Antoine was alive and his brothers weren't. He hated to deny her when her eyes sparkled with hope.

"I have some other concerns at the moment, but I assure you that I will do as I'm told and propose to Louise. Eventually."

"I suppose that will have to keep my spirits afloat for now." She sipped her hot coffee thoughtfully. "We'll just look at the contract to make sure it's ready when the time comes. And it's nice to have something to look forward to, isn't it?"

Antoine settled into an armchair and drank his coffee. He wasn't a romantic, necessarily. The moment didn't need to be right for a proposal like his. There didn't need to be any elaborate declarations or grand gestures. Just terms of a contract hashed out by lawyers and their parents. There was nothing romantic about it. He could save the romantic gestures for Charlotte, if she'd only let him.

It had been weeks since they kissed in the park; though the more pressure his mother put on him about proposing, the more he sought respite in the memory of her mouth on his. But he'd been consumed by her pages. Reading her stories, inhabiting her mind had been like a fever dream. Every word chosen, every phrase soaked in wit. He'd read through all four of the stories two times in one sitting and was weak in the knees when got up. He'd never experienced such pure and passionate affection. A life without this glorious sensation would be no life at all. However, the last time he saw Charlotte, she'd left abruptly, and Antoine still wasn't sure where he stood with her.

Later that afternoon, Antoine took the carriage to the offices of Martin, Barbier, and Marchambeau in the fifth arrondissement. A bell above the door chimed when he walked inside, just in time for his appointment with the lawyer he hoped would help him get money out of his father.

The office wasn't nearly as stately or impressive as his father's lawyer's. Instead of walls covered in shelves of leather-bound books, a thin rack of books sat behind his simple, narrow desk.

There was no view of the charming street from these windows. Even if the windows were low enough to see anything, the view was more likely to offer petty crimes than charm.

"Ah, Monsieur de Larminet." The lawyer's chair squeaked when he rose to shake Antoine's hand, which he did firmly.

"Monsieur Barbier. Thank you for seeing me." His youth was surprising. Not a gray hair on his head. Perhaps even younger than Antoine. He probably couldn't afford a nicer office because he hadn't been practicing for long. Still, Antoine was impressed by anyone who had to work to secure a living and position in society. It was something he would never have to do, even if he did give away all the money from selling the estate. He'd never have to do anything with his life except read and enjoy himself. This was why he believed the tenants who worked the land deserved a degree of security. And hopefully, this man was the lawyer to figure out how to do it.

"This is quite a generous request," Barbier said.

"My father doesn't think so."

"I'm sure not." When Barbier asked about Antoine's motive, Antoine explained everything as the lawyer nodded his head. They had drinks and talked about their childhoods. And they hashed out a plan that might work, if it didn't kill his father first.

By the end of the meeting, with a glass of whiskey in his system, Antoine had grown friendly enough with the lawyer to ask him about the plain gold wedding band he wore.

"I've been married for nearly two years now. We're expecting our first baby in a few months." He spoke with pride that seemed even more mature than his profession.

"Well, congratulations, to a man who seems to have it all."

"I am lucky."

"And your wife? She's perfect I'm sure."

His eyes gleamed. "She is. My best friend."

"That's nice. My marriage, which I'm putting off as long as I can, will be more of an arrangement than a friendship."

"I had a client in such a case recently. He became good friends with his wife eventually. They're still friends. Though no longer married."

"No? What happened?"

"No matter how much he cared for his wife, he couldn't seem to give up his mistress." Barbier shrugged. "It wore on the relationship. But because he'd befriended the wife, she understood. They'd been waiting until his mother died to divorce."

"My god." Antoine's gut sank. "That story slices a little close for my taste."

"Are you in love with your mistress, Monsieur de Larminet?"

"You could say that." His words came out distractedly. He was busy putting himself in the anecdote, imagining himself divorcing Louise after his mother's death because he had been in love with Charlotte the whole time. What kind of man lived his life in such a way? Not one that a woman like Charlotte would wait for, let alone tolerate. No wonder she seemed so annoyed with him.

"My wife keeps my hands too full to pursue any others, even if I wanted to. So I can't help you with the heart in that respect."

Antoine thanked him and stood.

Barbier stood as well. "Let me know when you're ready to write your will. And, of course, I'll be in touch."

# *Chapter Twelve*

*Charlotte sat on* her bed with her latest rejection letter in her hand. The rejection letter that meant she wouldn't have the money to pay her rent for July.

The rejection letter that meant she'd have to leave Paris.

She hadn't been frivolous with her money, but her expenses were higher than she'd anticipated. She'd bought a dress and a secondhand pair of shoes. That and paper and a typewriter ribbon. A few books. But the rejections had piled up faster than the checks. She had been waiting to hear back from a few magazines, hoping for an acceptance to save her. But her time was up.

She never expected being a writer to be easy, but did it really have to be this hard? Maybe she wasn't cut out for Paris.

"Good morning," Nadine said, passing Charlotte's open door. Aside from Madame, who was scrubbing the dining room floor with a deck brush, and the staff, they were the only ones home. Nadine had slept in and missed breakfast because of a late performance. Creases from her pillow lined one side of her face.

"Good morning." Charlotte set her letter aside. "Do you have a minute? I actually want to ask you something."

"Of course." Nadine came into the room and sat next to Charlotte on the bed. Her wrapper hung loose on her thin shoulders, and her long, auburn hair was tousled and curly from the braid she wore at night. "Is everything okay?"

"Well, not really." Charlotte shrugged and her eyes stung. "I'm short on rent for next month."

Nadine stiffened a little at the mention of money, but that was probably because she didn't have any. Charlotte would never ask any of her housemates for money because they were likely living on as little as she was.

She continued, "Very short. And I was wondering if Madame ever gives a boarder more time?"

"Never. Not since I've lived here. And she can be a bitch about it too. Once I had to borrow five francs from one of the ladies next door. From the house of ill repute! Because she wouldn't give me an extra day."

"That's what I was afraid of."

Nadine looked over her shoulder at the door and lowered her voice. "Maybe you have a gentleman friend you could ask for the money?"

Charlotte could ask Antoine. And he'd give her the money for sure. But she couldn't do that. He'd already given her so much, and she shouldn't get in the habit of relying on him. "I don't think I do."

"Or you could sell something?" Nadine's gaze crossed the room and landed on Charlotte's desk. The typewriter.

"I was hoping I wouldn't have to do that."

"It happens," Nadine said without judgment. "I know a pawn shop. They'll hold it for you for a month. So if this is only a rough patch, maybe you can get it back as soon as things turn around."

Could things turn around? Or had she not been realistic about the writing trade from the beginning? "It might not turn around until I have a book published. And I think I'll be able to do that soon, but it won't be in the next week."

Nadine reached across the bed and put a firm hand on Charlotte's shoulder. "You can't leave Paris. I have to say that because it's the best place in the world. But for you, leaving Paris could be temporary. You are smart, and you have a loving family who can keep you while you save up and get your book done."

"That's true. I can carry on writing in Vernon without so much expense." She sniffed. "Paris will always be here waiting for me to come back."

"I had to move back in with my aunt twice before I learned enough and earned a good enough professional reputation to afford to be here on my own."

Nadine was right. "I just like it here and don't want to leave. Vernon is so dull in comparison."

"Nobody wants to leave Paris."

"Why didn't you ever find a gentleman friend to help you? I mean, there's no shame in it. And so many actresses do it."

Nadine rolled her eyes. "Oh, that's not my style. I'm probably the only actress in town who doesn't moonlight as a courtesan. But that's the way my mother lived, and I've always told myself that I never would. I saw how those men treated her. Not always, but sometimes. Life is much more stable and less risky when you can provide for yourself." Nadine held up her hands. "Not that I begrudge any woman who does it that way. It's just not for me."

"That's admirable of you—providing for yourself."

"It's something."

Charlotte picked a piece of string off her friend's dress. The world was a harsh place. Her mother had warned her of this many times. It wasn't personal. It was harsh. All the editors who'd stroked her ego and then put her off or rejected her outright or asked her to send something a little more this or a little more that; it wasn't that they didn't like her or didn't like her work. Publishing was business. Just business. There was no sympathy or handouts or easy wins. And no matter how much she loved Paris or the idea of living the writer's life here, that didn't mean her life would happen that way. This didn't make her less of a writer. Just not a rich one. And one day, she might be able to return. The only thing she could do was keep working. She told herself all of this, firmly and with emphasis, but then crumpled back onto the bed and moaned, "I don't want to leave Paris, though!"

"Well," Nadine patted her knee. "You've got a little more time to figure it out. Rent's not due until Monday."

"I do." The typewriter gleamed on her desk. Selling it would be awful. But would it be more awful than admitting defeat and going home? Where her mother would keep her busy and finding time to write would be her greatest struggle. In theory, she could write anywhere. But she'd never been able to write in Vernon the way she was writing now in Paris. "Where's that pawn shop?"

"It's on Pernette du Guillet." Nadine stood up from the bed. "Are you hungry? I'm going to see if there's anything in the kitchen. I can bring you something."

"No, but thank you."

As she was leaving Charlotte's room, Nadine stopped and said, "Try not to worry. It will all work out in the end exactly as it's supposed to."

The next day was Guillaume's party. According to Antoine, there would be some people from publishing there, and so this would be another chance to further her career. But the only real reason she'd been invited was because of Antoine. Not because any of these supposedly powerful publishing friends wanted to meet her. She was just another writer trying to get a break. And the breaks, she knew for a fact, were not widely available. Now that she knew her departure from Paris was more or less inevitable, she didn't care so much about career opportunities.

She'd gone to sleep the night before planning on pawning the typewriter. But in the light of the new day, she couldn't bring herself to do it. She pulled the box down out of her bureau, but couldn't pack up the machine. If she pawned it, it would buy her more time; but she probably wouldn't be able to get it back for much longer than that, if ever. And she might have to go home anyway.

As the day unfolded and Guillaume's party approached, Charlotte realized that there was perhaps good reason to leave the city. Leaving Paris would make things easier between her and Antoine. If she was gone, then he couldn't tempt her with his offers. And he could get on with marrying Louise. This was why she had to go. She needed to make a clean break. The party at Guillaume's would be their last.

So Charlotte dressed in her new dress and the feathery hat that Antoine had sent. Nadine curled her hair, producing another fashionable success. She arrived at the stately residence in a cab among luxury private carriages. The house was lovely with a spacious foyer and ballroom. The sound of string instruments carried from some ensemble deeper inside. But there were no ostentatious fountains or cascading staircases. The dresses were more casual, the jewels lighter. Charlotte didn't stand out here the way she had at other parties with Antoine's crowd.

Standing inside the door to the ballroom with Guillaume, greeting guests with two people who appeared to be Guillaume's parents, was Antoine. Charlotte's throat tightened, and she swallowed hard as she approached them. Guillaume greeted her first, with a kiss on each cheek. Then Antoine greeted her the same, lingering next to her left ear to whisper how happy he was that she'd come. He was dressed handsomely as always in a black suit with a white tie. He had a red rose pinned on his lapel. A rush of sadness hit her as she stood next to him. This would surely be one of the last times they'd spend together.

After introducing her to Guillaume's parents, Monsieur and Madame Allard, Antoine left the hosts and led her toward the refreshments. "You look beautiful. I've been waiting at the door for you to walk through it."

"From what I've heard you say about Guillaume, the event sounded promising."

"His father has invested in some publishing businesses, and he's friends with Monsieur Bouche, the publisher of Étoile Books. I want to introduce you to him. But let's get you a drink first."

A well-dressed server passed Charlotte a glass of champagne. She filled a small plate with petite fours and mini quiches—one of each variety available because they all looked so delicious. Then they found a small table on the edge of the ballroom. The music swelled as she sipped and bubbles broke on her tongue. The quartet was playing on the far end of the room, underneath a stunning circle window assembled from what had to be a thousand smaller petal-shaped pieces. It looked like more a window in a cathedral than a home. It was too dark to see anything through it, only a reflection of the room cut into slices. Several couples were dancing, and many small groups stood around the perimeter of the room. People milled about, visiting and cramming bites of food into their mouths.

"You're awfully quiet this evening."

"What? No. I'm just taking it all in. This is a lovely room." She needed to tell him about her plans to go back to Normandy, but she didn't want to ruin the evening.

"Ah, I see Monsieur Bouche now." Antoine waved to catch an older gentleman's attention, and they stood when Monsieur Bouche came over. He was much shorter than Antoine, with red hair streaked in gray. And he wore small round glasses.

"This is the writer you've been telling me about?"

"Charlotte Devereau, this is Monsieur Bouche. She's working on a collection of stories that portray modern French life with such biting wit and clarity."

"It's a pleasure, monsieur."

"Well, my wife remembered your story in the paper. As soon as Antoine said your name, she knew who you were."

"I am fortunate that so many people read it."

Monsieur Bouche raised an eyebrow. "It was a good story, I'll say that. But is it the start of a career, or a flashpoint? That's what I have to consider as a publisher."

"Her stories have already been published in another paper. *La Fronde* searched her out to write something for them. She's very much in demand."

"Monsieur de Larminet is being too generous." It was too generous, considering she hadn't been able to sell anything else. Since her realization that she couldn't afford to stay in Paris and her writing wasn't actually going to sustain her, her emotions had been swinging between everything being okay and feeling like an embarrassing imposter.

"I'm not being generous." He smiled at her earnestly. "She's being modest."

"Well, if you have a manuscript, I'd be happy to take a look at it. Books of the feminine nature sometimes don't sell as well because the potential readership is that much smaller when it doesn't include men."

"Oh, I assure you her work will appeal to anyone who enjoys reading." Antoine argued with his characteristic magnetism. "Her charm is universal, and the stories aren't entirely feminine, I wouldn't say."

"You know we might consider publishing it under a man's name," Monsieur Bouche said thoughtfully. "I've heard that can work."

Charlotte's mouth dropped open. She'd heard of this sort of thing, of course. But she'd already published under her own name.

"I assure you, monsieur," Antoine said, aghast. He stood up straighter, emphasizing their height difference. "Charlotte Deveraux's name is an asset. Whatever imprint debuts her book will be greater for it."

Antoine, though smiling politely, was turning red. What had she done to deserve this man? Antoine's dedication to Charlotte and her work couldn't be denied, or attributed to purely physical attraction either. He wasn't saying it to get her in bed, but hearing him take up for her like this made her very much want to be in bed with him. She swallowed the last of her champagne with a gulp.

She turned to Monsieur Bouche, suddenly eager to be away from his company, and said, "I've promised a first look of my collection to Monsieur Patenaude at Palace Books. And now, Antoine and I are heading to the dance floor. It was a pleasure to meet you, Monsieur Bouche."

He nodded and slipped away, perhaps as eager to get away from them as she was to get away from him.

Antoine was staring at her in his openly adoring way. "Were we going to dance? Because I didn't remember that."

"I don't feel like sweet-talking publishers tonight." She grabbed his hand and pulled him toward the dance floor. The musicians were just starting a waltz.

"You don't have to sweet-talk. Your work stands," Antoine argued as they wove through the crowd. "But it probably helps if he can put a face with the name on the manuscript when it comes across his desk."

Her eyes met his when they found a spot on the dance floor, and it was like his attention snapped into place. His gaze swept scandalously over her. Then Antoine wrapped an arm around her waist and held her close. Far closer than was appropriate for friends, or anyone in public. His throat was dangerously close to her nose and mouth. The vanilla and cedar aroma of him snagged her attention. She straightened her back but didn't pull away, her whole body tingling with awareness and melting into flexible submission. The violins took off as they spun and pulled apart and bowed and pulled back together again. He was watching her, smiling mischievously. Around and around they swung in a seductive dance. And every time they came together, he seemed to get closer to her. By the time the song ended, she was hot and entranced in his physical nearness. And thirsty.

He didn't remove his hand from the small of her back until they had fresh flutes of champagne and were seated at one of the little tables around the edge of the room. He wasn't shy about touching her, not the way he had been at other events.

When she caught her breath, Charlotte asked, "How many dances have you promised to these other ladies?"

"Not a single one." He sipped his champagne.

"So you can dance with me again?"

"If we can dance the way we just did." He tugged at his collar.

"And how was that?" She awaited his description, even though she'd been there herself.

"You know what I mean. That was… quite exhilarating. Almost scandalous."

"Do you regret being seen in the throes of dance with a commoner?"

He caught the brush of his mustache with his lower lip, like he was contemplating taking a bite out of her. "No."

"How can you be so sure there isn't a gossip columnist lurking around taking notes?"

"I'd be surprised if there wasn't."

The tension swirled around them like smoke. She almost asked about Louise just to break it. But that wouldn't accomplish anything. Charlotte was leaving town anyway. Perhaps it was time to throw caution to the wind.

"I'm happy to dance with you, Antoine."

"I feel the same."

Charlotte drank a mouthful of her champagne. She should tell him now that she was leaving. But the room was so warm, especially after dancing. "Do you want to step outside? Maybe smoke?"

"I would like that very much."

The air outside was only slightly cooler than it had been inside. But a whisper of a breeze brought some relief.

"Ah, my good friend the vicomte," Guillaume cheered good-naturedly from where he was leaning against a balustrade. He was surrounded primarily by women, but also a few young men and a cloud of smoke.

"Surely you have two cigarettes to lend such a good friend."

"Surely." Guillaume extended his enamel cigarette case, and Antoine took it, removing a cigarette and passing it to Charlotte before removing one for himself and returning the case. The little crowd shifted to let them join in. A post lantern glowed above their heads, and moths circled the light. Crickets chirped from their hiding spots, the sound mingling with the faint music coming from inside.

Antoine struck a match, cupping his hand by Charlotte's face to shield the flame and light her cigarette. Then he used it to light his own before extinguishing it with a shake. The low light cast shadows across his profile, enhancing his already handsome face. He had a face she could look at every day. Could, but couldn't.

Charlotte inhaled and exhaled a puff of smoke that rose into the night. And they fell into the conversation that had been happening before they arrived, about a show that opened the weekend before. A woman in a corset-style dress and long black gloves said the star actress had been a disappointment. She was a famous singer with a reputation for capturing deep emotions in her performances. But not this time. Charlotte hadn't seen it, and probably never would, but she'd heard about it. She'd imagined seeing a show with Antoine because any daydream of Paris apparently included him, but now it was too late. Proximity to culture was perhaps what she'd miss the most about life in the city. Aside from Antoine. She'd miss him terribly. The stimulating conversation, the art, and the shows—she'd miss all that too.

Vernon wasn't ugly, but the beauty was harder to find. Or it was difficult for her to see because she'd grown up there. And it would all be the same when she got back. Two months wasn't long enough for the place to change. She hadn't moved to Paris, so much as come for a long visit.

"She lived up to all of my expectations," Guillaume said of the actress. "She had me practically on my knees in those ending scenes."

"I liked her too, but for more reasons than her singing, if you know what I mean," the young gentleman to his left chimed in. His lanky youth helped the joke land, or twisted it around on itself, because no matter how wealthy this young man was, the actress's outsized success put her far out of his realm of possible dates.

The woman next to Charlotte wore a heavy floral perfume that wasn't unpleasant. Her dress was pretty and blue, but not brand new. And her jewelry was simple. She smiled and extended a hand to Charlotte.

"I'm Natalie."

"Charlotte." She smiled warmly.

"How do you know Guillaume?"

"Through Antoine."

"Really? I thought everyone interesting knew Antoine through Guillaume." Natalie looked teasingly at Antoine, biting her bottom lip.

"I can interest people," Antoine said feigning defensiveness. "It does happen."

"Just this once, you mean?"

Antoine laughed along with everyone else, and then the conversation moved on to some juicy piece of gossip about the end of an affair involving people Charlotte didn't know. Even so, they explained so she could laugh too. This was a better crowd than at the fancy ball. They were friendlier. Not as stuffy. Rich, probably, but not because a king gave it to them. Charlotte liked Guillaume, but seeing him in his home, surrounded by his favorite people, she liked him even more. And thank goodness Guillaume was Antoine's closest friend to balance out his snobbish family. It was the kind of party that reflected well on everyone involved, and if she put off telling Antoine about leaving the city, then they could have a lot of fun.

# *Chapter Thirteen*

*Antoine broke away* from the group slightly to lean against the balustrade. The waxing moon hung in the dark sky, illuminating the garden below the terrace in a cool glow. The cigarette tasted sharp and sweet, the smoke mingled with the rosy scent of Charlotte's perfume. The fact that she'd come thrilled him. Her company was always his deepest pleasure, and at Guillaume's, he didn't have to worry so much about everyone watching him and forming harsh opinions the way he did in other settings. He could relax and enjoy Charlotte. And she could see that his life wasn't all stuffy balls and social expectations. That they could be together in a world like this no matter what was happening in his other world.

The feather on her hat quivered as she tilted her head back and blew out her smoke. The lantern light cast a pale light on her skin. She'd been quiet so far that evening. Not distant. Quite the opposite, especially on the dance floor. But quiet, like she had something on her mind.

"Have you seen any shows since you've been in Paris?"

"I haven't."

"We should see something together. Maybe the opera they were just talking about? Or something else, if you like." He offered this and immediately realized that once his engagement was official and announced, he wouldn't be able to take Charlotte to society venues even as friends. People would say it was in poor taste, which was precisely why he had to put all that business off for as long as he could.

"That sounds nice," Charlotte said noncommittally.

A server came around with a bottle of champagne, topping off everyone who held out their glass. Olivier Arnaud, a family friend of Guillaume's whom Antoine had met a few times, called for a toast to Guillaume's hospitality and servers with champagne. Everyone cheered with half-hearted good-nature. And the conversation carried on. The air and the group buzzed with latent energy, like the night was, despite the hour, just getting underway.

Not surprisingly, less than thirty minutes later, Guillaume came up and tapped on Antoine's shoulder. "Ready to get out of here?"

"What do you have in mind?"

"Some of us are going to Moulin Rouge. Charlotte, we'd love it if you'd join us."

"Can you leave your own party, Guillaume?"

"My parents' party, you mean. And yes. I can absolutely leave. They can hold their own, believe it or not, without my supervision."

She smiled. "A cabaret sounds like fun. Count me in."

"Wonderful." Guillaume gave Antoine another hard pat. "Give me a minute to gather everyone and then we'll take the metro."

Antoine nodded and, after Guillaume had gone, said to Charlotte, "I'm so glad you want to go. I wasn't sure you would."

"Why wouldn't I?"

"You're always scampering off early, going to bed so you can wake up before the sun and write during the quiet hours. At least I assume."

"That's an astonishingly close guess. Except for all the nights I simply had a different party to attend and made excuses about work to avoid hurting your feelings."

"Oh, really? Well, we can drop you wherever you like, if you have somewhere better to be."

"I do not. At least not tonight," she teased.

"Then I'm in luck." He offered her his arm, and she took it.

It seemed to take forever for the little group to separate from the party proper. There were goodbyes to be said, excuses to be applied, logistics to consider, and decisions to be made. Then there were the last pieces of gossip on which to get snagged on the way out the door. The group lost two who came up with a better idea on the short walk to the metro station. By the time it was all said and done, eight of them descended the stairs and boarded the underground train.

The carriage was lined with wide windows, which looked out on the dark walls of the tunnel. Inside it was sparsely occupied. Two women in domestic uniforms were seated toward the front, an older gentleman and younger man who looked like he could be his son boarded along with them and took seats in the back. An older couple who may have been heading home from dinner at a friend's glanced at their lively group and then silently returned their quiet conversation.

Antoine sat next to Charlotte on one of the little benches. Guillaume fell into the seat in front of them and shifted so he was facing back at everyone. Natalie Fornier and her friend, whose name Antoine had regrettably forgotten, sat on the bench across the aisle from Guillaume. Yves Beaulieu, a lawyer friend of Guillaume's who knew how to have a good time, and his wife

Anais sat on the bench behind Antoine and Charlotte. And Olivier took the bench across from them.

When the train started moving, Guillaume smiled the way he did when they were kids about to embark on some grand adventure.

"Guillaume has fully embraced the metro as a mode of travel," Antoine said mostly to Guillaume and Charlotte, but loud enough for the whole group to hear.

"I'm a little surprised," Natalie said. "I thought fancy carriages were the only way to go."

"Or one of those ones with the motor," her friend said.

"That would be fun, wouldn't it?" Olivier said.

"Ah, but this is the future of travel around the city. And I welcome it," Guillaume said.

The Paris metro was such a big deal that it made headlines even in Vernon. Cities all over the world were building underground trains to alleviate crowded streets. And it made it easier for people to get to and from work. Many of the city's workforce couldn't afford to live where the jobs were most plentiful. So it seemed to be worth the fuss over the construction and cost. It made the city smaller by being better connected. If people could overcome the hesitancy to go underground, then it was comfortable enough. The sparse carriage lacked cushions and armrests and other luxuries, but for a quick ride across town, none of that mattered. And it didn't have to stop or slow down for traffic.

"But you don't have to take the metro. You can afford your privacy," Natalie said.

"And wait in traffic like everyone else? Public transportation will never work unless everyone uses it. Even the people who can afford not to."

"That's very progressive of you, Guillaume," Charlotte said.

"Have you invested money in underground transportation?" Yves asked.

"No. I'm merely a citizen in need of a ride. But that's not a bad idea."

"So you don't mind the giant holes in the streets?" Olivier said.

"I heard him complain about that just the other day." Antoine chimed in.

"Building it is messy. But the result is worth the trouble. This is nice." Guillaume gestured at the carriage. The tunnel walls passed on the other side of the windows. "And we'll be on the other side of the city in no time."

"This is my first ride," said Charlotte. "But I don't know the city well enough to know where the metro can take me. Perhaps I should have been more adventurous."

Antoine quirked an eyebrow at her use of the past tense, but let it pass like a slip of the tongue.

"Moulin Rouge will be an adventure, for sure," Natalie said. "Forget about the metro. This is nothing."

When they arrived at the Blanche Station in Montmartre, the group exited the metro and made their way up onto Boulevard de Clichy. Antoine had been to Moulin Rouge a few times with Guillaume. These weren't the sort of outings he told Mother about, because he was supposed to be different than the people who hung around the clubs. But how could a person not love a raucous night of burlesque entertainment? It was wildly fun. And he was excited to be here with Charlotte, who would surely love the wildness of it. Except what she'd said in the park that day about men and their mistresses still tugged at his brain. This was the sort of place a man might bring his mistress and not his wife. And here he was with Charlotte, surely proving right some universal truth about the plights of mistresses and wives.

The red windmill, illuminated with spotlights, turned slowly above the rooftop. People congregated around the cabaret's entrance, waiting for friends or waiting for rides to get out of there. Music from inside carried out onto the street. Placards listing upcoming shows and events flanked the red door. Guillaume pulled open one side and held it for everyone. Charlotte smiled up at Antoine as they passed through, and he winked joyfully at her.

Inside Guillaume went to look for a maitre d' about service. The ceiling was draped with bold striped fabric and rimmed with strings of lights. Dinner tables set with white cloths and little lamps spread out around the stage, where a scantily clad dancer was swinging through the air and singing about love. Heavy red velvet curtains rimmed in gold fringe hung from the stage and along the walls. And an orchestra played from a balcony.

"What do you think?"

Charlotte squeezed his arm a little tighter and said, "It's amazing, Antoine. I'm too amazed to think."

"Charlotte! I thought that was you, Charlotte!" A woman emerged from the crowd, towing another woman behind her by the arm. "Diane didn't believe me."

"It's not that I didn't believe her. But you never come out! I'm surprised to see you is all." They were American, judging from their accents, and maybe sisters. Then, as if just noticing that Charlotte wasn't alone, the women surveyed him.

"We've only just arrived. I was at a party in the seventh, and then we took the metro here. Catherine and Diane," she introduced the women, "This is my friend Antoine de Larminet. Antoine, these are my housemates. They're sisters. That gentleman over there is Guillaume, who was hosting the party. A group of us came from his place."

"You again," Diane said to Guillaume, who looked as surprised as she was.

"We were just arguing about leaving and apparently met your friend Guillaume," Catherine said. "I'm ready to go and she's not."

"But now that Charlotte and her friends are here, you can take a cab home and I'll stay with them."

"Can't you stay, Catherine," Charlotte asked.

"I almost feel like it, now that you're here," she said regretfully. "But I have to work in the morning."

"So go home. I'll be fine!" Diane assured her sister.

"I'll keep you company." Guillaume, suave as ever, stepped forward and volunteered. He kissed their hands in turn, lingering particularly over Diane's. "I need to make up for the poor first impression I fear I left with your friend."

Her scowl faltered. "It will cost you dinner, monsieur."

"Good, then it's settled," Catherine said. "I'll get out of here and you can stay with them. Will you see me out?"

"Of course." Diane turned to Charlotte then. "I'll meet you back here in a few minutes?"

"Okay."

"We'll get a table outside," Guillaume said. While Catherine and Diane headed for the exit, they went outside and found a table with enough seats for everyone. Antoine, Charlotte, Guillaume, Olivier, Natalie, and her friend sat. But the group started to disperse a little. Yves and Anais headed off for the dance floor. Then Olivier, Natalie, and her friend left the table for a closer look at the elephant that towered over the courtyard. Moulin Rouge was truly a magnificent sight, more like a circus than a dance hall, or a unique combination of the two. A cocktail server took their drink order, and then Charlotte's housemate returned.

"Were you and Catherine here for long?" Charlotte asked.

"A few hours. We were dancing almost the whole time. I must look like a disaster."

"Don't be silly," Guillaume said. "You're the most stunning woman here. Are you American?"

"I am. But we've been here for months and have no plans to leave."

The server returned with drinks and asked if Diane wanted anything since she'd only just joined them.

Diane declined with a flick of her feather boa. "I should eat something before I have any more wine."

"Dinner is still being served inside, mademoiselle. Let me know if you want a table."

"Maybe. Thank you."

After the server had gone, Guillaume commenced flirtations with Diane, asking about her hometown and what she'd done since coming to Paris.

Across the table, Charlotte raised her eyebrows.

Antoine laughed. Guillaume was always meeting the next love of his life. Sometimes that thrill of finding someone new left after getting to know the person, but being with Charlotte had only become more compelling the more Antoine got to know her. And he wanted to know absolutely everything.

"Let me buy you dinner," Guillaume said. "We've eaten, but you must be starving."

Diane looked at Charlotte, who shrugged.

Antoine shrugged as well, hoping they'd take off so he could spend some time alone with Charlotte. "We'll probably stay out here with the others, but you two should go ahead."

"Absolutely. We're fine here. You two go ahead."

In seconds, Diane and Guillaume were up from their seats and headed inside.

"Guillaume isn't usually drawn to Americans," Antoine said after they were gone.

"Diane is a lot of fun. She and her sister are the first Americans I've ever really known, and they have a different way of seeing things for sure. I think her family is quite wealthy. They didn't want Diane and her sister to come to Paris, and they don't pay for much. So Diane and Catherine both have jobs. And they work all the time. Not like most wealthy girls I know."

"Do you know a lot of wealthy girls?" Antoine said.

"Not as many as you, I'm sure."

"Touché. So what do you think of Moulin Rouge?" Their table was off to the side and secluded behind a potted palm from the main action. But a row of cancan dancers on the little stage held their skirts aloft, exposing lacy stockings and ruffled undergarments. On the floor below them, dancers in long gloves and minimal clothing kicked right along with them. Clowns in full face paint galavanted through the crowd. Costumed revelers coexisted with men in top hats, black suits, and white ties.

"It's quite the experience. Do you come here often?"

He nodded. "Guillaume likes it."

"So does Diane. But I won't ask about Guillaume's intentions."

“Well, I’m sure they’re not the purest. But Guillaume is a gentleman.”

“Does that mean he’s promised to someone with an inheritance?”

The question hit him like a dart. She could bite so unexpectedly when something was bothering her. Not that he didn’t deserve it. The reality of his existence was always with him, whether he was in Montmartre or Faubourg Saint-Germain. There was only one way to deal with such a reality, and that was to face it and power through with honesty and forthrightness. “Not Guillaume. His family made their money. And they aren’t as traditional.”

“Ah.” Charlotte looked down at her hands. They were bare, but her arms were covered in the shimmery blue fabric of her dress. The wide neckline scooped down seductively far so the curls of her hair fell on her bare shoulders. It didn’t matter how well Antoine faced his reality, though, if she wasn’t willing to do the same.

Suddenly he wanted to sweep her away from it as fast as possible. “Charlotte, I think we should dance.”

She lifted her bright gaze to his. “I think we should too.”

# Chapter Fourteen

*Eight dancers in* red and blue dresses and feathered hats lined the stage, kicking their legs, swinging their ruffled skirts, and showing off the lacy lingerie underneath. They danced in a circle formation, kicking so high it looked like their legs might fly out from under them. Then they all kicked up their right legs and held them aloft almost vertical with their right arms. Holding this pose, they stomped their standing legs and spun like tops. Around and around they went, longer than seemed humanly possible, until their legs dropped and the dancers fell into the splits on the stage.

Charlotte kicked and tried to follow along with the others. Antoine did quite well, though the men didn't do as much leg throwing as the women. He was the kind of man who could let his ego go and have fun. He didn't care that he didn't know what he was doing. He smiled and laughed the whole time. And when he pulled her in after a particularly fast and rowdy combination of steps and held her waist and hand, a sense of loss struck her. They might never dance together again. This might be the last time he puts his arms around her. Her whole body crawled with anticipatory grief. Everything was so fleeting. Every sensation. Every moment.

It overwhelmed her. Then she caught his gaze, swirling with desire. Everything that existed between them—even the fact that he hadn't changed his mind about marrying someone else—fell away. Like this, she loved him. And she wanted them to be simply a man and a woman one time before reality swooped back in to prevent it.

She put her hands on his chest to stop him from flinging her away in a spin. She clutched his lapel, and then she lifted on her toes and kissed him. Right there in the middle of the dance floor, all those people around. If he was surprised, he quickly recovered. He put his arms around her and kissed her back. His mustache was soft and his mouth welcoming. When he parted his lips, she swiped her tongue along his teeth, kissing harder. Everyone around them disappeared into a noisy blur, and her head swam in delight until some expedient patron whistled and a few others joined in with applause and whooping shouts of ooh la la.

When she pulled away, most of the onlookers had already lost interest in their show of affection and carried on dancing. Antoine was looking at her as if he was in a daze. His dark eyes. His smiling face. His solid shoulders and chest. He was so perfect. And she had to leave him. She had to tell him she was leaving. She had to do it now.

"I'm leaving Paris."

"What?"

"I'm going home to Vernon."

"For how long?"

"I don't know. But probably for a while. For good, maybe."

Antoine's brow furrowed and he took her hand, leading her off the crowded dance floor and back toward the tables. Theirs was occupied, but he found another. He dropped into a chair like he couldn't stand for another second. Then he and looked up at her, still holding her hand. "I don't understand. When? Why?"

"I'm out of money, simple as that. Rent is due on Monday, and I don't have it." She dropped his hand and sat across from him. "It's been harder to sell stories than I thought it would be, and maybe I wasn't very realistic about how much I could earn that way. And so my time is up."

"Charlotte, don't be silly. How much do you need?"

"More than I've been able to earn or feel comfortable asking my parents for. They'd rather I came home anyway."

He stared at her, open-mouthed and wide-eyed.

"It's not that big of a deal. I wanted a Paris experience, and I got it. I've had a lovely time, thanks to you. And now my time is up. Back to real life. At least for now."

"This is what you want?"

"Not exactly. But I can't always get what I want." She imbued the words with as much double meaning as she could muster. She couldn't have him. "It doesn't work that way."

"Don't be silly. I will give you the money to pay your rent."

"Now you're being silly."

"I'm not at all. Establishing a writing career takes time, I'm sure. And I want you to succeed. I want to buy you the time you need. I'll give you the money. We can go to my house and get it right now."

"What? You've got fifteen francs just sitting around back at your place?"

"Yes."

After she'd lost sleep over the money for days, it seemed unfathomable that he could produce it with a quick stop at home. "Antoine, you know I can't let you do that."

"Why not?"

"Because. What will people think?"

"Who cares? No one has to know. I'll give you the cash."

"Antoine." The dancing on the stage finished with a roar of cheers from the dance floor. Then the band began a slower number and the throng of people fell into step.

"Charlotte. Please," Antoine said after a moment. "Let me do this for you. I am your friend, am I not? I have money. You need money. It's as simple as that."

"But it's not as simple as that, and you know it."

"If it's not simple, then you're the one who is complicating it." There was an edge desperation in his words. He leaned back in his seat.

"I don't know when I'll be able to pay you back."

"I don't care if you never pay me back."

"Maybe not. But what will I do next month?"

"By then you will have sold another story." He said it so confidently, as if it could only be true.

"Maybe. Or maybe my departure is inevitable."

Antoine put his hat on the table and his head in his hands. The music swirled around them, and Charlotte didn't know what to say. This was more painful for him than she anticipated. When he looked up, his ruffled hair fell over his forehead and he smiled weakly at her. He reached across the table and took her hand. He held it in both of his and played with her fingers a little, lovingly examining the little callus where she held her pencil too tight and the faint ink stains that she'd scrubbed at earlier. His white gloves were soft against her skin. Antoine was a different sort of man than she'd ever met, and his feelings for her ran deep, deeper than Pierre's lusty admiration. Leaving Pierre had been easy. This was something else entirely. She never felt so admired and loved.

Antoine loved her. It radiated off him. It wasn't a game for him, or a fling. The crumpled, tired look on his face was heartbreak. Charlotte's eyes burned with a surge of tears, which she blinked away. And when that didn't hold them off, she wiped her eyes with her free hand. He raised the hand he had to his mouth and kissed the back of it. He held it there, breathing her in. Then he turned her hand over and kissed her wrist quickly before enclosing her hand in his and setting it back down on the table between them. The delicate gesture entranced her, wiped her thoughts and worries from her mind.

"Is this what you want, Charlotte? Vernon?"

"No. It most certainly isn't."

"*Let's go see* if we can find Guillaume and Diane." Antoine stood up and gently tugged Charlotte's hand so she'd stand too. The loud, boisterous music pounded against his brain. The crowd around them had become oppressive. And he had to convince Charlotte to stay in the city. He had to show her how much she meant to him. He laced his fingers in hers and maneuvered them through the partying crowd. When they made it inside, he searched for their friends at every table.

"I don't see them," Charlotte said. "I don't see anyone we arrived with."

"I don't either."

They checked the bar area and went to the other side of the dining room for a different angle, checking every face they passed.

"Could they have gone back outside? Or left?"

"Maybe. I should check with the maître d'."

Without releasing Charlotte's hand, he explained the situation to the man at the front door.

"Ah, yes. Monsieur Allard left a message for you. He and Mademoiselle Talbot left not long ago, and Monsieur Allard is seeing the lady home."

Charlotte shrugged. And then she didn't argue or even ask where they were going when Antoine led her out the door and onto the street. He didn't quite know the answer himself. He just couldn't stand to be in the cabaret for one more minute, surrounded by all those people when everything inside him screamed for Charlotte alone. He hailed a cab, helped Charlotte into it, and gave the driver his home address before sliding in next to her. As the carriage jolted forward, he removed his gloves and tucked them in the interior pocket of his jacket. Then he took Charlotte's soft, small hand again.

The shadows from the streetlights moved across her face, and he held her gaze for a long moment. Then her eyes flicked down to his mouth. She put her free hand on his thigh and used it as leverage to reach him. She paused for a second, a breath away, and then kissed him.

Antoine moved his hands to her waist and pulled her closer, nearly into his lap, and held her there. Charlotte wrapped her arms around his neck and tipped her head to kiss him deeper. The fabric of her dress rustled as she pressed against him, and the only other sounds were the rhythm of the horses' hooves on the street and Charlotte's soft little moans. She tasted like champagne and the scent of smoke from the club clung to her and mingled with her floral perfume. It drained him of every thought and sensation besides desire.

He had snuck women into his parents' house on an occasion or two. Not that he could get in any sort of real trouble; he was a grown man after all. But everything at his parents' house was simpler when he kept his affairs as private as possible. And so when the cab dropped them in front, he led her around to the side entrance and ushered her upstairs to his rooms. With the door closed behind him, he lit two lamps while Charlotte stood timidly against the wall, seemingly taking in every detail of his lodgings.

"I spend most of my time in here reading and corresponding. My bed and dressing room are through there."

The housekeeper had been through and neatened his piles of books and papers. The surface of his desk had been cleared. He didn't have company often, though the thought of bringing Charlotte back had crossed his mind a million times. Having her here now, in his space, felt more intimate than the other times they'd spent together, perhaps even more so than their carriage rides.

"It's quite grand," she said quietly. "Can anyone hear us talking?"

"No. We are alone. But first..."

He left her and went to his closet, where he kept cash in a carved wooden box. Among his rows of suits and shelves of shoes, he counted fifteen francs, then twenty, off the stack. Then he counted what was left. Thirty-four francs wasn't a small amount of money, but it wasn't that much either. So little to him and so much to Charlotte. He'd give it all to her. He closed the box and returned to Charlotte in the sitting room.

"I brought you here to give this to you. And so I want to do it right away, before anything else happens." He put the money in her hand and closed her fingers around it. "Because no matter what happens next, whether you stay or go or what we do or say, I want you to have this money. Think of it as a donation in support of the arts."

She looked at the money like she wasn't sure she should take it. Antoine was prepared to argue. But then she put it in the pocket of her dress. He could have collapsed with relief.

"Would you like a drink? I have whiskey, and can probably drum up some wine in the kitchen if you prefer that."

"Whiskey is fine. Thank you."

"Please sit."

She did, on the leather settee, while he poured the drinks. He served her, and then sat down next to her, as close as he could get without smashing her. Settling in, he propped his arm on the back of the settee.

Charlotte sipped the whiskey, shuddered, and then set her glass on the edge of the table. That shudder delighted Antoine. He took a drink, savoring the burn as he swallowed.

After a few quiet minutes, Charlotte spoke. "This is a pretty nice place you have here, Antoine."

"Merci. It's been in the family for generations."

"I would assume nothing less," she said with a wry edge. She turned in the seat to face him. Pulling her to him would be so easy, he was so close to her mouth. Their nearness, the amicable silence, seemed to be building. But it was something tenuous, something he should approach with caution. He should wait for her to make the next move, even if his need for her strained in his chest and his pants.

Another quiet minute ticked by. The lamp flickered and shot shadows across them. Antoine took another swallow of his whiskey, and when the glass left his mouth, she took it and set it next to hers on the table. Then she placed her hand on his leg and looked up at him with a cloudy, desirous haze in her eyes.

"Charlotte, are you sure?" He managed to get the words out even as her hand slid up his thigh, closing in on his aching crotch.

She rubbed and whispered, "Yes. I have wanted this for quite some time, perhaps more than I've ever wanted anything else."

She stood, and he mourned the absence of her warm hand as he watched her remove the pins holding her hat to her head. She set them on the table, and then stepped out of her shoes and kicked them away. She unhooked the buttons that held her dress in place. Then she pulled her arms loose and let the whole thing fall to the floor. Catching the strings of her bodice in her nimble fingers, she untied and loosened the laces. She undressed as if she were alone, slowly and without show. It was so simple and so sexy, her self-possession so compelling, that all he could do was watch it all unfold. She bent down to pick the dress up, and then draped it on the back of the wingback chair with her bag. Then she stood before him, straddling his knees with her legs, wearing nothing but a thin chemise, lacy underwear, and the garters holding her stockings. She unclipped them, placing her toes on the settee next to him and sliding the stocking down.

He'd never seen anything like it. He'd never met anyone like her. Her getting naked in his room was like jumping off a cliff, something that he could never undo. His life changed when she entered it. She'd thrown everything off.

With both stockings discarded on the oriental rug, Charlotte pulled the satin chemise over her head, stepped forward as it fell from her hands, and straddled him in nothing but her drawers.

The scent of her enveloped him as his mouth met her soft bare shoulder, his hands met her breasts. He would never be the same.

*"Oh, Charlotte, I'm* done for," Antoine whispered into her skin. His warm hands explored, soothing and torturing her at the same time. Charlotte moaned and tilted her hips, rubbing against the fabric of his suit. She laced her hands through his hair, finding his mouth with hers. Her whole body throbbed and her mind focused on him, his lips, his neck, all his layers of clothing between them. She was done for too.

Their lips fused and his tongue dipped into her mouth. Her hands moved down the back of his neck to his shoulders and then to his tie. Tipping her head, desperate to deepen their kiss, she unknotted his tie and slid it free from his collar. The silky fabric slid from her fingers, and she began opening the buttons of his shirt. He moved his hands to her hips while she worked. When she couldn't feel any more buttons, she pushed his shirt down over his shoulders and pulled it free from his pants. He wrapped an arm around her to hold her in place, then bent forward to slip out of his jacket. With her help, he pulled his arm free.

"Let's go to the bed, Charlotte."

She nodded eagerly and stood. As he stood, he removed the rest of his jacket and shirt. Then he pulled her against his bare chest and lifted her. She wrapped her legs around his waist as he carried her toward the bedroom. He bumped into a table on the way, and she cringed at his sharp intake of breath.

"Are you all right?"

"Of course, I am, darling."

They passed through a little hall into his bedroom, which was dark and shadowy. The moon shone through the windows that lined one wall, and that's all Charlotte noticed before he set her gently down on the bed. In a quick swoop, he had her drawers down her legs and off. And then he knelt before her and parted her knees. Charlotte quivered when his tongue met her flesh and pressed against the place where all her nerves came together. She wiggled underneath him and he put his hands under her to hold her in position and licked in firm swipes, then tenderly bit and sucked until her brain glitched and blacked out in pleasure. She cried out his name and writhed against him until her whole body was reduced to a puddle.

Before she could recover, he pecked her inner thigh, stood, and stripped away his pants with remarkable speed. In a second, he was naked and gleaming in the shadowy light of his bedroom. Then he was over her kissing her mouth and pressing between her thighs. After wanting this man for so long, and even knowing he'd never truly be hers, Charlotte gasped as he slowly, gently pushed inside her. It was finally happening. She was as close as she could be to this man.

"Oh, Charlotte," he whispered, pausing for a moment to kiss her jaw before he started moving his hips in a slow, devastating rhythm. Focusing only on that, she forgot about all the other complications of their situation. There were no parental expectations. No society. No gossip. No traditions. It was just Charlotte and Antoine, and the physical act of love.

She wrapped her legs around his waist and ran her hands down his strong, muscled back. His skin was so smooth, silkier even than his fine clothes. As their bodies moved together, her mind softened and the world disappeared. His mouth found hers again, found her tongue, and he kissed her so deeply that something stirred within her. When he came up for air, he groaned and pumped harder and faster, grinding against her until she exploded again into a million tingling stars. Antoine's body tensed then and shuddered as he pulled out fast, spilling onto her stomach. He made the most delightful, guttural sound and then collapsed over her.

Panting and messy and slicked in sweat, he kissed her ear and laughed. "Charlotte, that was marvelous. You're marvelous."

"It was fun, wasn't it?" Over his shoulder, the window cast a pale wedge of light across the ceiling. The chandelier hanging over them hung from the center of an ornate tin medallion. What could it be like to wake up under such elegance every morning? She'd never imagined herself in a room like this. Or with a man like Antoine. She'd scoffed at such fantasies. And here she was, in his huge, satiny bed. Perfectly comfortable. Perfectly in love.

After cleaning up and taking a break, Charlotte and Antoine repeated the performance twice more before falling asleep. But Charlotte didn't sleep for long.

She awoke in the blue morning darkness. Antoine was lying on his side, facing away from her, breathing slow and steady with sleep. She listened to him and tried to fall back to sleep in the pocket of his warm bed. But she couldn't. When the little clock on his bedside table advanced to six in the morning, she gave up and slid as stealthily out of bed as she could. Her legs were still weak from their passionate activities. The air in the room was cool against her bare skin. She moved through the rooms, collecting each piece of her clothing, and redressed herself. The curtains of the sitting room were open, and so the oncoming sunrise cast the room in a pale, creamy light. She'd never slept in such fancy rooms before, and she took in every detail of his space, his habits. When she found his cigarettes on a side table, she took one and held her breath as she slowly opened the glass door that led to the balcony.

Outside was quiet and still. The balcony looked over a garden below. From that vantage point, all the other windows appeared to be dark except for one on the bottom of the other side. The kitchen, perhaps. She'd had too much to drink last night. And she'd practically thrown herself at Antoine. But as the smoke billowed around her, her mind felt clear and open and satisfied. Who knew what would happen next? What Antoine would say after the night they'd had. None of it worried her now. They were in love. Madly. She just had to trust that Antoine would know it meant he couldn't marry anyone but her. When the cigarette was finished, she put it in the cast iron ashtray and went back inside.

Antoine hadn't moved, so Charlotte slowly opened the door that led out into the hallway. Creeping back the way they'd come the night before, she walked quickly and as quietly as possible. The floor was covered in a floral rug with big red roses and greenery. It had been dark when they'd come in, but she found the service stairs easily and made her way down. His house was quite magnificent, as magnificent as the others she'd visited in his company. Until then, his wealth was abstract, at least somewhat. Seeing it firsthand secured the understanding that he was a different sort of person than her.

As she was stepping down onto the landing and the exit, a man in a livery came around the corner and started when he saw her.

"Pardon me, mademoiselle. Bon matin." He recovered himself quickly and smiled.

"Apologies, monsieur. I was just leaving."

"Can I send for a carriage?"

This was a tempting offer, but she was afraid of drawing undue attention to the fact of her existence in the de Larminet mansion. And the shame of being caught was beginning to burn. "No, thank you."

"It's no trouble, and I'm sure Monsieur de Larminet would insist."

"That's okay." Monsieur de Larminet. No doubt this man knew exactly what she was doing here.

The man nodded and stepped forward, opening the door for her. "Au revoir, mademoiselle."

Outside, daylight greeted her harshly. Charlotte was tired and sore and a little hungover. But the air was cool and a light breeze blew off the river. Instead of looking for a cab, she walked back toward Rue de Fortuny, regretting only that she hadn't thought to leave Antoine a note.

# *Chapter Fifteen*

*As Charlotte walked* across the bridge and up Avenue d'Alma, the city around her awoke with the determination of a busy day. The bouquinistes were arriving at their stands, unlocking their boxes, and uncovering their wares. Delivery wagons were easing into slim parking situations to unload. Domestic workers were starting their errands. Seeing everyone moving about, Charlotte became increasingly concerned about getting back into the house and up to her room without having to explain her whereabouts. Cook would be in the kitchen inside the service entrance, finishing breakfast. Madame would be lurking around the drawing room, reading the papers, drinking coffee, and making her plans for the day. They might not realize she wasn't in her room, but there was no way they'd miss her coming in dressed in the same clothes she'd worn out the night before. It would be obvious she'd stayed out.

She was passing a boulangerie when a plan started to formulate. She could say she'd been unable to sleep and gone out early for a walk. The ruse would be better if she had a coat to make her clothes less conspicuous. When the shops started opening, she stopped in one that specialized in workwear and bought a lightweight, utilitarian sweater that hid her from neck to waist. It was like the one her mother wore to do garden chores on cool mornings. Charlotte tucked her feathery hat into the paper bag from the shop. She also picked up a box of croissants to distract anyone she might encounter.

Back on Rue de Fortuny, she scurried around the house and rose on her tiptoes to peek quickly in the window at the top of the door. Cook was there, stirring something at the stove. And so was Vanessa. Charlotte pasted on a smile and opened the door with an overly cheerful, "Good morning!"

They stared at her as she set the box of croissants on the table and launched into her planned story about not being able to sleep. Cook listened and chose a croissant. But Vanessa eyed Charlotte with suspicion. It wasn't a threatening look, but it conveyed a lack of belief in Charlotte's little tale. And perhaps some amusement that she'd gone to all this trouble.

"Did you get a new sweater?" Vanessa said.

"No. I've had it for some time."

"Oh."

"I'll just go up now and see if I can get some work done."

Seeming to have satisfied them, Charlotte slipped away and up to her room. She removed her sweater and hung it over the back of her chair. It was a good sweater. And then she removed her dress. Her feet were sore and her legs tired, not only from her night's activities but also the long walk home. She disrobed and put on a dressing gown. Then she took a book with her to bed. Hers was considerably smaller than Antoine's, and the sheets were only soft because they were old, not because they were made of expensive cotton. But her bed had never felt so good. Charlotte got comfortable and opened her book. Her eyes followed the lines of text on the page, but her mind was still back at Antoine's house. The uninhibited sex, the waking in a strange room, the hangover, and the knowing look the valet or butler or whoever gave her on the way out. All the looks from the serious people as she walked home. Oh, the horrors of being seen! None of this quelled the ache she still felt for Antoine. She lay there for a long time going over the details of him. The soft skin of his back, and muscles of his arms, his body stripped of all his fine clothes. Wishing she hadn't left his bed at all. But as far as complications, sleeping with Antoine had only made things between them more complicated.

Over the next few days, Charlotte steeped in her memories of him on top of her, inside her, bringing her to the height of ecstasy. It was like a haze that she moved through. He wrote her the most romantic letter, which she read countless times, and she wrote one back to him. Then she wrote two sex scenes in the story she'd been working on even though it only really needed one.

Giving the rent money to Madame on Monday morning cast her memories in a transactional light, further complicating her feelings. Even though he'd said it was simply a friend helping a friend, he'd asked her before to be his mistress. And he hadn't given her any indication that he'd changed his mind. At least not before they had deliciously plot-thickening sex. She didn't want to inflate her bedroom attributes, but it had been incredible. Together they worked like a well-oiled machine. They had laughed and talked and given themselves completely. They were more than friends now. But the question remained whether or not he still intended to marry someone else.

She worked for the rest of the day and didn't see any of the newspapers until she came downstairs late in the afternoon. The drawing room was empty, but Cook had just brought up a pot of coffee. Madame often liked to sit and have a cup to get her through the end of the day. Charlotte poured herself a cup, stirred in enough cream to lighten it, and then went to sit by the window that looked out onto the sidewalk and street. Absentmindedly, she picked up a copy of the paper where Vanessa worked and started paging through it. Then a headline stopped her cold: "The Amorous Future Vicomte and His Literary Darling."

Charlotte put down her coffee cup and read frantically. The story named both her and Antoine, and it wove a narrative from all the occasions where they were sighted together and mentioned in the various papers that built up to a romantic evening in his mansion that "kept the literary lady out all night long, according to the paper's exclusive sources." Her skin prickled as the words and their not-so-subtle implications jumped at her: lady, night, exclusive sources. Exclusive sources? To accompany the piece, some enterprising artist had sketched what was meant to be Charlotte and Antoine in the throes of a scandalous embrace. A rush of shame engulfed Charlotte, followed quickly by anger. She quickly folded the paper, tucked it under her arm, and took her coffee upstairs.

*In a luxurious* drawing room on the other side of the river, Antoine was also sitting down for coffee and a look at the papers. Just as he was raising the hot cup to his mouth, his mother burst in with a newspaper clenched in her raised fist.

"My son, I have always allowed you your private affairs. But when your private affairs are recounted in such salacious detail, I can no longer turn my head."

"Bonjour, Mother," he said, unfazed. He liked pleasing his mother, but this wasn't his first scolding.

She dropped the paper in front of him and put a sharp finger on the offending headline. "What am I supposed to say when the Montmorencys ask for an explanation?"

As Antoine read, his back stiffened. This was considerably worse than the other little mentions they'd garnered, more of a direct hit. Exclusive sources? Had someone been following Charlotte? Had Charlotte seen it? It would no doubt make more trouble for her than it would for him. Not that he could tell Mother that. "It's just a bit of gossip, Mother. The family legacy will surely survive."

"This is no way to set up for an engagement. How will Louise feel when she sees this? Reads about your, 'tender embraces' and 'passionate glances'?"

"I am sure it will be fine. We're not engaged yet."

"Well, that ends today. I insist you head this off at the pass. Go to her, explain yourself, and ask her to marry you."

"Mother, I refuse to do that."

"You can't refuse. It's too late. Your father and I have courted this girl and her family for months. We've made promises. And now it's time to settle things."

"No."

Adeline de Larminet clutched her chest and gasped, making such a show that one of the servants came and helped her into a chair. "How could you, Antoine? This is the one thing we've asked of you, your one duty as a privileged member of the titled class."

Then she started to cry. Real, genuine tears poured from her. Her words came out choked. "Have you no respect for hundreds of years of tradition? Of our way of life? This is like losing my sons all over again!"

Because if Antoine didn't carry on the family legacy and tradition, then it was like every aristocratic ancestor ceased to matter. All the suffering and work to maintain society's superiority would be for nothing. It was complete bullshit logic, but Mother's agony always weakened Antoine. Seeing her so upset reopened the wounds he'd suffered losing his brothers, his heroes, his best friends. It stirred up his survivor's guilt. And it hardened his sense of duty.

He had the power to ease his mother's suffering in this way. Marriage didn't have to be that big of a deal. That's what it was, after all, just a deal between two families. Many people of his class married for the same reasons. It wasn't about love. It was about business. And when it was over and done, he could do whatever he wanted.

What he shared with Charlotte, what was described in the article, was love. The passionate glances had been genuine. Now that he'd shown her exactly how much he loved her, maybe she would be more amenable to his situation. At least he hoped she would be. After the night they had, Antoine couldn't live without her. No other woman, and there had been a handful, had ever ignited his soul the way she did. And she was incredibly sexy. Echoes of her gasps and cries of pleasure still tickled his ears. Everything about her made his pulse race. Marrying Louise wasn't ideal, but Antoine wasn't exactly an idealist. Plus, if he did what his parents asked as far as this marriage business, they might be more open to settling fairly on the suit he and his lawyer were working to build against them. Charlotte would understand.

An hour later, he and his mother were ushered into the Montmorencys' drawing room. Louise sat primly on a settee in a cornflower blue dress. Antoine bowed and kissed her hand.

Everything would be so much easier if he felt a fraction of the desire and admiration for her that he felt for Charlotte. But there was nothing. Not a stir or a tingle or glint of attraction, though she was perfectly attractive in all the conventional ways. Her mother, just as prim, sat across from her. Antoine bowed and kissed her hand too.

"I'm afraid you've seen the papers," Adeline said, diving right into the pool of her worst fears.

"I hope you aren't too concerned about that," Louise's mother said, clutching the pearls around her neck with her thin, pale hand. "We know how unkind and creative the press can be. And this isn't the sort of thing that should come between years of friendship."

Antoine's head tipped to the side. His mother's mouth fell open. This was not exactly the reaction they'd anticipated. Louise's mother looked on anxiously while they processed her response to the news. But Lady de Larminet never missed an opportunity to sweep trouble under the rug. "Oh, that's such a relief. And not a word of it is true. Isn't that right, Antoine?"

"Charlotte Deveraux and I are good friends. I'm reading some of her manuscripts for her, and the reporter misconstrued it."

"I knew there would be a simple explanation. Isn't that right, Louise?" And then without waiting for an answer, she turned back to Antoine and said, "I told her there was no need to worry."

"Now that that's behind us, Antoine told me this morning that he was hoping for some time alone with mademoiselle. Would you mind showing me your hothouse again, Lady Montmorency? I've been dreaming about those hibiscus flowers of yours."

"Oh." Madame Montemorecy jumped into action. "Absolutely. The yellow one is blooming now; you must see it. We'll leave these two alone."

When the mothers had gone, Antoine turned to Louise. Another woman in his life to disappoint. Everything inside his head screamed at him to run out the door, to escape. Except for the part of him that would do something, anything to make his mother happy. And although he didn't like it, and would loathe to admit it, there was perhaps a flicker of a sense of responsibility to the tradition inside him. Because it was true that once people stopped caring about something, then it would lose meaning. Marriage didn't have to be a big deal. "I suppose you know what it is I'd like to ask you?"

"There has been some hinting around at it, yes."

"Well, Louise, we don't know each other well. And so I feel like I should clear up some things, as far as my offer goes." Just business.

"Your offer?" She blushed sweetly and looked down at her hands.

"Yes. If you marry me, Louise, I will do my best to be a dutiful husband and father to the heirs I'm sure we'll be pressured into producing." He paused, unsure how to say it without being hurtful. "And I'm sure my feelings for you will grow with time…"

"But…" Expectation clouded her eyes.

"But there is some truth to that article my mother rushed me over to apologize for. Charlotte Deveraux is very dear to me. And while I am prepared to enter into marriage with you, I am not prepared to give up my relationship with her."

"I see."

"And seeing as this is not the first time our names have been put together by the press, it probably won't be the last. Though going forward, I will try to be more discreet."

"I see."

"I know that my private affairs will affect my future wife, and I will do everything in my power to minimize that for you."

"I admire your honesty." She wasn't blushing any more. She'd hardly flinched. "Would you like some coffee? It was rude not to ask when you arrived."

"No, thank you."

"You can smoke if you like." She stood and poured herself a cup from a silver decanter, and Antoine was grateful for a moment to gather his thoughts. There was a pianoforte by the window and a potted fig tree that grew almost as tall as the ceiling. At least Louise didn't seem to be the hysterical sort or a romantic. She was a child of the aristocracy, after all, just like him.

When she returned to her seat, he continued clearing the air. "You should also know that I'm getting ready to sue my parents for the proceeds of the sale of our family estate. The viscounty. I intend to give away the money."

Her eyes grew wide. "Really?"

"Yes, but it doesn't have to involve you. Your support might help, but that's up to you. I just thought you should know."

"I have to say, Antoine, that this meeting has gone quite differently than I had anticipated it would."

"My parents don't know yet, about the lawsuit, so I hope you'll keep that between us for now."

"Of course." She watched him with renewed interest. Then she laughed shyly. "Do you want to know the reason my mother was so happy to forgive your indiscretion?"

"No, though I did notice."

"Because they caught me in bed with my English teacher."

"Ha. You're kidding?" Louise was full of surprises herself.

"I'm not." She looked directly at him when she spoke, laying out her own proposition.

"Do you love him?"

"Absolutely not. I don't love the gardener who I've been sleeping with either. But that doesn't mean I plan to discontinue either relationship after marriage."

She didn't ask if he was in love with Charlotte, though it may not have mattered. Her parents were probably pushing her as hard as his were to make an appropriate match. "I see. Then it appears we have a deal, don't we?"

"It appears so."

"In that case, Louise Montmorency..." He cleared his throat, but the words stuck there. The muscles in his hands twitched and his palms were slick with sweat. He coughed and something acid burned his tongue. This proposal was a matter of business, and yet he was physically unable to say the words. He cleared his throat again. Finally, he managed to croak out the question, "Will you be my wife?"

Louise watched, mouth hanging open as a combination of pity and humor played on her face. "I suppose I will since it didn't kill you to ask."

As if on cue, their mothers returned then from the hothouse tour. They both teared up and cheered when they confirmed the news. And for a brief second, Antoine was able to let his mother's happiness overshadow how physically uncomfortable and wrong everything about this engagement felt.

"We'll have the announcement in tomorrow's papers," Mother said as soon as her rush of joy subsided enough to speak complete sentences.

"Is there a rush?" Antoine asked. He needed to talk to Charlotte first. He hadn't even seen her in person since their night together. They'd written, so he was no longer worried by the fact that she'd left without waking him. But they were in a precarious relationship position. After denying each other for so many weeks, they'd been intimate. Finally. If he wanted to be intimate with her again, and he did, then he had to talk to her before she found out about the engagement in some other way. She couldn't read about it in the papers; she might never speak to him again. He paced the room as the women ignored his question about delaying the announcement. He twirled the right edge of his mustache in his fingers. He had to reassure Charlotte of his feelings for her, which were a deep, bottomless chasm of desire and appreciation and admiration. He needed an extravagant gift. He needed a carefully crafted explanation and proposition.

While the mothers and Louise fell into aspirational wedding plans, Antoine excused himself and walked home along the river. The water sparkled in the setting sun. A garbage barge slid past, trailing the foul aroma so ubiquitous with modern life. Or maybe it was life in general. He'd been hoping for more time with Charlotte before having to tell her about the engagement. This rush was not ideal. He'd hoped to prime her for this conversation with enough kisses and pleasure to make her forget all about Louise.

When he arrived at the house, he hurried up to his room, took off his hat and jacket, and settled at his desk. He restarted the letter three times, before catching the right thread of thoughts and words. He loved Charlotte, and he believed she loved him. And even though she had refused him before, he would appeal to that love and try again. The words poured out of him and onto the page. He didn't reveal any details except an urgent need to see her that evening. Then he called up one of the servants to take his message to her on Rue de Fortuny right away.

# *Chapter Sixteen*

*Charlotte read the* letter twice and refolded it. Then she unfolded it and read it again.

*My dearest Charlotte,*

*I write to you with a hasty proposition, which must come in two parts. First, since our intimate evening, I have existed in a state of bliss. Every breath I take is infused with memories of you. Every movement I make elicits the sensation of you. Every flower I see is a reminder. You have ruined me. I have never felt life at this level of sensation, of craving and complete admiration, before. I have read your words over and over again, searching for some relief. But everything only serves to deepen my feelings. I must see you again, most urgently today, and then every day after.*

*It's important that you read these sincere words and know them deep within your heart. And then please meet me in the park tonight at five. As you may have seen in the paper, our attachment has reached the public eye. If you have been unaware of this recent development, I regret to inform you. The second part of my proposition—the most important part—can only be expressed with both your hands in mine, face to face, with all of my being on the proverbial line.*

*There is no need to respond. The post won't make it in time, and I don't want my messenger lingering suspiciously outside your door. I*

*will be at the little bridge like always, waiting only for you. Please come, Charlotte. And I promise you will be happy.*
*Yours always,*
*Antoine*

She had imagined several scenarios in response to the gossip column. Antoine distancing himself from her. Antoine bucking tradition and marrying her instead of the Louise woman his parents chose. Charlotte's mother racing to the city and hauling her back to Vernon. She'd tried to write to Antoine after seeing the article, but she didn't know what to say and decided to wait for him to write to her. Now he had. And he was promising her happiness.

She tried to work, but she couldn't seem to keep herself in her chair. She tried reading, but as her eyes scanned the rows of text, her mind wandered. So she fixed her hair and went out. Charlotte walked down Rue de Fortuny, taking her time to look at all the little details of the neighborhood. It had so quickly begun to feel like home, like she was no longer an interloper or wannabe, but walking down her street in her arrondissement.

If Antoine hadn't given her that money, she'd be leaving it all in a matter of days. She was grateful to him, even if the idea of sleeping with a man for money repulsed her sensibilities. But that's not what she'd done, she reminded herself for the hundredth time. It was as he'd described, a friend helping a friend. She'd slept with him because she loved him. Because she wanted to. And because she'd been so afraid that she'd have to leave him and then so relieved that she didn't have to. As foolish as it sounded, she felt much closer to him as a result. But not in a cheap I've-seen-you-naked sort of way. It was a deeper knowing of him as a person, a closeness that they'd achieved not only in the throes of passion but also in the time they spent. She'd seen his room, been in his bed, observed the setting of his private life. The closer she got, the more of him she wanted.

She reached the end of Rue de Fortuny and turned onto Rue de Prony. It was a mild day for so late in summer with puffy clouds marching across the sky. Domestic workers were finishing their errands. The afternoon papers were arriving at the newsstands. The restaurants were getting ready for dinner service.

Antoine had provided her more time in the city, but publishing was slow and making enough money to stay forever was beginning to seem like a fantasy. And lingering somewhere in her mind was an understanding that her time at Madame's pension was going to end.

*Please come, Charlotte. And I promise you will be happy.*

Those words gave her hope of staying in Paris permanently. Of being with Antoine. As risky as it could be to dream, she could picture them living together in an apartment. It would be a nice, spacious place because he was rich, but not as opulent as his current residence. She didn't consider how he might feel about moving out of his family home for a more modest existence because, most importantly, it would be theirs. They could fill it with books, and she could have an office. And they could make a life together there, with dinner parties and conversations with friends, but also with quiet Sundays reading by the fire. With plenty of I've-seen-you-naked too, of course. She shouldn't, because dreams never work out the way we dream them, but as she walked, she dared to.

She reached Park Monceau early and found a bench along the path that led to the bridge where Antoine said he'd be. The green lawn spread out before her. Two children were chasing a little black dog with curly hair and a leash dangling from its neck. A man and woman were lying on a picnic blanket and reading from the same open book. Beyond the grassy area, the glassy pond reflected the pale sky. A few minutes later, Antoine appeared around a bend in the path. Slim and handsome in his suit. But as he drew closer, there was something worrisome or anxious in his eyes and the set of his jaw.

Charlotte stood up from the bench when he reached her, and Antoine greeted her with a kiss on each side of her face.

"My darling, I was so worried you wouldn't come. Please, sit."

"Why wouldn't I?"

"Because of that horrible article, of course. You've seen it, haven't you?" He sat close to her on the bench and took her hand. "I was worried you'd never speak to me again."

"I did see it." And she was almost certain that her housemate had something to do with it. Vanessa worked at the same paper and had been conveniently present when Charlotte came in that morning. Even more suspicious was the fact that she hadn't seen Vanessa since. But that didn't matter now. The damage was done. Though she might never speak to Vanessa again.

"I fear everyone in the city did." Antoine looked stricken as he spoke, his eyes tired and regretful. He wasn't as dismissive of this article as he had been about the others, which worried her even more.

"What is it that you need to ask me?"

"I need to tell you, Charlotte, that seeing you has been a dream. One I desperately want to continue. But now that everyone in the city is reading about our intimate glances, things are more complicated."

"They are."

"And I'm afraid I don't know how best to say what I have to say, so I'm just going to do it. I've asked Louise to marry me."

"What?" Charlotte pulled her hand away. This wasn't one of the scenarios she'd imagined. Foolish Charlotte.

"The engagement will be announced as soon as tomorrow." The words looked like they hurt coming out. His brow crumpled and his eyes closed to the unbearable. "I wanted you to hear it from me before you found out from someone else."

"I can't believe this." Charlotte ached like her ribs might collapse.

"Charlotte, my dear. I know you said you wouldn't become my mistress, but that was before. Before we knew how wonderful we are for each other. And I understand that the timing of this is a disaster. I would much rather we had more time together without a wedding getting in the way. But it doesn't have to change anything between us."

"What do you mean it doesn't have to change anything?" Could terrible news break a person's ribs?

"I've spoken with Louise. She understands our connection perfectly and won't interfere. She's sleeping with her family's gardener, for goodness sake. And if you can't stay at your current place, then I want to get you an apartment. Anywhere you want in the city. A place all your own where you can work and have company. A place where we can be together undisturbed."

"An apartment?"

"Yes. Anywhere you want."

The ache in her chest grew into something sharper, a stabbing pain. Her heart shattering. And a flame sparking in its place. “Where we can be together, separate from the life and family and home you’re building with your wife?”

“Charlotte,” he said soothingly. “I’ve told you about Louise and my commitment to my family. It’s not exactly what I want either, but it’s a way for us to be together. People do it all the time.”

“I don’t.”

“But Charlotte, I love you. And I believe you love me. So I’m asking you, because our love is so real, to try it. To let me try to make you happy.”

Suddenly, everything clicked into place. His mention of his fiancée sleeping with a gardener, and the fact that he would put his relationship with his precious family at risk to sue them but not to marry her. He was never going to change his mind. No matter how modern his mind, his heart lived somewhere far more traditional. Charlotte’s hands trembled in her lap. And then a hot rage surged in her like she might explode. She stood up from the bench and faced him.

“You asshole. I can’t believe you’re asking me this. I can’t believe you’re using our love as an excuse for your infidelity. You act like you’re powerless against this arranged marriage, but you could just not marry her. You could have not proposed to Louise. You could have stopped kowtowing to your mother because you feel guilty that your brothers died and you didn’t. But you didn’t do that, when if you really truly loved me, you would have. No, Antoine. No. I will not be your mistress.”

Charlotte turned and stomped away as fast as she could.

Antoine called after her and followed. But when he came up behind her, she turned and shot him a look filled with so much vitriol that he stopped short and let her go. A white rage consumed her as she walked so fast she was almost running. Her shoes scraped angrily over the sidewalk, hands fisted at her sides. Not even the exertion of her walk eased her fury. She just made it back to Rue de Fortuny and upstairs into her room before she burst into tears.

Charlotte cried until she was numb. And then she lay there for a long time, splayed on her stomach, face to the side so she could breathe. She'd left her window open, and the sheer curtains moved with the breeze. The sounds of carriages passing on the street below carried in. And the occasional sound of movement or conversation penetrated the walls of the house. The light in the room faded. But she couldn't bring herself to move.

A knock came. Probably dinner time. She wasn't hungry. But when she didn't answer, Nadine opened the door and looked in. "Charlotte, dear, is everything okay in here?"

"No. But yes. I'm fine."

"It's dinner time."

"I'm not hungry."

Charlotte hadn't moved. She couldn't see Nadine, but her footfalls crossed the room and then a hand landed on her back.

"What's wrong, Charlotte?"

She inhaled and exhaled a sigh. Then she rolled over and sat up. "Nothing," she said, smoothing her hair.

"It's obviously not nothing."

"If I say it, I'll start crying again." She wiped her eyes with the back of her hand.

"Come down for dinner. Cook made a lovely salad."

"I'd rather stay here."

"Vanessa won't be there, if that's what you're worried about."

Charlotte suspected Vanessa had been the gossip columnist's source. The fact that Nadine suspected the same only made it more clear. The column, like a gun going off, had set her whole day in motion, and her housemate pulled the trigger. Charlotte hadn't truly been able to care about that part of her mess yet. "It's fine. I'm unwell. Tell Madame and Cook how sorry I am."

"Can I put on your lights?"

"Sure."

Nadine lit the lamp on Charlotte's desk, patted her on the shoulder, and left. Charlotte rubbed her eyes as they adjusted to the light. Her room was neat as always, except for her stacks of books and papers. She should try to work or read or do something to distract her mind. But she couldn't move. She just sat there, taking in the space of her Paris life, everything she'd worked so hard to create, everything she stood to lose. Antoine had never been to her room, but his presence was everywhere. His notes on her manuscripts, the pile of his letters that were too sweet to dispose of, the typewriter. All of it paralyzed her.

She lost track of how long she'd sat there, swirling in an eddy of thoughts until another knock came on her door.

"Yes," she said without moving from her spot on the bed. The same spot where she'd rolled over and sat up to talk to Nadine over an hour before.

It was her again. "I brought you a tray."

"Okay."

Nadine stepped inside and set the tray on Charlotte's bed. There was a salad, bread and butter, a cup of coffee, and a familiar-looking envelope.

"Your fancy man's messenger came during dinner," Nadine explained.

When Charlotte didn't respond, didn't even move, Nadine patted her shoulder again and left the room.

There was no way Charlotte was going to read that letter. Nothing Antoine could say would make this situation any better. And so after a few minutes of staring at the tray, she picked up the coffee cup. It was strong and still warm enough to perk her out of her daze. After a few sips, Charlotte got up and took off her dress. She wet a hand towel in her pitcher and pressed it to her face, which she caught sight of in her little mirror. She was red and swollen in the most miserable way. Tears—still more of them—welled in her eyes as she undressed and unpinned her hair, but she blinked them away. She ate a forkful of salad and a bite of bread. Then she set the tray aside on her dresser, put out her light, and crawled into bed, where she stayed for the rest of the night.

*All the windows* on the third floor were dark, and only one was open. Antoine didn't know for sure that any of them belonged to Charlotte, though she had mentioned residing on the third story. Two women wearing lipstick and walking arm in arm eyed him as they passed and mounted the stairs to the house next door. Antoine nodded and pretended to move along until they were gone. Then he quickly circled back to pass under that open window again.

He'd sent a letter right before dinner, and whoever received the messenger had refused to call Charlotte down so he could put it in her hand, as Antoine had instructed. And so now he was here, lurking under a window he wasn't completely sure was hers.

His carriage and driver were parked down the street. He hadn't known how stupid he'd been until that sharp look from Charlotte hit him like a dagger in the chest. Of course, Charlotte would not stay with him if he married another woman. She had told him so in as many words. He'd been an idiot, and yes, an asshole, to think that she would change her mind on such a fundamental point.

Although Charlotte could have been somewhere in the house asleep, Antoine felt in his gut that she wasn't. So where was she? As a result of his foolishness, Charlotte could be out with another man. She could have her hand on another man's arm right at that moment and be laughing at his jokes. The thought of it implanted in his mind and from it grew a desperate jealousy.

He could knock and present himself properly to whoever answered. He'd been introduced to Diane, but there was no guarantee that she'd answer or receive him well if Charlotte had told her what he'd done. Based on what Charlotte had said about the woman who ran the place, she would be highly suspicious of a gentleman knocking on the door and asking for one of her tenants. He didn't want to make any more trouble for her.

When the front door of Charlotte's house pushed open, Antoine turned away and walked as if he was leisurely passing by and not lingering. Someone was leaving. Antoine turned casually over his shoulder to see if it was Charlotte, but it was Diane and her sister, laughing and talking, heading in the opposite direction. They hadn't seen him, but Antoine kept walking toward his waiting carriage. He couldn't hang around like this any longer. But he also couldn't accept that this was the end. He needed to speak to Charlotte, make his case one more time. Ease her into the idea slowly. She would come around. She had to. When a connection as powerful as theirs, a relationship so deep, existed, then the discussion of how to navigate it would be ongoing. It couldn't ever be a closed issue. Their love was a living thing. Their relationship. And he'd warned her that this was coming. The sting she felt now would surely subside. He couldn't lose her, could he?

The next morning, Emile came to Antoine's room early to help him dress. Antoine and his parents were supposed to have breakfast with the Montmorencys and then spend the day at the club. Antoine, still hopeful that he could remedy the situation with Charlotte was disappointed not to find a response from her in the morning's post. Disappointed, but not surprised. This was what she did. When she was mad, she didn't respond. It would be fine. It had to be.

"You're quiet this morning, monsieur," Emile said, helping Antoine into his coat.

"I'm a little distracted. You're sure nothing else came in the post? I was expecting something."

"I can check again, if you like."

"No. It's fine. Sorry."

"It's natural to be distracted by such an important step as marriage."

"Believe me, things would be much easier if that were all it was." The words came out sharper than he intended. "I'm sorry for my tone. I'm just upset because not everyone is so thrilled about my engagement."

"Do you mean Mademoiselle Devereaux?"

"I do. How did you know?"

"I read the papers, monsieur. And am I to presume that the lady I encountered on her way out the other morning was Mademoiselle Devereaux?"

A chill fell over Antoine. He didn't even know all the details of Charlotte's departure. "Did she seem upset? When you ran into her?"

"No, monsieur. Startled and embarrassed, but not upset."

"Well, she's upset now, to say the least. She's breaking ties with me because of the marriage, though I'm holding out hope that she'll change her mind."

"May I speak freely, monsieur?"

"Please do."

"Perhaps it would be best to give her some space. You're the one getting married, after all. Not to her. I'm sure she is quite disappointed."

"But I was honest with her from the start. She's always known that I have to marry someone from a titled family. She's aware of my duties to my family."

"But does that make it any less disappointing, if you consider it from her perspective?"

"No. It doesn't."

"Will you need anything else, monsieur?"

"No, thank you."

Emile left the room. He was right. Even though Charlotte knew about Louise, she had perhaps hoped for a different outcome. Just because you know something terrible exists on the horizon, doesn't make it any less terrible when it arrives. Antoine hated himself for causing her this pain. He absolutely couldn't bear it. Emile was right about her anger; it wasn't going anywhere fast. But Charlotte had to come around. All Antoine wanted was her, every day for the rest of his life. While there were occasional sacrifices, he more or less always got what he wanted. Didn't he?

He couldn't stop reaching for her. Before leaving for breakfast, he wrote a short note and sent for a messenger.

"Try again to put it in her hand yourself."

"Should I await a response?" The young man's mother worked in the kitchen, and he came a few times a week to run errands. This wasn't his first trip to Rue de Fortuny, and Antoine made sure to tip him well for his long journey.

"No need for that. Just take note of how she reacts, if you will. But I'll give you extra money to stop and buy her flowers on your way. See if you can make her smile."

# Chapter Seventeen

*Charlotte hesitated and* then knocked twice on Vanessa's door. When nothing but silence came from the other side, she tried the knob. Locked. It had been for three days now. The article was published and Vanessa disappeared. No explanation or apology. Nothing. Charlotte was taking this as an admission of guilt, but she still wanted a confrontation.

After listening for another moment for Vanessa, Charlotte retreated downstairs to try filling the pit in her stomach with some breakfast. She'd not only lost her love, but Antoine had also been her friend. Every thought was followed by a desire to know what he'd think. He was there every time she sat down to write, not only in his messy margin notes, but in every character and situation she imagined. She missed him terribly. She'd gone to the park the other afternoon, and when she passed the places where they'd been together, she nearly burst into tears. When she walked down the street, she searched every face in the crowd for his. Paris wasn't the same without him. But she'd also been hardening these past few days, ignoring Antoine's multiple letters and searching the papers for his wedding announcement. Every time it wasn't there, a feather of hope that maybe he'd reconsider tickled her insides.

In the dining room, there were three croissants on a platter in the middle of the table. Madame Tremblay stuffed the last bite of hers into her mouth as Charlotte was sitting down and helping herself to one. Madame smiled as she chewed and swallowed. Then she held out the morning copy of *Le Figaro*.

"I've finished with it, dear. And I'm afraid I can't sit with you. Cook and I are off to the market in a few minutes." She put a hand on Charlotte's shoulder as she left the room. Charlotte poured herself a cup of coffee from the carafe on the table and unfolded the newspaper. That was when one of the little preview headlines under the fold caught her eye: "Future Vicomte to Marry and Other Society News, page 8."

Dread filled her as she frantically turned the pages, even though she knew exactly who the headline referred to. And there it was, on the top of the page, Antoine's wedding announcement and several columns worth of text about his and the bride's esteemed families and connections to long-dead royalty. She read it twice while numbly eating her croissant. So he hadn't changed his mind after all.

After breakfast, Charlotte went upstairs and closed her door. She sat on her bed for a long time, staring at the sky through her window. The beautiful summer day taking hold of the city. For the first time, she couldn't stand the sight of it. She wanted to rip up every feather of hope she'd ever felt over that stupid man. Desperate to be anywhere but in the city where her life had been so wrapped up in his, she got up and packed her things. She wrote a note to assure Madame that she'd be back or at least send word before the next rent payment was due. Then Charlotte walked to the train station and bought a one-way ticket to Vernon.

She rode in quiet agony with her head against the rest, staring out the window as city transitioned to outskirts and then countryside. She hated to leave, but she couldn't stay another minute. And his wedding on the horizon. It was nearly dark when Vernon came into view. And despite herself, relief fluttered through her. Maybe it always felt a little good to be home, no matter how badly you'd wanted to leave. When she stepped off the train and onto the platform, a porter helped her with her bags and to find a cab. And when her mother opened the door and saw her standing there, they both cried.

Two days later, Charlotte met her friend Marie for lunch at the inn in downtown Vernon and told her everything that had happened.

"I saw in the Paris papers that you'd been seen out with him," Marie said. Her hair was curled and more sophisticated than Charlotte remembered, but otherwise Marie hadn't changed. Even her dress was familiar and comforting to see. "I thought for sure you'd be marrying him."

"No fairy tales for me, sadly," Charlotte said. She'd written to Marie a few times when she first arrived in Paris, but they hadn't corresponded for a month. She'd walked into the shop on Charlotte's first morning back in town, and the two women had squealed and hugged each other. If there had been any hard feelings about losing touch, neither one of them mentioned it.

The server arrived at the table with bowls of soup and bread, and both women were silent for a few minutes while they ate. It was strange how easily Charlotte fell back into the rhythms of her life before Paris. It had seemed like a lifetime, but she'd only been gone for a few months. Everything was just as she'd left it. That first morning back in town, she woke up early and wrote before the day started. Then she helped in the store through the busy morning hours. All day, familiar faces came and went, curious as to how long she'd be back and about her experiences in Paris. No one seemed to care that she was back because she'd failed to make it on her own, though they may have been gossiping about her as soon as they left the store.

She'd left the stack of Antoine's letters boxed up with some other papers on her desk in Paris so she wouldn't be tempted to keep reading them. And she'd given the bouquets of flowers he'd sent to Cook and Claire. Aside from the hat stuffed in her parents' hall closet and the typewriter, which she hardly associated with him anymore because she used it every day, the physical reminders of Antoine were gone. Her parents and brother were happy she was home. And something about the return to this rhythm made her appreciate the fact that she'd been to Paris at all.

"I didn't want to say anything because you're so heartbroken, but I can't stand to keep quiet," Marie said with a bashful smile. "I've met someone. And I think it could be serious."

"Oh, that's wonderful! Who is he?"

"Don't worry. It's not Pierre, though they do know each other."

Charlotte rolled her eyes dramatically. "Oh god, stop it. Who is he?"

"He's in town for the summer, so you won't know him. But he's almost finished university. He's studying law. And he thinks he'll have a place here in town in his uncle's law firm. That's what he was doing here, working for his uncle. It's the same firm that Pierre works for."

No matter how many times Marie said Pierre's name, Charlotte didn't experience any pangs of longing or even much curiosity. Antoine had dwarfed anything she ever felt for anyone else. "Will he have to go back to school?"

“Yes, in a month.” Marie sipped her red wine. “I'm devastated by it, but he can take the train in on the weekends so we can see each other.”

While Marie shared all the details of her new romantic entanglement, Charlotte finished her lunch and tried not to feel jealous or sad or disappointed by her own situation. But some awful feeling must have shown on her face because Marie cut her story short.

“Oh, honey,” she said emphatically. "I'm sorry it didn't work out with your aristocrat.”

“I am too.” Charlotte didn't want to dampen her friend's excitement. “But I'll be fine. Paris was a great adventure. I don't regret going.”

It was true. Charlotte would do it all over again, even knowing how devastating losing Antoine would be. She was writing—less than when she was in Paris, but she'd managed a few pages every day since she arrived—and she had enough material to keep her busy revising and shaping stories for months.

“I'm glad you don't regret it. It seems like such a waste, going to Paris only to come home broken-hearted. Though I suppose that means you went to Paris and found love.”

Charlotte had. And it wouldn't always hurt this bad. She missed Antoine. Not a minute passed without thoughts of him. But she no longer searched the crowds for his face. He was so Parisian, she couldn't even imagine Antoine in Vernon. Charlotte would write to Madame to give up the room and ask her to forward her boxes of papers to her in Vernon. And she could go to Paris again when it didn't hurt as much, when they really could be friends and nothing more.

*Antoine paced the length of his balcony, watching the street for the* return of his messenger and hopefully word of Charlotte. It was past breakfast time, but his face was unshaven and he still wasn't dressed. His life had also fallen into a pattern since he'd last seen Charlotte. Without fail, he wrote to her twice a day, and often more. And although it was difficult for him to tell, the letters had become increasingly desperate. On the days when his messenger wasn't able to see Charlotte and report back, Antoine often found himself staring up at the pension on Rue de Fortuny from inside his carriage. When there wasn't a spot to park discreetly on the street, he made the driver circle the block three or four times before relenting and allowing him to move on. And because he couldn't sleep, he'd been drinking more. After a boozy dinner with Guillaume last night, he slept through tennis this morning, which had only perpetuated his foul mood. His head had been such a mess not knowing what she was up to, what she was thinking.

So today, he paid the messenger three times his normal carrying fee to wait for a reply before returning, thinking the boy could sit on the stoop until she either came out or returned. He didn't like pressuring Charlotte like this, but his messenger hadn't seen her in days. When the boy came running down the quay, Antoine was both relieved and desperately anxious to hear what he had to say. Antoine hurried downstairs to meet him.

"I'm sorry, Monsieur de Larminet. I can give you back some of your money since it didn't take so long as you thought."

"It's fine, my friend. Just tell me what she said."

"I didn't see her. That is, Mademoiselle Deveraux's not there. The lady who answered said she probably wasn't coming back either."

"Where has she gone?"

"I asked twice, monsieur. The lady wouldn't say. I'm sorry."

Antoine put a reassuring hand on his shoulder. "Don't worry about it."

The boy nodded and hurried away. Antoine hadn't considered that she'd leave the pension altogether, especially not after he paid for her to stay out the month. He would gladly pay her rent every month if she'd let him. It killed him that she was mad enough to leave the place altogether. What if she'd left Paris? All of these thoughts swirled around Antoine's mind as he made his way back up to his room. When he reached the third floor, Emile was at his door.

"Ah, there you are, monsieur. Your mother has been quite anxious since you didn't show up for breakfast. Remember you are supposed to have lunch with the Montmorencys. Can I help you get ready?"

Wordlessly, Antoine shaved and dressed with Emile's help. And when his mother came up to see if he was ready, Antoine followed her downstairs and into the carriage.

He drank his coffee dutifully in the Montmorencys' drawing room, and he smiled and nodded whenever any comments were directed toward him. But his mind never stopped ruminating on the problem of Charlotte's departure. Where could she have gone? When? Had she even been reading his letters?

Later, after their mothers had scurried off in hopes that they'd fall madly in love, he and Louise were walking alone in the garden.

"You seem distracted," Louise said. "You haven't responded to my last two questions."

"Oh? Sorry." Antoine scrubbed his face with his hand. "I am distracted."

"By what?"

He looked at Louise, perhaps for the first time that morning. She wasn't nearly as much trouble as most women in her position would be. Most brides would take such absentmindedness personally, no doubt. "My lover has fled, apparently, and I don't know where she is."

"That's unfortunate," she said serenely.

"To be sure."

"The writer, correct? Charlotte Deveraux?"

Antoine nodded.

"She's not happy about the wedding, I take it?"

"No. She's refusing me because of it."

"Ha. Imagine that."

"You're not surprised?"

"Most women would be upset."

"I haven't cast her aside. Quite the opposite. But she says she'll never be my mistress."

Louise stopped walking then and turned to face him. Her brow furrowed, but her face was filled with humor. "That's because she loves you."

"How do you mean?"

"Are you so foolish? A woman in love won't be happy to share." When he didn't say anything, she continued. "Antoine, are you and Charlotte in love?"

He sighed as if he were deflating. He was the dumbest man alive. And he still didn't know what to do. "I believe so, yes. I mean, I love her. And I think she loves me. That's why I was so sure this would work. That you and I could marry and come to an agreement, and Charlotte and I could live happily ever after."

"You are a fool. I'm sure of it now." She started walking again. The gravel path was narrow and lined with waist-high box bushes cut into uniform cone shapes. "Tell me what happened."

Antoine told her everything, from the chance meetings to the deep friendship to the breakup and Charlotte's disappearance. When he finished, Louise was quiet for a moment, thoughtful. And then she said, "Antoine, why are you marrying me?"

"For the same reason you're marrying me. Because we're expected to marry someone with a title. This is what my parents want. This is what everyone wants and expects."

"All of that is fine. And for me, people do expect this. But marrying a peer is important to me too, not just my parents." She spoke with a calm, measured tone. "It's something I want, and you are as good a choice as any. But I'm not in love with anyone else. I don't have anything to lose."

"You don't?"

"No." Her curls bounced merrily when she shook her head, but her words were serious. "Whereas it seems as if you have quite a bit to lose. Do you see what I'm saying, Antoine?"

He ran a hand along the slanted side of the box bush, the leaves scraping pleasantly against his skin. "I suppose I do."

"What do you want, Antoine?"

He didn't have to think about an answer to that. "I want Charlotte."

She swatted his arm with the back of her hand. "So what are we doing here, then? Really? You can't please everyone, Antoine. And not to be so dark about it, but your parents are going to die eventually, and likely long before you do. They made their choices and got to live their lives. You get to live your life too."

"It sounds simple. Why does it feel so hard?"

"Because we've been told our whole lives that this is the way it is, that tradition is of utmost importance, that it's a sacrifice we have the privilege of making. But it's not always a privilege. And it's the twentieth century! Tradition isn't the only way."

"But if I don't marry you now, it will be a scandal. Your reputation will be damaged by my mess."

"Yes, people will talk." She shrugged and looked off into the distance for a moment before turning back to him. "I'm not exactly happy about taking the collateral damage of your inconstancy. But I'm not sure I can marry you when it's so clearly wrong for you. I'm also pretty confident that the fault here and the resulting scandal will land primarily on your shoulders."

"I think you're right. And it's definitely my fault." He scrubbed his face with his hands.

"Definitely. But that's okay. It's your life. Sometimes we have to disappoint people so that we can be happy."

"Is my happiness so important, though? In the grand scheme of things? I mean, no one ever died of a broken heart."

"You're more than some pawn in a game, Antoine. You're more than your title. Your happiness should be important to you. And it should be important to your parents as well. You're their last surviving son. Shouldn't they want you to be happy?"

"Can I use that? When I tell them the wedding is off?"

"Yes. Though probably nothing you say will do any good. At least not at first. They'll have to come around to the idea. After they stop seething with rage."

They'd circled the garden now and came to a stop in front of the door. "We'll still be friends afterward?"

"Of course. And I can't wait to meet Charlotte."

"Yes. Charlotte. I will have to figure out what to do about that. Right now she's the one seething with rage, I fear."

"Well, whatever you do, include lots of groveling."

Rather than tell everyone together and ruin what had been a perfectly civil lunch, they decided to tell their parents respectively in private. So the two families said their goodbyes and made loose plans to get together again soon, and Antoine and his parents walked home together in companionable silence. Then, when they made it back, Antoine asked to see them for coffee in the drawing room.

"The wedding is off," he said when they'd all assembled. Best to get it over with fast.

His mother yelped and dropped her coffee cup onto her lap. She stood up quickly so the hot liquid wouldn't seep through the fabric of her dress and burn her. His father, equally as shocked, threw his arms up as if in surrender. Antoine passed his mother a towel and after a few minutes of blotting and cussing, she looked at him again, her bafflement fully sunk in. "Tell me you're joking, Antoine, for the love of god."

"I'm sorry. But I'm not marrying Louise. We decided just now that we don't suit because I am in love with someone else. Charlotte Deveraux. It's my fault, and I accept all responsibility for it. I have apologized profusely to Louise, and I will do the same for her whole family as soon as possible."

"You're refusing a perfect match in favor of that girl writer? That commoner?"

"Hack is more like it," his father chimed in cruelly.

"How could you do this? Do you not understand what you're throwing away?"

"Mother, really. What does 'commoner' even mean? Class isn't important."

She gasped and clutched her chest, reeling anew. "If you don't continue the tradition, then it negates everything that came before it. It brings the whole history down and makes it all for naught. Our whole lives, the sacrifices that we've made, will be worthless if you don't keep it up. It's just how things are done."

"But this is my life. I have to live it. And I deserve to be happy. You made your choices. And I won't cease to be a vicomte regardless of who I marry. I won't cease to be your son. And I refuse to let some outdated tradition run my life. If living a respectable life means side-lining love, then I'm not interested."

His sense of urgency grew as he took his stand. What started by releasing Louise, strengthened as he told his parents. His decision became real. He was making it happen, creating a future rather than letting it fall into place according to someone else's ideas of how it should be. And the stronger and more certain he became, the bigger his problems with Charlotte got. She was gone. He didn't know for sure where she was. And it had already been days.

Both his mother and his father were talking at increasing volumes, arguing with each other and him about the way things should be, seemingly unaware that Antoine was still in the room. The scene was a perfect metaphor for much of his life. When he stood up and excused himself, they didn't notice.

Just before closing the door to leave, Antoine looked back at his parents one more time.

"By the way," he yelled. They both paused to look at him, anger flaring in their eyes. He had one last shot to fire before he was in the clear. "I'm suing you for the money from the sale of the viscounty. My lawyer will be in touch."

With that, he closed the door.

# Chapter Eighteen

*Antoine left his* parents in their drawing room and took the carriage to Rue de Fortuny. Traffic was heavy through the city center, and the ride seemed like the longest he'd ever taken. After so many angsty days of passing her house and sending off letters, he was taking definitive action. He'd waited long enough, so long he may have already lost Charlotte. She could be somewhere in the city, in the company of another man. She could have gone to another city altogether. He'd given her enough money to leave France if she wanted. When the carriage reached the house, Antoine didn't let the driver come to a complete stop before he jumped down onto the pavement.

He took both stairs at once and knocked on the door before he could think better of it. But there was nothing to think better of anymore. He was here with the purest, highest intent for Charlotte. There was nothing to hide. Now there was only his rush to finally remedy the situation. After a long minute and no response, he knocked again, harder this time. After another long minute, the door swung open and a red-haired woman in a flimsy gown was standing there.

"Bonjour." She dragged her eyes up and down his body without indicating her thoughts about what she saw. "How can I help you?"

"Bonjour. My name is Antoine de Larminet, and I'm looking for Charlotte Deveraux. Can I find her here?"

"You can't." She stepped back and made to close the door.

"Wait! Please. Can you tell me where I can find her?"

"I don't think so." The woman started closing the door again, but another woman appeared. She was older and conservatively dressed.

"Nadine, who is it?"

"A gentleman looking for Charlotte."

The older woman faced Antoine through the door. "Are you the one who's been sending the messenger around at all hours?"

"I am." He couldn't tell if this would help or hurt his cause.

The older woman apprised him and squared off. "Monsieur, you should be ashamed of yourself, chasing after a young woman like that. Have you no decency?"

Antoine raised his hand to protest. "I beg your pardon, Madame, and with the utmost respect. I am here with the most decent intentions. I wouldn't have knocked on your door if I didn't. I want to marry Charlotte. She doesn't know this. I have recently behaved very badly toward her, and I must make it right. I must see her. Please. Tell me where I can find her."

The first woman, Nadine, shrugged. "That's not what it said in the paper."

"The paper is wrong. Rather, it's no longer accurate. I am not engaged to anyone and only want to be engaged to Charlotte Deveraux. Is she still in the city?"

A third woman appeared now. This one had blonde hair and was dressed in a light gray suit. "She's gone home to Vernon."

"Stop it, Vanessa. I wasn't going to tell him," Nadine said.

The blonde woman, Vanessa, shrugged. "I can't keep my mouth shut apparently."

Nadine laughed wickedly. "You're terrible."

"And you," Vanessa said, pointing over the threshold at Antoine. "You are terrible too, from what we've heard."

"I am aware of my flaws, mademoiselles, thank you. But I have to go. I have to get to Vernon."

Antoine took the carriage directly to the train station and then sent his driver home. The station bustled around him and the line for the ticket counters was exceptionally long. When he finally made it to the window, the attendant smiled and greeted him with an artificial sweetness.

"I need a ticket on the next train to Vernon, or thereabouts."

"Of course, monsieur. Is it just you traveling today?"

"Yes. When does the next train leave?"

"Well, you're missing one right now. But another leaves in two hours."

"There's a train leaving now?" Antoine gripped the ticket counter.

"Yes, monsieur. It's leaving now. You'll have to take the next one."

He rose on his tiptoes to see around her, but there was no way to see down to the platform from there. "Can't I try and catch the one leaving now?"

"Oh, there's no way you'll make it." The woman's doe-eyes masked her lack of helpfulness.

"I'd like to try."

"I'm sorry, monsieur."

"While we're standing here arguing about it, I could be catching the train. Please." He opened his wallet and put the money for the ticket on the counter. "Keep the change and give me a ticket. I'm going to try to make it."

"Yes, monsieur." The woman relented and rang up his ticket sale without another word.

Antoine, ticket in hand, thanked her and took off running for the platform. Dodging other people and moving as fast as he could through the station, Antoine made it to the platform just as the train was pulling away. Nearly crashing into a gentleman, Antoine moved as fast as he could, like he was after a tennis ball and about to beat Guillaume. The train picked up speed, and Antoine's chest ached from running so hard, but after a few tense moments of pursuit, he leaped onto the departing ride. He grabbed the handle on the side of the car and slipped in the most undignified way, but he recovered his footing for a graceless landing.

The ground beneath the train whizzed past at increasing speed, and Antoine went inside the cabin. He found a seat and caught his breath, watching the city pass by through the window.

"You almost didn't make it there," the gentleman across from Antoine said after a few minutes.

"It was close." Antoine straightened his jacket and placed his hat on the empty seat next to him. "Do you know when we're scheduled to arrive in Vernon?"

"Should be about two hours."

Antoine nodded and sighed.

"So, since we've some time to pass, perhaps you can tell me what business in Vernon is worth running for?"

"A woman." Antoine smiled at the thought of soon seeing Charlotte.

"Ah! Of course. The best reason." The man was neatly dressed in a brown suit, though the seams of his clothes showed wear.

"She's very angry with me at the moment."

"Well, then it sounds like you have good reason to be in a hurry."

"I do, yes."

A coffee cart came around then, and Antoine ordered a cup for himself and the gentleman. When they'd been served and the attendant moved on, the gentleman said, "I ran after a woman once."

Antoine listened to the gentleman's story and told him about Charlotte and how he hoped to win her back. The gentleman, who was a butcher from Vernon, even knew of her parents' bookshop and gave him directions on how to find it from the train station.

Antoine had traveled by train before and enjoyed it immensely, speeding over the landscape, arriving at a destination in a fraction of the time it would take by horse and carriage. Railroad expansion was one of the greatest accomplishments of the modern world. But there hadn't been time to purchase a first-class ticket or private cabin, which was the way he'd always traveled before. This would have made his parents crazy, riding next to the regular people and not sequestered away in some catered experience. He could imagine Mother, nervous as a cat in a hand-basket in the company of the lower classes. It was as if she could hear them sharpening the guillotine. But a sense of well-being and deep connectedness came over Antoine. He'd never spoken with a butcher at length before. And here they'd conversed without preconception or prejudice for over an hour. He wouldn't tell Charlotte about this feeling, because it was probably snobby of him to notice. However, he recognized class as an invisible barrier to meaningful experiences and social connection. And that life was far more interesting when those boundaries came down.

Just when they should have been closing in on Vernon, the train jolted and ground to a stop. Everyone in the car looked around curiously for some sign to indicate the cause of the delay. Some, including the gentleman, speculated about the holdup. Cattle on the tracks, a broken this or that on the engine. After nearly ten minutes, an attendant walked through the carriage, telling people that there'd been a mechanical breakdown and they were working to get the train moving again.

When the attendant passed Antoine, he asked, "How far are we from Vernon?"

"About seven kilometers, monsieur."

Gently rolling green hills and fields surrounded the train. In the distance was a little farmhouse and barn, the only dwelling in sight. It was no bother. Technical failures were a normal part of technological advances, and this sort of minor delay was to be expected. They'd surely be on their way in a few minutes. Antoine remained unbothered until someone on the other side of the car shouted with disbelief, "They're getting off the train!"

Antoine and everyone else moved to look. People were stepping down from the cars up ahead, milling about in the grass on the sides of the track. Then another attendant came through, apologizing and asking everyone to exit the train in an orderly fashion. With no choice, Antoine disembarked. The attendant didn't provide many specifics, but information traveled among the passengers the way it did when something was happening and people were talking. The train couldn't be fixed right away. They were waiting for help to arrive. Another train would take them back south to Mantes-la-Jolie temporarily. They would likely miss dinner. And they might not see Vernon until morning.

The grass was soft and dry under Antoine's feet and the sky above was clear and liquid blue. Some were sitting in little groups on the grass, commiserating. His former seat mate, the butcher, was gingerly squatting down to take a seat next to a family that he seemed to know. Standing there, Antoine grew more anxious. He wanted to be moving toward Charlotte. Antoine's gaze swept the horizon and landed on the little farmhouse, straight across the field. If he could borrow their carriage, he could be in Vernon in an hour.

"Thank you for your company," Antoine said, shaking the butcher's hand as he passed him. "I'm going to head on from here."

The butcher nodded knowingly and wished Antoine luck. And Antoine set off across the field.

At first, the going was easy. The soft swish of his feet against the grass was pleasant. The train and his fellow passengers shrank into the distance. But he came to a place where the soft field was bisected by a thick bramble. Unaware, he stepped high and tried to go through it, but his pants snagged on a thorn. And when he tried to work himself free, he cut his hand on the sharp weed. When he emerged, scraped and bloody, a thick cluster of nasty burrs had attached to the arm of his tailored jacket. They were so sharp, he had to find a twig to wrench them free. His clothes were no longer pristine, but he pressed on. Not long after that, he stepped in a deep and well-camouflaged puddle that soaked his left foot completely up to his ankle and coated it with what Antoine could only hope was mud. His new Italian leather shoe, singular, was destroyed, and he was officially a mess.

When he reached a fence on the other side of the field, Antoine spotted the corral's inhabitant. A dappled gray horse stood in the shade of a some sort of tree. The beast seemed content chewing on whatever it had in its mouth, but there was a menacing rhythm to its swishing tail. Rather than contend with the animal, Antoine followed the fence all the way around and approached the house from the side. A man was standing in the yard, partially obscured by a buggy. Antoine called out to him and the man waved. He looked kindly enough to give a desperate man a ride. Antoine, sloshing in his shoe, strode across the yard and greeted the farmer.

The man's weathered face cracked into a broad smile. He was dressed in rugged workwear, with shirtsleeves rolled up to his elbows and patches on the knees of his trousers.

"Monsieur, pardon the intrusion. But I've arrived here on the train." Antoine gestured toward the distant tracks, where everything still appeared to be at a standstill. "I'd do anything for transportation into Vernon, including paying you whatever you want for the favor."

A woman came out of the house then, suspicion on her brow. "What's this about?"

"This gentleman's from the train."

"It broke down, as you can see." Antoine carried on jovially. "They're waiting for a ride back to Mantes-la-Jolie, but I am in the middle of a critical errand upon which my future depends, and must continue to Vernon. I'm begging for your assistance and the use of your carriage."

Antoine pointed at their humble conveyance.

"You can't do that, I'm afraid. Not at least until I can fix the wheel." The man tipped his head toward the side of the house where a broken wagon wheel was leaning against the stone wall. "But if you can give me some sort of insurance that you'll see to the animal's return once you arrive in the city, I'll let you borrow the horse."

"You don't have another carriage? Or a cart even? That you could drive for me?"

"Afraid not, monsieur."

"How far from Vernon are we?"

"About six kilometers or so."

"Do you have any neighbors who might have a carriage?"

The woman made a demonstration out of looking around. There was nothing anywhere except for a broken-down train.

"Afraid not, monsieur."

"A bicycle?"

"No, monsieur."

"Any other sort of conveyance besides a horse?"

"Not today, monsieur. But our son will be back with our wagon tomorrow. Coming from Vernon, in fact. And there's always the chance that someone will come by on the road."

"You're welcome to stay here with us until we can get you off." The woman offered, not unkindly. "I can make coffee."

Antoine knew how to ride a horse in theory. He'd taken riding lessons as a boy like all upper-class youths did. But after being bitten by an ornery stallion at the equestrian club stables, his skittishness hardened into something more like fear or hateful tolerance. He didn't trust horses. Dogs and cats, he could manage and predict with some authority, but horses were not his animal. They were dangerously large. Each one had a mind of its own and an expressionless face that revealed nothing. But could he really let that stand in the way of his mission? He'd made it through a treacherous course in wilderness survival. His clothes were ruined. But the sense of urgency within him hadn't eased off through any of it. As nice and hospitable as these folks surely were, Antoine needed to carry on. There was no messenger for him to send, no cab to hail or servant to summon. A horse ride might take thirty minutes. He could be in Charlotte's arms in no time. They could be back in Paris tonight.

"Damnit. I'll take the horse." Antoine fisted his hands. "I'll pay you for the trouble, and believe me, I have no intention of keeping the beast."

In no time, the farmer had the gray horse saddled and standing ready in the drive.

"Don't worry. I know how to ride a horse," Antoine said, though no one had asked.

"A gentleman such as yourself, monsieur, I assumed so."

"It's just been a while, is all."

"Don't worry, monsieur. It's like swimming. Once you learn, you can't unlearn it. Diablo here is a fine horse. Very easy to manage. I trust him to get you there." The man patted the horse's haunch and the animal flinched.

Antoine took a step back. "Does he bite?"

"Not unless necessary." The farmer laughed. "Just follow this road into the town center."

Antoine shuddered, accepting his fate. Then he put his hands on the saddle. The animal shifted its weight. Antoine took a deep breath and exhaled slowly. Then he raised his muddy foot into the stirrup, stepped up, and slung his other leg over. Shifting onto the saddle, his heart thumped in his chest. His hands were sweating in his filthy gloves. Again, the animal shifted under him. Antoine's stomach dipped like the earth was spinning off course. But Diablo didn't buck or bolt or throw him off. The horse knew what to do, even if Antoine was not so sure.

He gave the steed a gentle squeeze with his legs and Diablo started forward. Antoine waved and thanked the people as he and his mount trotted out onto the road and headed toward Vernon, toward Charlotte. After several minutes of trotting, he cued the horse into a canter and they were off, to Antoine's dismay.

With each step, the animal surged under him, warm and alive and terrifying with its strength. Antoine was wildly uncomfortable. His wet, filthy shoe only amplified it. He would give anything for a hot bath, clean clothes, and enclosed carriage. Not that he wasn't grateful to Diablo. He told the horse several times during the ride that, if he could just get him to his destination this one time, he would never ride another horse again for as long as he lived.

The horse's feet thumped with sickening power on the ground underneath them. And before long, the green landscape gave way to clusters of houses outside town.

When they were coming over a bridge, the horse came down hard enough to knock Antoine's hat from his head. He'd carried it so carefully from Paris, and it was his newest hat, so he stopped the horse and circled back to grab it. It took a moment for Antoine to overcome his hesitation about getting off the horse. Anything could happen if he dismounted—Diablo could take off and get away. Antoine might not be able to get back on the saddle for any number of reasons. It seemed safer to stay mounted where he was. But he really didn't want to leave that hat. Just as he stepped down and found his footing, the horse stepped back onto his hat and crushed it flat. When Antoine threw a frustrated fist at the sky, the horse flinched and whinnied ominously. But the animal didn't protest when Antoine mounted him again.

Aside from that minor delay, the horse got him to the Central Vernon Bookshop on Rue Carnot in downtown Vernon. But Antoine was so out of breath when he arrived that he may as well have run there himself. He managed to dismount and tie up the horse, and then Antoine collapsed flat onto the sidewalk with relief. They'd made it six kilometers, but the trip had done nothing to reduce his fear of horses. Absolutely nothing.

The bookshop loomed over him. It was a tall, narrow building with a pretty storefront and painted sign. Charlotte could be in there right now. Or upstairs where she lived with her family. The sun came out from behind a cloud and flashed in Antoine's eyes. She was so close. A woman approached, then gasped and swerved away from Antoine in a wide arc. Vernon was a quiet town, and not many people were on the street. But they apparently weren't used to filthy well-dressed men washing up on horseback. Antoine, remembering his manners, stood up in a hurry and brushed himself off. He was so dirty it didn't matter.

He might be able to find a hotel and get cleaned up, but he'd still have to wear his dirty clothes. So Antoine went inside the shop to see if she was there.

The walls were lined with shelves of books, and a counter sat to the left of the door. Charlotte wasn't there, but a handsome woman who looked like an older version of her was. She was alone and looked up when he stepped toward her. She smiled at him, and Antoine extended his hand and introduced himself.

"I'm looking for Charlotte Deveraux. I'm her friend. I've come from Paris."

"I'm sorry, monsieur. But Charlotte isn't here." She was looking at him harder now, taking in the spectacle of his dishevelment. "But you're welcome to wait for her. She's gone out with friends but shouldn't be long."

The bookshop and this woman were perfectly welcoming, but Antoine had never felt more out of place in his life. Not because he was in a bookshop in Vernon and not Paris. But he'd stepped into Charlotte's life. Her real life. Something that existed, until this moment, completely without him. And the weight of his actions fully settled on him while he was standing there, wishing he were clean. They really were from two different worlds. "I would like that very much, if you don't mind, madame. And please forgive my appearance. I started on a train, and it was all very civilized. But the last leg of my journey here was something more akin to that of a cowboy."

Though she made a face like she was trying to hold it in, the woman laughed aloud at that. And Antoine laughed too.

"I'm not kidding. My horse is right out there. And I'm not sure I'll ever be the same."

She laughed even harder and then apologized. "Come with me, I'll get you some coffee. And we'll see about getting some water for your horse. I'm Charlotte's mother, by the way."

Antoine followed her up the stairs in the back of the shop to the family's home, where he met Charlotte's father and brother. Despite Antoine's apprehensions about being rude or indecent, Madame Deveraux insisted that he remove his wet sock and shoe so they could dry on the hearth. Then they all sat around the kitchen table and had coffee together. And it wasn't long before he felt completely at home. That was until, nearly two hours later, the sounds of Charlotte entering the shop downstairs and calling out a cheerful bonjour carried up to the kitchen, and Antoine's heart began to race anew.

# Chapter Nineteen

*"Where is everyone?"* Charlotte called through the empty bookshop. Someone had closed up already, and so she made her way upstairs. Voices from the kitchen carried out into the hallway. They had company, which explained the strange saddled horse tied up in the courtyard. Everyone was seated at the kitchen table when she turned the corner. But there was also Antoine, standing next to the fireplace. His tie had been loosened and there was dirt on his shirt and pants. And he was standing there, like he belonged, with one bare foot.

"Antoine."

"Charlotte." He seemed frozen for a moment, as if her presence were the surprise. Her family, now thoroughly invested, watched on.

"How long have you been here? What are you doing?"

"Long enough to meet everyone, check the train schedule, and make arrangements for Diablo. I came as soon as I found out you were no longer in Paris. I need to speak with you Charlotte."

"Don't worry, dear," her mother chimed in. "We've kept Monsieur de Larminet well while you were out."

"I'm sure." It was hard to tell what her parents might be thinking about this man. Or what he may have said to fall so easily into their good graces. "Everyone looks quite cozy."

"The stew is almost ready. Why don't you settle in and eat something, then you two can take a walk or go down to the café to talk," Charlotte's mother suggested.

Charlotte nodded and excused herself. She hurried up to her room, took off her hat, and put away the notebook she'd picked up while she was out. Her motions were normal, but her mind was fraught. Antoine was here. At her house. What could he have possibly come here to say that he had the gall to face her parents with? Unsure of what to think, she sat in her chair and looked at herself in the mirror on her dresser. Her hair had loosened during her afternoon out, but it would have to do. Antoine was seeing everything about her now, her natural state. The place that made her. It had been over a week since their final meeting in the park. All these days, she'd been miserable and trying so hard to get over him. She hadn't made much progress. But finding him in her parents' kitchen would likely impede it completely. A part of her still wanted to kill him. Laughter carried up through the stairwell then, and Charlotte hurried back down.

Antoine was his most charming self during dinner, asking question after question about the book business and talking up Charlotte's work at every opportunity. After filling her in on his treacherous journey to Vernon, he told the most darling story about a horse biting him as a child. Everyone laughed and seemed quite sad to see Antoine go when he and Charlotte finished their dinner and excused themselves for a private talk.

Charlotte led Antoine downstairs and out the back door. Diablo had been given a room for the night in their stable and would be picked up by the farmer's son in the morning before he headed out of town. Antoine's train back to Paris was leaving that night at 9:30. When they were out on the street and out of her mother's earshot, Charlotte finally spoke the question that had been on the tip of her tongue for the last hour.

"What are you doing here, Antoine?"

He looked down at her and offered her his arm. "I hoped it would be obvious."

"It isn't. Not at all." He had charmed everyone, but Charlotte's hurt feelings and anger were far from soothed. The sun was low and setting fast, but they weren't the only ones out taking advantage of the cool night air. They came to an empty bench at the edge of the town center and Antoine pulled her toward it.

"Charlotte, I've been a complete fool." She dropped his arm as he sat down. He patted the spot next to him, but she didn't take it. He continued, looking up at her. "The engagement with Louise is off. I've told her and my parents. Everyone in Paris knows by now. I am here in Vernon to present myself to your family and father as a proper suitor, which I have done. And, of course, to beg your forgiveness for being such a stupid, stupid fool and not standing up to my family before now."

The words stunned Charlotte, and her mouth dropped open.

"I want to marry you, Charlotte. I want to wake up with you every day and make a family and never leave your side. I want you to be my wife. And if I ever made you feel like you weren't worth that, or that your feelings didn't matter, then I'm sorry. I will spend the rest of my life righting this terrible wrong."

"I don't know what to say."

Antoine dropped his head for a moment, then looked back up at her. "You don't have to say anything now. You can think about it. I don't expect you to come rushing back into my arms after what I've done. But I had to see you and tell you how I feel and show you how serious I am."

Charlotte sat down next to Antoine on the bench. A big moth fluttered around the streetlight over them. And a carriage passed slowly by. "I've missed you, Antoine."

"Oh, my god, Charlotte, I've missed you too." Antoine took her hand and raised it to his mouth, breathing her in and kissing her knuckles.

"What happens now?"

"We sit here just like this—and perhaps closer than this if I'm lucky—until I have to catch my train. And then I will take the train back and forth from Paris to Vernon every day until I can convince you to come back to the city with me."

"You'll take the train to Vernon and back every day to visit me?"

"Charlotte, I would ride bareback on that cursed horse from Paris to Vernon if it meant I got to see you."

"Diablo hardly seems cursed to me."

"He didn't wreck your hat."

"You can hardly blame the animal for that."

"I absolutely can blame him. He had a wicked glimmer in his eye as he brought down his hoof."

Charlotte laughed. Antoine was making light of things, but it couldn't have been easy for him to forsake his parents' wishes and all their precious traditions. She decided not to ask if they'd ever accept her. Not yet. She squeezed his hand. "Well, I suppose I'm glad you're here. Even if it took you a ridiculously long time to arrive."

"I love you, Charlotte."

"I love you too, Antoine."

He pulled her closer to him and didn't stop until his mouth was on hers. Charlotte nearly cried with relief. His kiss was soft and gentle and reacquainting. Then she put her arms around him and parted her lips with his. Antoine's tongue tangled with Charlotte's and the kiss deepened with gratitude and desire. They kissed for some time, but he slowed down every time the passion got heavy. They kissed and chatted, and he showered her with love until it was time to walk to the train station.

There, they kissed on the platform until his train was in motion and he couldn't kiss her any longer. Both their lips and faces were red from so much kissing. He let her go and stepped onto the train as it pulled away. And Charlotte stood there on the platform, elated beyond belief and completely love-sick. She waved pitifully and he blew her a kiss. Then he was gone, and everything had changed.

Antoine returned to Vernon the next day and took Charlotte to dinner and a show at the Vernon Theater. Then the following day, he came early and they went to the park. He came three more times the following week. On his last visit, he brought a diamond ring and a receipt from Madame Tremblay for six months of rent paid in full.

"That should be more than enough time to plan the wedding, shouldn't it?"

"I'm sure it will be."

"So it's a yes, then?" He bent his knees down to her eye level and watched her anxiously. He'd worn the suit she liked and a stunning peach rose on his lapel that had held up remarkably well on the train.

"It is. As long as that's not the same ring you gave Louise."

"I didn't give Louise a ring." He smiled with relief as he slipped it on her finger. "I bought this for you."

"Then yes, Antoine, I'll marry you."

That evening, Charlotte took the train back to Paris with him as an engaged woman. But he didn't take her to Rue de Fortuny until after he'd kept her in his bed for two days. His parents had gone to the beach for the rest of the summer, along with most of the house staff. They had that big place all to themselves. And when Antoine took her back to Rue de Fortuny, he introduced himself properly to Madame Tremblay as Charlotte's fiancé. Madame eyed him coldly and then took Charlotte's left hand for a look at the engagement ring. She nodded approvingly and told Antoine that he was welcome to visit Charlotte in the drawing room whenever he liked.

# *Epilogue*

## ***Paris, April 1902***

*Charlotte lifted onto* her tiptoes and pressed her face awkwardly against the glass to see as far down the alley as she possibly could see. Still no delivery truck.

"Darling, I don't think watching will make it come any faster. I've been looking all over for you."

Charlotte turned and Antoine was standing there bemused. The only reachable window with a view of the back of the building was in the dry stock pantry off the kitchen. She had flour on her sleeve where she'd bumped into the sack.

"I thought I might be able to see further from here than I could standing on the ground in the alley."

He laughed and reached for her hand. "Come with me. I have something that will make you forget all about that delivery."

He led her back out through the kitchen. They'd been in the apartment since the wedding in January. It was in the Gros Caillou neighborhood, not far from Antoine's parents' house. They had a concierge who lived on the first floor of the building, and the view out the front windows included a sliver of the Eiffel Tower. And although Charlotte insisted it wasn't necessary, Antoine had floor-to-ceiling shelves built along two sides of her office so she'd have room for all the books she'd write. It was a stunning backdrop for her typewriter and the workspace of her dreams.

When they came out of the kitchen into the hall, Monsieur Patenaude, publisher of her forthcoming collection of short stories, was standing with a blue clothbound book in his hand. When he saw them coming, Monsieur Patenaude held the book aloft and smiled.

"Oh, you've got a copy already!" Charlotte rushed forward, clapping with glee.

"They brought them to the shop first thing this morning. I came right away because I wanted to see your face when I put it in your hands."

"I've been hanging around our back alley waiting for my box of them." He passed her the book. The bright blue fabric was embossed with a medallion design and the words: *Little Portraiture; Stories* by Charlotte Deveraux. Charlotte ran her fingers over the letters, hardly believing that a book of her work was truly there in her hand. Tears welled in her eyes. "It's the most beautiful thing I've ever seen."

"It's lovely." Antoine put an arm around her and squeezed. "My brilliant wife is an author!"

"She is indeed," Monsieur Patenaude agreed. "But I must be on my way. I want to drop a few copies at the papers to see if we can get some more early reviews."

As Antoine closed the door behind the publisher, Charlotte examined her book again. "I can't even think about reviews yet. It's all so exciting and scary at the same time."

"Everyone will love it. And anything the papers say, good or bad, will increase sales."

"I'll keep that in mind."

The truth was, she'd gotten used to ignoring the press. After news of Antoine and Louise's broken engagement and the reasons behind it spread, Charlotte lost track of her growing list of critics. She had a lot of fans too, which helped. She'd heard from nearly a hundred working-class women who loved and identified with Charlotte's work. It bolstered her against the critics, including the de Larminets.

Charlotte and Antoine married at the Mairie de Farschviller in the Tuileries Garden. For weeks ahead of time, his parents refused to attend. In the end, though, they were there because his mother couldn't stand to miss her last living son's wedding after all. They shook hands with Charlotte's parents and paid for dinner at Buffet de la Gare de Lyon afterward. During the meal, everyone was polite and pleasant, even Vicomtesse de Larminet. The two families expressed interest in each other's lifestyles and experiences, and at least for the duration of the meal, class barriers ceased to limit understanding and human connection. Since then, the de Larminets had gotten to know Charlotte a little better and were perhaps getting over the sting of Antoine not doing what he was told.

They weren't as mad about the lawsuit as they were about him calling off the wedding to Louise. As soon as the papers were served, Antoine's father agreed to put the proceeds from the sale of the property into a trust for the tenant families. Not only because Antoine was right, that the people deserved it, but also because Adeline de Larminet couldn't handle one more scandalous headline. Antoine's lawyer was overseeing the distribution of the funds and helping the people use it to establish themselves in new places and positions.

With that taken care of, Antoine, who poked around Monsieur Deveraux's old printing press in the back of the shop every time he came to Vernon, was helping make repairs and a few upgrades to the machine. He was determined to have Central Vernon Bookshop and Press publish Charlotte's first novella before the end of the year.

Charlotte was in her office a little while later when Antoine brought in the box of books she'd been waiting for. Seeing the one had been a treat, and the whole box was even better. Antoine began unloading the books a handful at a time, lining them up on one of the many empty shelves of the spacious library.

"They look so small on that towering shelf," she said, looking up toward the ceiling. He'd installed a rolling ladder so she could reach the highest shelves. Right now, her collection barely filled three shelves.

"But look how beautiful, Charlotte." He smiled at her and then turned back to gaze at the neat row of pretty blue books on the shelf. "And this is only the beginning."

# *About the Author*

Melinda Copp is a writer based in Bluffton, South Carolina. Her work has been published in newspapers, magazines, and literary journals, including *HuffPost*, *The Rumpus*, *The Cleveland Review of Books*, and *The Petigru Review*.

Melinda has a bachelor's degree in journalism from West Virginia University and a master's degree in creative writing from Goucher College. She writes essays about books, culture, and life in her monthly e-mail newsletter, *Melinda's Letter*. Like a note from a friend, new essays arrive on the first Tuesday of every month. Subscribe for a free short story that follows Louise Montmorency to the last place she expects: deep in love. Get your copy here: melinda-copp.com/newsletter.

Let's keep in touch!

On Instagram: instagram.com/melindacopp/
On Threads: threads.net/@melindacopp
On Facebook: facebook.com/melindacoppwriter/

And please consider reviewing this book on all your favorite book review sites.

# *My Scandal Season*

***Louise Montmorency Finds Love…***

Jilted and scandalized, Louise Montmorency retreats from Paris society to her family's isolated country home in southwestern France. For weeks, she wallows in self-pity and shame, refusing all visitors. Until her cousin and her husband arrive with a strangely compelling companion. But is falling into the arms of another man really the answer to Louise's trouble?

Against the stunning backdrop of the Loire Valley, Louise tells her side of the story as you've never heard it. And she gets another chance at happily ever after.

For a free copy of Louise's story, subscribe to *Melinda's Letter* at melinda-copp.com/newsletter.

Printed in the USA
CPSIA information can be obtained
at www.ICGtesting.com
CBHW020502150924
14363CB00008B/145

9 781964 546001